The PUGLY Truth

A Second-Chance Romance by

TIFFANY ANDREA

Paperback ISBN: 978-1-990724-37-4
eBook ISBN: 978-1-990724-36-7

Cover Design by: Burden of Proofreading Publishing featuring Graphics by Msanca, Leonido, and A7880S via DepositPhotos.

Interior Graphics by Design & Beyond via Canva

www.boppublishing.com

To Desirea,

Thank you for being the cheerleader I never knew I needed and for pushing me so far out of my comfort zone, I can never return. Without you, none of my books would have seen the light of day, and I'm forever indebted to you.

To Otis,

We never met, but I know you were a precious pug who was deeply loved. Thank you for being my inspiration for Akili, and for allowing your love to live on through her.

TABLE OF CONTENTS

PREFACE

As with all of my books, they are free from explicit sexual content and violence, but they often dive into more serious topics. This book, while it is light-hearted and sweet, which I always strive for, it does have mention of a few darker subjects. If there is potential for anything like that to bother you, please read the warnings below. If not, happy reading, and I hope you enjoy Caleb and Hannah's story.

A portion of this story focuses on the effects of domestic abuse. There is also minimal mention of having a narcissistic parent. If either of these could be upsetting to you, either proceed with caution or consider whether this book is right for you.

HANNAH

Don't You Pretend

Unemployment isn't all it's cracked up to be. Or maybe it is. I'm not really sure what people are saying about it, but I do know I'm not enjoying it.

I quit my job five weeks ago, and despite having a degree in culinary arts, years of restaurant experience, and the drive to make my mark anywhere willing to take a chance on me, no one wants to. I'm feeling hopeless, because even though I'm living in the most populated city in Canada, finding a new suitable job seems impossible. Sure, I could work in fast food or somewhere just to earn a paycheque, but I have worked too hard to give up on my dreams by selling myself short.

Plus, I live with my parents, so I'm not worried about getting evicted.

So that's me, Hannah Parker, in a nutshell. Twenty-eight, unemployed, living in my childhood bedroom, and tragically single. The single part doesn't bother me, though, because I'm lucky enough to have the real love of my life curled up on my feet. My pug, Akili, is keeping my toes warm while I stare at my empty email inbox, waiting for a job offer to roll in.

"Hannah?" My mom's shrill voice calls from across the house.

Instead of shouting back, I get up, much to Akili's dismay, and walk out to the kitchen. My mother's hearing is not what it used to be.

"Yes, Ma?"

"Oh, good. You're home."

I'm unemployed and single. Where else would I be?

"Help me with these groceries, please? I got everything on the list."

My eyes light up when I spot the fresh produce and butcher-wrapped cuts of meat my mother purchased. I'm so desperate for something to do, I asked—okay, begged—Mom to invite some of her friends over so I can cook for them. I'm afraid if I don't use my skills, I'll lose them. Plus, I get a lot of excitement from watching people enjoy the things I create. I could use a little excitement right now.

"These look great. Good choice," I commend.

Her soft brown eyes stare up at me as a smile tugs at her lips and creases her face. "Thank you for doing this. It's been too long since I've seen some of these ladies. They're all looking forward to it."

"I'm happy to, Ma. This internet job search is getting old, and I can't face another in-person rejection."

My mother pulls me in for a tight hug. "Don't worry, beautiful girl. The right job will turn up. You were too good for *Harvest*, anyway."

That's an understatement. Not only was management a joke, the kitchen staff were incompetent, their health and safety practices left a lot to be desired, and, let's just say, I wouldn't eat there unless the entire world's supply of canned beans had been consumed. From the start, I knew I was better than that place, but I got complacent. Maybe even a little stubborn, wanting to prove to myself I could save a failing restaurant. Not everything is worth saving, though. That's something I keep learning the hard way.

I push aside my disappointment in my stagnant career and focus on the task ahead: creating an epic meal for a group of women who will probably be more interested in the wine selection.

I swipe away the sweat dripping from my forehead with my black cotton shirt. My long, ash brown hair was in a tight ponytail before I started; now, I can feel tendrils coming loose, tickling my neck and ears. Irritating, but I will persevere.

My mother's friends have started to arrive. They're giggling and talking over each other in the living room. Thankfully, our mid-century bungalow isn't open-concept, so I can maintain some peace and privacy in the closed-off kitchen.

Once I put the finishing touches on the butternut squash ravioli appetizers, I call out to my mom for her assistance. Her less-than-stellar hearing means she doesn't respond. I peek my head into the living room to find my mother and eight women—only half of whom I recognize. One of the four familiar faces sparks with recognition when she spots me. Now it's too late for me to duck back into the kitchen.

Why would Mom invite her?

I take a deep breath as the woman approaches.

"Hannah Parker. How have you been?"

If I thought for one second Noa McNamara genuinely cared about the answer to that question, I'd respond more favourably. Her stunning coffee-coloured hair with subtle highlights is pulled back into a tight twist. Her nails are done in a tasteful French manicure, and her outfit looks like Coco Chanel herself. But her poised appearance doesn't hide the hatred radiating from her.

"I'm great, thanks. Just looking for my mom." I attempt to walk past, but Noa blocks me with her arm.

"Catherine said you're currently unemployed. That's too bad."

We stand in silence for a few seconds. I shouldn't care what she thinks, but the last thing I want is to be viewed as some pathetic deadbeat, which leaves me unsure what to say. I send Akili a pleading look when she opens one eye from her bed by the fireplace; her reaction says I better sort this out myself, because she's not about to intervene.

So I take matters into my own hands and reply, "Well, my old boss cared more about his business than he did about people. I'm sure you can understand that's not an ideal scenario to dedicate your life to."

Based on Noa's brief scowl, she understands the point I'm making.

"If you'll excuse me. Food will be ready in a minute." I sidestep her arm and walk over to my mother, then lean down to whisper in her ear.

She interrupts the chatting by shouting, "Everyone, our food is ready. You ladies get seated at the table, and we'll bring out our first course. I hope you're hungry."

My mother and I walk back into the kitchen with her clasping my hand and bouncing with each step. A sure sign she's dabbled in the wine offerings already.

We each carry out three dishes at a time and place them around the table for mom's guests, then I return for the last three. I could have asked my friends, Angel and Vida, to come help, but they both have actual social lives and jobs. I wasn't about to ask them to give up a Saturday for an unpaid gig.

"Here we have butternut squash ravioli with a brown butter sauce. This is just the appetizer, so there's plenty more to come. Please, enjoy." I race out of the dining room so I can hide behind the kitchen wall and listen to their reactions.

There are squeals—honest to God squeals—of delight as several voices gush over the appetizer. This is a good start. I've missed this. Even during my time at *Harvest*, I never experienced this. Their menu was an embarrassment.

As I'm working on final touches for the main course and finishing up the salad, my mother brings nine empty pasta bowls back to the kitchen. Not a crumb to be found. Akili will be disappointed, but because of her rebuff earlier when I could have used her help, I don't feel bad.

"That was a hit. Everyone loved it."

A huge smile splits my face. Those words are everything to a chef.

We carry out the next course, which I present as a baby kale salad with pears, candied walnuts, and goat cheese. The ladies *ooh* and *ahh* over the presentation. I sneak away, again pausing for a few seconds to hear their hushed chatter. Things like "She's so talented," and "That was the best thing I've ever tasted" buzz around the dining room.

That sparks my excitement over presenting the main course. The *pièce de résistance*. Beef Wellington, herb-roasted fingerling potatoes, and wilted greens. I plate the final dish as my mother returns with the salad bowls.

"Hannah, this smells divine. The ladies have loved everything," my inebriated mother compliments.

I never had any doubt, but this—cooking for these women and bringing them so much joy through food—is where I belong. This is what I'm meant to be doing. It's just too bad the only place I can do it is my mother's 1980s kitchen. What I wouldn't give for a gas stove right about now.

The main course is as well received as the rest of the food, making me feel like a rockstar.

Until Noa stops me on my way back to the kitchen after delivering dessert. "Hannah, I've heard through the grapevine that *Hibiscus* is looking for new kitchen staff. Maybe you should apply."

I pause and stare at her, questioning her intentions. Noa McNamara doesn't do things out of the goodness of her heart for me, considering our history. But *Hibiscus* has the potential to be great, and would definitely be worth putting in the effort to save. With a twelfth-floor location on the waterfront, its recent renovations made local headlines, but the food fell flat. If I could be part of the team to rebuild their reputation—something I failed to do at *Harvest*—it could catapult my career to new heights.

Even with the suspicious look on this woman's face, it might be worth the risk to apply.

Behind These Hazel Eyes

Taking over an established restaurant and revamping the menu is a huge endeavour. Especially a place that underwent a million-dollar renovation almost two years ago and hasn't had the revenue to break even ever since. Despite an elaborate advertising campaign and people coming just to say they did, the food is not winning anyone over. More meals are being sent back than eaten, and no one is sticking around for dessert.

That's where I come in.

Out with the old; in with the new. Sayonara to the head chef who was stuck in the 80s with his old-school techniques, and in with me, the up and comer.

That's not to say I'm better than the former head chef, but my modern style and years of training in France make me a better match for a restaurant marketing itself as modern. Okay, no; I am better.

The downfall is that I have to find several new staff members to fill in the gaps. The kitchen has to work as one cohesive unit. If one person doesn't know what they're doing or doesn't do it well, we all suffer. That can't happen. It's majorly inconvenient to replace fifty percent of the required kitchen staff in my second week on the job, but we're booked solid and need to recuperate *Hibiscus'* reputation. The missing half of my staff either quit out of loyalty when the old chef was fired, or they didn't hack it and I've since let them go.

The restaurant owner, Sergei Antonov, keeps setting up interviews with people who don't meet my standards. He insists on vetting each new candidate and only sends through the ones he thinks are worth my time, but our expectations of new staff members are not at the same level.

Today I have two back-to-back interviews with people Mr. Antonov insists are "cream of the crop," which he's said about seven people so far. Not one of them could even make toast. My twin sister Sophie, who could burn water, would be a better fit for my kitchen.

I look out at Lake Ontario from my spot at an unset table by the south-facing windows, waiting for the first of my two interviewees to show up before the restaurant opens for the day. Five minutes late, a tall, gangly guy with blond hair and weathered skin struts across the room in my direction. I'm already annoyed by the time he reaches the table. To be fair, I was probably annoyed by the time he entered the building, because if he was serious about this job, he would have been here early. Strike one.

His oversized, wrinkled T-shirt and ripped jeans don't give me a lot of hope either, but I'll give Sergei the benefit of the doubt and at least talk to the guy. Even if he looks like he'd rather be travelling along the California coast in a station wagon with surfboards strapped to the roof.

"Good morning, Chester. Have a seat," I instruct.

He walks past me to drop into the chair on the opposite side of the table. "Yup."

Zero pleasantries or common decency. Strike two.

"Let's cut to the chase here, yeah? Why should I hire you at *Hibiscus*?"

He leans forward and places his elbows on the table, holding his chin in his hands. "I've been working in kitchens for two years and nothing challenges me. Safe to say I can nail anything you need me to cook."

Right. As if training and experience have nothing to do with the ability to cook anything, and he can master it all just because he's awesome.

"Why did you leave your last job, Chester?"

"Uh… it was time to move on. Like I said, nothing was a challenge." He tugs at the collar of his wrinkled tee as his eyes search the room. They stop on something that brings an obnoxious smile to his face.

I do my best to reroute his attention, but he seems intent on staring at whatever caught his eye. I spin so I can see for myself and just about fall out of my chair.

Hannah Parker is standing next to the hostess stand, with her long, silky brown hair falling to her waist. *My* Hannah Parker. Though, I lost the right to make that claim a long time ago.

I swallow hard to choke back the surprise of seeing my high school girlfriend and first love. "Well, Chester, I don't want to waste your time, so I'll tell you now, I don't think you're the right fit for us. Maybe with a few more years' experience."

Chester doesn't seem bothered by my abrupt dismissal, because he's still staring at Hannah as he replies, "That's cool, bro."

Strike three.

I push out my chair and walk toward the restaurant entrance, blinking until I know for sure what I'm seeing is real. "Hannah?" I greet once I'm within speaking distance.

She's so startled, she trips over her own foot and nearly falls into the large half-wall planters affixed to the floor. I almost reach out to stop her, but that might result in me getting a busted lip or black eye.

"Caleb?" She steadies herself, swatting away the hibiscus plant by her ear, then smooths down her blouse, brushing her hands over her chest.

Don't watch. Don't watch. I can't help it. Twenty-eight-year-old Hannah has a womanly figure that eighteen-year-old Hannah did not. She also has a long scar running down her right cheek that I want to ask about, but I don't. Otherwise, she looks the same—minus the tears she had streaming down her face the last time I saw her.

It may have been a decade since then, but apparently I still get the same rush from her presence. My heart is racing and I feel a distinct draw toward her.

"What are you doing here?" I ask, hoping she's lost and ended up on the twelfth floor by accident. I'm not stupid, though.

"What are *you* doing here?" she counters. "You're supposed to be in Europe. Not here, crashing my job interview."

This is the kind of surprise I get for not preparing for interviews beforehand. In my defence, the interviewees Sergei has sent my way haven't warranted any more of my time. But it's unnerving standing across from the woman who has always been *the one who got away*. Or rather, *the one I left behind and regretted every moment since*.

"I'm the new head chef here. I got back from France in January."

Hannah looks behind me, as if she's hoping someone else will pop out and tell her this is all a mistake. "The website says the head chef is Miguel Santorino. If it had said Caleb McNamara, I wouldn't have shown up."

Ouch.

"It's new." I could say something to acknowledge our past. Apologize or ask how she's been, but the safest bet right now is to get to business, hope she bombs the interview, and then I'll have a legitimate reason to refuse giving her a job. "Let's take a seat over here and get through your interview. I don't have time to waste."

She scoffs beside me as I raise my arm toward the table I sat at with Chester, which he has thankfully vacated. Anyone else, scoffing would be strike one; with Hannah, I can forgive it. She walks in the direction of my raised arm, and as soon as she steps ahead of me, like the *dawg* that I am, I take in the curves that teenage Hannah did not possess. Her hair reaches well below the middle of her back and sways like a sheet of satin. Her fitted charcoal pants and deep purple blouse look no different from every professional woman in the downtown core, but it's distinctly Hannah. A little edgy, and even though it should look plain and subdued, she makes it stand out.

We sit opposite each other in the off-white upholstered chairs around a gold and glass table. For a long moment, I stare at her while she glares back. Like we're both trying to figure out where we start.

Finally, I decide to dive into business, like I'm supposed to be doing. "So, tell me in sixty seconds or less why I should hire you."

Her gorgeous hazel eyes narrow in a flash, but her anger disappears as quickly, returning her to the picture of profession-alism. "No one can match my work ethic or my passion. And I don't say that to be arrogant; I say it because it's true. Kitchen staff, wait staff included, need to work as a unit, and I'm committed to making that happen. I'm a team player, and while I do believe I'm a talented chef, I am also dedicated to learning more. I'll absorb what you want to teach me, and I'll do it well."

She never faltered once. I'm not sure if she practiced that answer beforehand, but it's exactly what I wanted to hear.

Shoot.

"If I call your last employer and ask their opinion of you, what would they say?"

Hannah barks an alarming laugh before clapping her hand over her mouth. "You're welcome to call if you're curious, but I can promise he won't say anything good."

As terrible as it sounds, this offers me a glimmer of hope. "Why's that?"

"Because of how I left. For two years, I put up with a lot. I was the only female in the kitchen, other than our head chef, and the guys acted as if I was there for their entertainment. Beyond that, none of them could make a fried egg, so I spent my days cooking three times more than I should have to pick up their slack."

My posture stiffens at the thought of anyone viewing her as 'entertainment'. I'm not sure what that means, but I don't think I want to. "So what made you decide to leave without another job lined up?"

"Short version? A good friend of mine worked as a server there. She was dealing with a table of handsy clients in the middle of our lunch rush. The manager came to see what the fuss was about, the guys lied, and she was fired. That was the final straw for me. So, I walked out in solidarity, but I may have caused a scene on the way."

That could be enough of a reason not to hire her. I don't have time or patience for drama, and causing a scene would qualify. However, it sounds like leaving was justified, and she always was one to stand up for others. That's one thing about her that clearly hasn't changed.

"Let's see how you get on making a bearnaise sauce."

3

I should have known Noa McNamara suggested *Hibiscus* for a reason. She's not the type to frequent the help wanted ads. But I genuinely thought Caleb was still in Europe and it didn't occur to me that he'd be the one I would come face to face with. This is like running into heartbreak and disappointment and contention all at once.

When he says *bearnaise sauce*, I know that's his way of testing me. He can probably make a bearnaise in his sleep, but it's widely known to be a challenging sauce to perfect. Making it isn't the hard part for me, though. The hard part is accepting the fact he seems to want to disregard the two years we dated—as well as the lifetime of friendship before that—and treat me like a virtual stranger. He's content to ignore the fact we represent a lot of firsts for each other, like that means nothing.

I guess it's easier to pretend I wasn't his first kiss or his first love—though, I doubt he ever loved me like he claimed he did.

It's not so easy for me to face the man I thought I'd marry and have children with someday. We may have been young, but I thought we were forever. Joke's on me, because he's obviously thrived while I've floundered.

Not only is he running his own kitchen, he's grown up. A lot. His hair is a few shades darker, so it's more similar to his father's—not that I'd ever tell him that. He's got a seriously sexy stubble enhancing his sharp jawline. And the black chef coat he's currently tugging on is like watching him slip into his teenage dreams. I know how much this means to him.

He hands me a pristine white apron, so I pull it on and tie my hair up, ready to get down to business. He may have had some knowledge of what I could do as a teenager in the kitchen, but he has no idea what I'm capable of now.

"Come. I'll give you a quick tour. You'll have to find your way around because I need to jump on the line and help with lunch prep." He turns for me to follow him and explains where all the main things can be found.

The immaculate kitchen is buzzing with activity as other cooks rush around, preparing for the influx of lunch guests. The space is divided into sections, with two long islands running down the middle and various equipment placed around the perimeter. Everything is made from gleaming stainless steel, and given the massive exhaust fans covering a large portion of the ceiling, the temperature isn't as bad in here as most kitchens I've worked in.

The entire space is spotless. It's not just cleaned to *get by* when it comes to health and safety inspections. There's pride in the shine of this kitchen.

"Stay out of everyone else's way and let me know when you're finished. This is your one shot. I don't give second chances," Caleb states before walking off.

That makes two of us.

It's obvious the kitchen is short-staffed if they're expecting to fill that dining room. As much as I'm desperate for a job, I don't want him hiring me because *he's* desperate. Nor do I want a pity hire because of our history; though I don't think that's on his mind at all.

So I get to work creating a perfect bearnaise that will land me a job. It is very finicky, so it takes skill and patience. It's something I've done at least a hundred times before. Never in a restaurant, because I haven't worked anywhere that had it on the menu, but I took Sunday brunches and dinners at home seriously.

It takes me a few moments to gather the equipment I need, familiarize myself with the stove, and find the right ingredients. I start by clarifying the butter, which a donkey with one bad eye could manage. Hardly a challenge. I skim off the foam, leaving behind a beautiful yellow liquid. Next, I tie up the tarragon and peppercorns in cheesecloth, chop a couple of shallots, and add everything to vinegar in a saucepan. It takes time to infuse the vinegar, and you can't skimp on this step. I glance up to see Caleb studying me from his spot at the far centre island. The heat in my cheeks is unexpected. I chalk it off to the warming vinegar mixture.

I continue to watch the flurry of activity as everyone dances around each other. It looks like they're all struggling. I'm not sure if it's because they lack the skill to accomplish what they're trying to, or if they're just overworked.

Once my vinegar is infused, I discard the cheesecloth and allow the mixture to cool. I hate wasting time in between steps, so while I wait, I ask another line cook if I can help her with any of her prep. She looks toward Caleb, who issues a sour-faced shake of his head.

"No, thank you," the timid ginger woman replies.

I thought redheads were feisty. She just capitulated so fast, it makes me wonder if it's the job or Caleb who has doused her flame. I contemplate that question until my vinegar cools and I can move on to the next step. After an arm workout from whisking, I've finished my task.

My first taste of it has me nodding in satisfaction. It's not the best bearnaise I've ever made, but I'm partial to one type of champagne vinegar. This will do.

I notice Caleb about to dart by, so I call out, "Chef? When you have a moment, the sauce is done."

Caleb's eyebrow raises, and the gesture leaves me wondering if he thought I could finish it at all.

My better judgement tells me to storm out and not look back. To walk away from the man who walked away from me, and now stands here doubting me without giving me a real chance. But, as he pulls a clean spoon from the utensil tray underneath the counter and dips the back of it in the sauce to test the thickness, logic loses out. I want to see his reaction when he tastes it. To see his surprise register when he realizes he can't sabotage me. I may not have studied at a fancy French school, but I know my way around a kitchen.

He tilts the spoon, taking a small amount in his mouth. His facial expression doesn't change. "You made a lot for a test batch."

My stomach drops. Does that mean he thinks it's bad? There's no way. "I figured since I was making it anyway, I'd save someone else the work."

"What if it's awful?"

His face might remain neutral, but mine doesn't.

I glare at him, angry he's doubting me like this. "It's not, and I *knew* it wouldn't be." I inhale deeply, trying to find the courage to advocate for myself. "Sure, this was supposed to be a test, but I'm good at what I do. I've never worked somewhere that allowed me to showcase what I'm capable of because I got complacent. It was never because I couldn't do it. If I'm not the right fit for *Hibiscus*, so be it."

Here I thought he'd come over and appreciate my initiative. He'd tell me the sauce was out-of-this-world amazing, then he'd help me find a chef's coat in my size. Instead, I'm leaving defeated. This entire situation was just a tax on my emotions.

The hope of finding a new job.

Seeing him.

Cooking in a restaurant kitchen again.

High highs and low lows. Too much for one day.

"Thanks for the opportunity, Caleb." I untie the apron and walk toward the exit, hanging the garment on a hook as I hang my head in defeat.

"Hannah?"

I turn back to look at my first love, hating that I feel like I'm at his mercy.

"Decent sauce." That must be his idea of a compliment.

"Thanks for your approval," I retort with more sass than I should. "See you around." Even though I'm sure I never will.

Rather than drowning my sorrows in a three-course meal my parents will complain about because they think I'm trying to make them fat, I curl up on my bed with my little pug. She's only two years old, but she came into my life at a difficult time and quickly became my entire world.

"What am I going to do? No one wants to hire me without references," I whine as she lies on the pillow beside me.

Akili stares at me with her soulful eyes, as if she's trying to tell me something. I imagine what she'd say if she could speak. *"Stop sitting around feeling sorry for yourself, Hannah. Pull yourself together. My dog food isn't cheap, so you better suck it up and get your life in order."*

She's harsh, but she's not wrong.

I feel a rush of disappointment recalling the events of the day. It's just another bump in the road that has been very bumpy over the last few years.

"*Move on, Hannah,*" Akili tells me with a tap of her paw.

At least, that's my translation.

"You're right. No sense crying over it."

Akili spins in a circle, digging at the pillow to fluff it up, and curls back up beside my right ear. I'll take the rest of the day to lick my wounds, but tomorrow I'll be back on the hunt.

4

CALEB

Trying to Help You Out

While seeing Hannah again was surreal, what I can't get over is how incredible that sauce was. I've had bearnaise sauce made by French chefs who were the best in the world, so I wasn't expecting Hannah to make one I even considered edible. But it was. Not only did she make a delicious sauce, she didn't break a sweat in the process. She didn't show the slightest hesitation at the challenge.

Serves me right for underestimating her. I used to know her better than anyone, and she could accomplish anything she set her mind to.

So what now? I was hoping she'd bomb my test so I had a reason not to hire her.

She'll be a distraction. A dangerous one. If she's here every day, within reach, proving her worth and tempting me with those hazel eyes, I'll slip. I'll make mistakes and I made enough of those in France, which literally resulted in me fleeing the country.

At the end of the day, though, I need staff, and she deserves the job. The remaining cooks I inherited have proven them-selves capable so far—minus one line cook, Ivan, who is the restaurant owner's nephew—but there just aren't enough hands to do the work. Even if Ivan wasn't prancing around with a healthy dose of nepotism and actually performed his job, we'd still be significantly understaffed.

I can set my personal feelings aside. Stick to professional boundaries and not blur them, no matter what. This is my future on the line, and I can't get wrapped up in my past.

I pick up my phone, opting to call. Good news shouldn't be delivered by email.

"Hello?"

"Hi, Hannah? This is Caleb McNamara." I pinch my temples with one hand, cringing at how idiotic I am. Like I needed to tell her my last name, as if we hadn't spent countless hours with our tongues down each other's throats.

"Oh." Her voice perks up, and there's some rustling and snorting in the background. "Caleb, Hi. What can I do for you?"

"Well, I was hoping you'd be on board for working this weekend."

She doesn't reply right away, which confuses me. I thought she'd be excited.

"Just for this weekend?"

Maybe that's why.

"No, no. Sorry. Yes, to this weekend—well, tomorrow and Friday too, so we can get you up to speed before Saturday—but I was hoping you'd accept a position at *Hibiscus*. Permanently."

She blows out a breath, and for a split second, I imagine how her lips look as she does. Stop it.

"I would love that. Is it easier to send details by email? Or I can come back in if you need me to sign any paperwork."

"Email is fine. Can you print the contract I'll send over, sign everything, and return it when you come in?"

"Sure. Yeah."

"Perfect. I'll see you tomorrow, then?"

"Looking forward to it, Chef."

An awkward pause lingers because I don't know what else to say, but for some reason, being stuck on the phone with her feels more important than anything else. It brings me back to a time we used to spend hours on the phone, even when one of us had fallen asleep.

"Caleb?" she asks.

"Yeah?"

"I won't let you down. Thank you for taking a chance on me."

Something about that statement feels personal. Is she telling me she won't let me down because *I* let her down? It stings as it rips open a wound I thought had healed a long time ago.

"I wouldn't hire you if I thought you would. See you tomorrow, Hannah."

Our dinner service has been a disaster. Overall, we've struggled to keep up with the pace of orders coming in, and I had to man the service counter on top of pitching in to cook. Everyone is exhausted by the time the kitchen closes at 11pm. My voice is hoarse from shouting instructions on repeat for seven hours. Safe to say, I'm ready to go home.

The lone dishwasher is the only other person left when I'm about to do just that, so instead of abandoning him to finish everything himself, I roll up my sleeves.

This is my kitchen. So if that means I have to scrub food pans and utensils to make it function its best, that's what I'll do.

Alejandro and I work in silence until well after midnight, making sure every surface is gleaming.

It's nearly 1am when I pour myself into my lonely house. I wash off the day with a hot shower and climb into bed. Much like last night, there's only one thing on my mind—and it's not perfecting my restaurant menu.

I admire the view of the rain falling over lake Ontario as I stand in the empty dining room Thursday morning. My plan is to have every open spot in my kitchen filled by next week. *My kitchen.* I'll never tire of saying that.

Hannah is a decent start, but I'll have to start poaching capable chefs and line cooks from other kitchens, because anyone worth their weight should already be employed in one of the city's 7,500 established restaurants. Money talks, and the owner here is willing to pay for quality staff. He's tired of running in the red and has put it squarely on my shoulders to fix that.

My phone rings, and when I break my gaze over the water, I see my mother's number on the screen.

I hesitate to answer, but she doesn't call just because, so curiosity wins out. "Hello, Mother."

"Caleb. How are you?" My mother's voice is cold and distant—her passive-aggressive way of making sure I know what a disappointment I am.

"Fine, but I have a lot to do today. Do you need something?"

"Did you like the surprise I sent you?"

I pinch the bridge of my nose, recalling if I received any packages recently. None. "Care to elaborate?"

"I ran into Hannah on the weekend."

Those seven words render me speechless for a moment. "And?" I finally prompt, attempting to sound disinterested.

"Caleb. Must you be so heartless?"

I almost laugh at that statement coming from my mother. From the woman who is married to a textbook narcissist who has no love for anything except money and power. That's rich.

"Mom, I'm busy, so can you get to the point of this conversation?"

She exhales a huff. "Catherine said Hannah was unemployed, so I told her *Hibiscus* was hiring. You're welcome." My mother's words come out a lot like a scheme she's cooked up to sabotage my efforts to defy her and my father. She may have been absent through most of our teenage years, but she would have had to be dead not to notice how in love I was with Hannah.

I also know how much my mom hates her.

"She cooked for us at Catherine's little house, and the food was amazing. Best I've ever tasted from a home kitchen. I almost considered hiring her as our personal chef if I thought she could get along with your father."

I clench my jaw a little tighter. It's nearing the point my teeth are about to shatter, and the only thing I'll be cooking for myself will be smoothies. "Henry doesn't get along with anyone. That's not Hannah's fault."

"You still have a thing for her?" she asks with condescension clear in her tone.

"No. My only 'thing' right now is my job, which I'd like to get back to."

A ten second pause holds between us until my mother replies, "You should stop by to visit sometime. We miss seeing you."

My teeth clench harder, reaching the limit for jaw tension. I guarantee there is no *we* in the equation. My father doesn't miss me. He resents my existence because I didn't follow his plan. I'm not ungrateful for what he did provide, but that doesn't mean I owe him a lifetime of being miserable in a job I despise. He could have chosen to be happy for me and we could have maintained a normal father-son relationship. Instead, he berated me, sabotaged me, and disowned me. He made his choice, and I've made mine.

So I reply to my mother without acknowledging that statement. "I have to go. Talk soon." Then I hang up and try to allow the calmness of the rain to wash away the flurry of emotions that conversation presented me with.

Hiring Hannah is a huge mistake.

HANNAH

Standing In front of You

With paperwork in hand, I return to *Hibiscus* at 1pm on Thursday afternoon. The restaurant is in an ornate fifteen-storey building that houses retail and office spaces. *Hibiscus* is the only restaurant, but it's not the kind of place you frequent for a casual lunch break, so I doubt the white-collar workers create much business.

I'm early on purpose. I want to get acquainted with the kitchen and deal with paperwork before my shift starts at 2pm, so I can jump right in on the action. The restaurant is a hive of activity with a crowded dining room and a short lineup at the hostess station.

This rarely happened at *Harvest*, and when it did, it was a disaster. It's refreshing to see the wait staff working efficiently, moving in and out of the kitchen with deft fluidity. My eyes land on the maître d', Alec Hogan, whom I met briefly on Tuesday. I wave to signal that I need his help for a moment. He smiles at me from over a black vinyl folio and walks the few feet to where I'm standing.

"Yes, Hannah? What can I do for you?"

"Hi, Mr. Hogan. Today is my first shift. I'm here early, but I have some paperwork. Can you tell me where I drop it off?"

"Oh, I'm so happy for you. You'll love it here." He takes a hold of my paperwork to glance at it, but a server calls for him, asking for his help. "Go back into the kitchen and see what Chef wants from you." Then he's gone.

That's exactly the kind of thing I like to see. Someone who is dedicated to their job and doesn't waste time when there's work to be done. I think I will like it here. Maybe aside from the minor issue of facing my former love every day—which wouldn't be so bad if I didn't still get butterflies from the sound of his voice.

I stuff the paperwork back into my purse, paste on my best confident look, and saunter into the kitchen like I belong here—because I do. As much as the dining room is buzzing, the kitchen is ten times busier. Pots clanging, people shouting, equipment beeping. There are eleven people by my count, but from the looks of the dining room, they're doing the work of twenty.

Caleb passes by, about to dart around the corner, carrying a massive chunk of what looks to be swordfish. He slaps it down on an empty stainless steel prep surface and turns around, locking eyes with me. Before he speaks, his eyes glance up at the digital clock over the stove. "You're early," he snaps.

Again, I straighten my posture, refusing to shrink back from his harshness. "I wanted to get familiar with the kitchen and get paperwork sorted before my shift starts."

"Next time you want to make managerial decisions, Miss Parker, I suggest you wait until you're management. I asked you to come at two because that's the earliest I'd have time to deal with you."

I fight to keep my jaw from dropping. "Sorry, Chef," I bite out. "At least give me something to do to pitch in since I'm here."

He doesn't look at me. He's busy sharpening a fillet knife. "Know how to prep a fish?"

"Yes, Chef."

He sets the tools down on the counter beside the sea creature. I pray that filleting a swordfish is the same as a salmon. Just bigger.

It's not like it's Fugu.

I grab an apron from the same hook I hung one on two days ago, determined not to ruin this opportunity. So if I have to scoop fish guts with my bare hands, that's what I'm going to do.

Caleb stands over me, scowling as I size up the massive fish. This thing must be over a metre long—and it doesn't even have a head. I couldn't guess the weight of it, but I doubt I could lift it as easily as Caleb did.

"This is our special tonight, so I need it sectioned into as many eight-ounce portions as you can get. Then I want them placed in a marinade. Garlic, olive oil, lemon, paprika, coriander, and cumin. It's straight from the Mediterranean, and I want our customers to walk out of here feeling like they are, too."

"Yes, Chef."

A less confident person might be nervous to handle the main protein for the evening before clocking in, but I'm going to show Caleb that my sauce wasn't a fluke. I'm not a one-trick pony. He can glare at the back of my head all he wants; I will not mess this up.

I grab a kitchen scale so I can section off a portion of fish and check it for weight, a mixing bowl to prepare my marinade, and a stainless steel prep container for the fish to go in.

Off to work. With swift, confident movements, I slice the fish into one-inch pieces, ensuring each one is clean and uniform in size. The Wusthof seven-inch fillet knife slices through fish like a warm knife through butter. After a few moments of watching me work without saying a word, Caleb wanders off to do something else. I don't spare anyone a glance as I work through the fish. By the time I finish, I have exactly ninety-six portions.

The marinade is next, but I make quick work of it, ensuring I keep track of proportions so each piece is seasoned equally. Then I grab the vacuum sealer and package each individual cut of fish, sealing it shut to marinate.

Seventy minutes after I started, I turn to find Caleb standing behind me and his face earning some premature wrinkles.

"We have ninety-six portions, so I've got ninety in the marinade and left six plain to accommodate food allergies. What can I do next?" I wait for Caleb's face to show a hint of approval, but it never comes.

He makes an awkward grunt sound and gestures for me to follow him.

I trail behind, wondering if it was his time in France or genetics that turned him into a curmudgeon.

We enter his chaotic office. There are files thrown around the room, an overturned waste bin with shredded paper spilled onto the floor, a cluttered desk—at least, I think there's a desk under the mess—and an entire bookshelf's contents strewn about the carpet. It's one of those rooms where you feel the need to stay standing because you want to spend as little time in it as possible.

"Close the door," Caleb orders.

That makes it even worse. Beyond the mess, I smell like fish, and being in close quarters with the grown-up version of the boy I once loved is not my idea of fun.

But I comply. I close the door and turn back around to face Caleb. My boss; not my first love.

"Sorry for the mess. When the owner told the last chef he was being replaced, he didn't take it well, and I haven't had time to deal with it."

That's the nicest he's been since I arrived. It's also a relief that he hasn't turned into a disgusting slob.

"That's fine. Can I help with anything?"

"I didn't hire you to be a housekeeper, Hannah."

Okay. I guess snappy Caleb is back. Note to self: Stick to the job you were hired for.

"Where's your paperwork?" he asks without looking up from shuffling random documents.

His foul mood has me nervous to tell him where it is. A non-answer won't help the situation, though.

"Sorry, Chef. It's in my purse. I tossed it aside to get to work."

"Go get it, then we'll go over the terms in your contract. We have about"—he looks down at his thick silver watch—"twenty minutes before we need to get back to dinner service prep. Make it fast."

I rush out of the office, speed walk toward my purse hung on an apron hook, snatch the paperwork, and return to the office in under sixty seconds. Somehow, I still feel as if that was too long for him to be kept waiting.

Caleb spends ten minutes outlining the basic terms of my contract. He emphasizes that I'm on a three-month probation period and any drama, lacklustre performance, or just because he wants to, is cause for my termination.

Basically, if I can't hack it, I'm out.

The scary thing about that is the fact Caleb's moods are as predictable as the weather, but I don't have billion-dollar satellites to help me forecast an oncoming change. I don't know what to expect from him. Frosty for now; beyond that, who knows? Though, I doubt I'll see any sunshine anytime soon.

Once the paperwork is dealt with, Caleb instructs me on dinner service. We get back to work and he spends the rest of my shift barking orders, demanding perfection, and chastising any small mistake. Luckily, none of those mistakes are mine, but that doesn't make me cringe any less as he berates people for their failings.

If we rated tempers in terms of Scoville heat units, Caleb McNamara's would be a ghost chili.

He'll quickly come to learn that my habanero-level heat is not to be underestimated.

5

CALEB

Breaking Your Own Heart

This Is going to be even harder than I thought. Not only is Hannah dedicated, her skill in making a bearnaise wasn't a fluke. The way she carved up that swordfish with expert precision had me doubting my own abilities. The entire weekend, she cranked out one perfect dish after the next. It was hard for me to focus on my work because I was so captivated by hers.

My plan to put on my best Gordon Ramsay, *Hell's Kitchen* persona is failing. I keep acting more like Gordon Ramsay from *MasterChef Kids*. Even when I'm trying to be harsh so she'll hate me, it feels like she's filleting *me* with her expressive hazel eyes. She just accepts what I say and gets back to work.

From a business standpoint, having Hannah in the kitchen is a major asset. From a personal standpoint, she's a liability.

But I will not be one of those idiots who allows his entire career to be derailed by a woman. Again.

I need to get my head sorted. I'm taking the morning off, which I've arranged as my regular weekly schedule—half a day off, once a week. Typical chef life. Today, my twin sister Sophie made me promise to spend some time with her. We've barely seen each other since I returned from France nine months ago.

The only reason we saw each other while I was there is because she made the effort to come to me. I didn't return home once. She's always taken her role as my big sister seriously. It never mattered to her that she was nine minutes older.

She texted me the address of a coffee shop that's so out of her way from work, I'm not even sure how she knows about it. Considering how far she travelled to see me, the thirty-five minute drive from my house is the least I can do for her.

Finding a parking spot is a nightmare. I end up half a kilometre down the road and have to walk a full city block to the cafe. If it wasn't for my sister's smiling face waiting outside of the gated patio, my mood would be foul. It's impossible to stay mad at her for anything. She really has been my lifelong best friend.

"Hey, baby brother." Sophie's brown eyes sparkle as she pulls me in for a tight hug.

"Hardy har har. That never gets old." I roll my eyes, but joking with my sister was the only thing to get me through my pre-teen years. It feels nostalgic and familiar. Comfortable. "What are you all dressed up for?"

She glances down as if she's forgotten she was wearing a dress that's not her typical work attire. She is always in a skirt suit and sensible shoes. Today she's wearing a figure-hugging black floral dress with strappy three-inch heels. "I'm not ready to give up on summer yet." She shrugs.

I would buy that if the heatwave we were suffering through was still happening, but it's a reasonable temperature today, and I know she wears her typical suits all summer long.

She doesn't give me the chance to press her for answers, dragging me inside the rustic-chic café with obvious intention.

"What are you getting?" I ask, while staring at the menu board.

"Oh, this place has the best flat white. I'm going to order you one. I only have thirty minutes left."

"Why would you ask me to meet here if your break was short? We could have met somewhere closer."

Sophie's eyes dart around and lock onto a target. I follow her gaze and notice a barista with dark blond hair and a distinct hipster vibe staring back at us.

It's important to note that my sister, historically, has the worst taste in men. Much like our mother. Only instead of the power-hungry megalomaniac type, Sophie goes for the guys with nothing to offer beyond zero career ambitions and debt. She spends her work life trying to impress our father—a pointless endeavour—and her personal life seeking men who are the complete opposite. Henry McNamara is driven by his perceived success in business. But for all his faults, he has an impeccable work ethic. Sophie goes for the guys with none.

"Soph, don't tell me this is why you brought me here. Because you have a thing for the barista?" I whisper.

"W—what are you talking about? No!" She tries to respond with indignation, but I can tell I've called her out for exactly what's happening here.

"I'm not going to tell you who you can and cannot date. Just please, don't let another Dean weasel his way into your life, yeah?"

She looks up at me like I've shattered her heart, and it's not a good feeling. "Drew. His name was Drew. And I won't." She sighs, deflating her normally confident posture. "It's stupid. I know."

"Just make sure you know your worth."

She looks up at me with a hint of surprise. "I do."

"I said I won't tell you who you can date. You're smart enough to make that decision on your own. But I don't want to resort to any more fist fights in your honour. I'm getting too old for that."

She chuckles and I realize how much I missed that sound in the years we've been apart.

"I love you, baby brother."

We step forward as I loop my arm through hers. "I love you too." I lean down to kiss the top of her head. Even in her heels, she's a few inches shorter than me. In this department, I'll always be her big brother.

She orders our drinks and we walk around to the pickup counter to wait. I study the object of my sister's affection, wondering what it is about him that appeals to her. Objectively, he's a handsome guy and seems to know his way around an espresso machine, but I don't know what else women look for. Not as if I have a stellar track record with relationships myself, so I'm hardly in a position to coach her through one.

We grab our drinks and find a table along the wall, where I spend the next five minutes watching Sophie sipping her too-hot-to-drink coffee, grimacing, and sneaking glances at the counter, but the barista seems to have disappeared.

"You really like him." I take a healthy gulp of my drink to hide my amusement.

She huffs a laugh. "I don't even know him. There's just... I don't know." She takes a tentative sip of her drink before surprising me. "Grandma said you hired Hannah Parker."

The mention of Hannah's name causes me to choke on nothing. When I can take a full breath, I reply, "How does she even know? I haven't spoken to her in over a week."

"No idea. I think Mom. Grandma seemed pretty excited about it."

I grumble and look over at the counter, hoping I can redirect this conversation back to Sophie's crush. No luck. "She's good at her job. That's all it is. We're not revisiting anything. Water under the bridge."

"Right. That didn't sound like a rehearsed statement issued by your public relations department. Have you been telling yourself the same thing?"

"She's just another cook in my kitchen, Soph. Nothing to curb your gossip craving."

"Then explain why your eyes lit up when I said her name, hm?" Her arched eyebrow raises as she gives me her best intimidating big sister face.

"They did not. Don't be ridiculous. If anyone here is going all goo-goo-eyed, it's you."

"At least I'm not afraid to admit it."

"There's nothing for me to admit. We're over. We were a long time ago. There's no redeeming what we had. Even if I wanted to." I take a sip of my coffee, trying to come up with a new topic to talk about. "This *is* the best coffee I've ever had. You were right."

"It's not the only thing I'm right about." She reaches her hand across to place on my arm just as a throat clears to my left.

"I'm sorry to interrupt. Can I get you anything else?"

Sophie's face flushes bright pink. I focus on the barista, evidently named Boyd, who is here to offer table service when no one else is getting the same attention. Perhaps Sophie's crush isn't one-sided.

"Thanks, man, but I'm good. Soph? You see anything *you* want? Anything at all?"

She kicks me under the table, which makes me laugh. "No, I'm good, thanks, *Caleb*." Her brown eyes flare at me, threatening to kick me again.

"Right." Boyd takes a small step back, like he's as confused with his customer service as I am. "Well, let me know if you change your mind." He rushes off and ducks back behind the counter, where a small line has formed.

Once Sophie's face returns to a normal shade, she blurts, "Stop living your life to prove him wrong."

I know she's referring to Henry. The man who has never supported anything that doesn't align with his best interests. A man who was never cut out to be a father, so I no longer view him as one.

"You're one to talk."

"I am. I know what you think, Caleb, but I like my job. Sure, there are things I want to change, and those will come with time. For now, I'm making the best of it, and I'm good at it. But I'm not trying to be good at it *for* Henry. I'm trying for me, and I'll succeed for me."

What can I say to that? I want to succeed for me too, despite my lingering motivation to prove Henry wrong. Motivation to show him that I've made something of myself on my own, without his help. I wish I could turn that off, but I can't. So I nod and enjoy the remaining time with my sister before she returns to her thankless corporate job, and I head back to my kitchen.

My kitchen. Take that, Henry.

7

HANNAH

Dance With Me

The lunch rush was killer today. Caleb wasn't here because Tuesday mornings are his scheduled time off, and while I think that's important, there's a remarkable difference when he's gone.

Most notably, Ivan, one of the line cooks, spent way too much time getting in the way, screwing up, and not pulling his weight. Honest to God, the man needs his own Remy the Rat under his chef's hat to motivate him. There's no way a man who spends his working hours cracking his knuckles and picking his teeth is here because Caleb vetted and hired him.

I refuse to work in another environment like *Harvest* where people don't do their job and expect others to pick up the slack. I put up with it there because I wanted to help that place get better. My reputation as a chef would have skyrocketed if I could have salvaged it. But my stubbornness to do so meant I dragged a lot of dead weight.

This is a great opportunity, and I won't let it slip through my fingers because one guy has the work ethic of a sloth.

Since I'm on probation and promised not to start any drama, I choose to focus on my own work and make sure the food that goes out is magnificent.

Every other day on the switchover from lunch to dinner menus, Ivan has made himself scarce. He often takes multiple cigarette and bathroom breaks like he's a nicotine addict with IBS. It's infuriating, but not as much as having him follow me around today. He's worse than Akili, and at least I like her. She's also a better conversationalist.

"So, Hannah, when are you going to let me take you out?"

Internal groan. If I told him I would also like to take him out, I'd mean it in a very different context. "Sorry, Ivan. I don't date people I work with." I don't date at all, but he doesn't need to know that.

He has the nerve to look hurt before a smirk appears. "Why not? I'm hot. You're hot. We can be hot together."

His *hot* rating scores around the same as applesauce as far as I'm concerned. Looks aside, the idea of going on a date with him sounds as painful as drinking pureed Carolina reapers.

"That's a very intriguing invitation—"

"Get back to work; both of you."

I tear my eyes from the sirloin I'm preparing and find Caleb standing a few feet away with his arms crossed, wearing a serious scowl.

Ivan stands upright and mirrors Caleb's gesture, but he's about six inches shorter. "She's getting her work done. I'm not stopping her. Plus, a little action could be good for workplace morale, if you know what I mean."

Those words make me drop the knife I'm holding and pause. I want to tell him off. Scream at him to leave me alone, but that could be considered drama and I'll end up being fired. So instead of standing up for myself with the same ferocity I would for anyone else I care about, I shut down. Mentally. Physically.

I don't know how long I stare off into space. The only sound I hear is my own blood pumping in my ears and my rapid breaths. A gentle hand on my shoulder makes me jump.

"Woah. Hey, it's just me."

After I blink several times, I realize the voice and hand belong to Caleb. Ivan is across the kitchen, onto something else that will waste his time. I stare at Caleb for a moment, trying to form words to explain what just happened. I haven't had an episode like that for almost two years.

"Sorry, Chef." I clear my throat and tug at my apron to smooth it out for no reason. "Won't happen again."

"Hannah," he says with a pitying note in his voice I don't want to hear. A note of tenderness that used to be so common between us. One that sounds like he cares.

He may see it as rude, but I turn back to my task, picking up my knife to prepare the beef that will be the star of our dinner special. I offer a "hm" in response, which is all I can manage now with the delayed emotions flooding my system.

Caleb exhales beside me, and I can almost feel the disappointment he breathes out. He says nothing, instead turning and walking into his office to my right.

I try my best, but for the rest of my shift, my head is off my game. My heart isn't in it, either. I'm cooking to earn a paycheque today, and I hate that. Passion has always motivated me, but today, it isn't enough.

By the time I get home, Akili is doing her dance, so we go for a walk to clear my head. That doesn't work, so I lie in bed with my furry life coach and dish all the hard parts of my day. She tells me to know my worth and not allow anyone or anything to ruin this opportunity.

At least, if my translation of her snorts is accurate, that's what she's saying. And she has a very valid point.

Rather than commiserating with my dog and attempting to decipher her canine sound effects as if she's dishing out decent advice, I decide to meet up with my human friends. Since it's a Wednesday night, we opt for a nightclub called *Lair* that none of us have been to before.

I arrive at quarter to ten and find Vida waiting outside the front doors. Before we properly greet each other, Angel gets dropped off along the curb across the street.

She dashes across the road in between slow-moving cars and reaches us with a wide smile. "I've missed you girls so much." And when Angel says something, I have full confidence it's true.

"Me too. It sucks not working together anymore. You guys kept me sane."

"Sane is a stretch for any of us, I think, but we hide it well," Vida replies, stepping forward to hug Angel.

I was always closer with Vida than Angel was until we stormed out of work together and all ended up unemployed at the same time. Ever since that fateful day, we've formed an unbreakable trio. A bond forged by our unrelenting hatred for our former boss, Mr. Harrington.

I feel so at ease in their presence again, I have to stop myself from blurting out that my high school boyfriend is back in my life. Granted, only in a professional capacity, but it still has me all emotionally twisted. My thoughts surrounding Caleb are as straightforward as a funnel cake.

"Come on. I need a drink," I say, dragging them both inside the door.

"New job is going that well?" Vida asks, holding a finger up and turning to the hostess before I can reply. "Table for three, please."

The svelte blonde woman directs us to follow her, so I answer while trailing behind Vida, and walking in front of Angel.

"Let's just say we have a few staff members who belong at *Harvest*, and I can use a night to forget."

We're seated in a booth at the edge of the dance floor, where both of my friends cast me a concerned look from their side of the table. But I don't get to elaborate before the hostess informs us they serve food for another hour, then the space becomes rowdier with people coming in for dancing and drinks.

All of those things—food, alcohol, and dancing—sound like exactly what I need. I missed out on partying with friends for most of my twenties because I was either too afraid to or too busy. Also, I didn't have any friends. These girls have been instrumental in helping me learn how to have fun again; in healing my heart that I'm now wondering if it ever really mended.

"I love you girls," I blurt after the hostess walks away.

They exchange another look before Vida replies, "We love you too. Were you pre-drinking before you got here, or…?"

"Stone-cold sober. Scout's honour." I hold up three fingers to prove I mean it.

"I don't think that counts unless you're a Scout, but I believe you," Angel adds. "So, how's the new job? Everything you dreamed of?"

Before I can explain that it's more of a nightmare, our waitress comes to take our drink order. I go right for the hard stuff and ask for whisky. I'm not driving.

Our conversation is such a hodgepodge of random topics, we never seem to get back around to our discussion about my job, and before I know it, I'm pleasantly buzzed, swaying in the middle of the dancefloor, sweaty and content.

Call me a snob, but I never love food from other restaurants and find myself critiquing it, rather than enjoying it, so I didn't eat much. Pair that with the alcohol coursing through my veins, and you have a recipe for some epic dance moves.

This is just what I needed. A night to unwind and let loose without fear of consequences. To be my happy drunken self.

But this is going to hurt tomorrow.

"We're at *Lair* on the corner of Bathurst and Dundas. She's..." Angel's words trail off as she paces the sidewalk in front of me. "... don't want to send her in a ride-share..."

My head is buzzing as I sit on the bench at the bus stop. There's no way I'm taking the bus right now. I may have indulged a little too much, but after the situation with Ivan this week and the complicated reality of having Caleb back in my life, I needed a distraction.

Vida leans me against her and wraps one arm around my shoulder. "You're going to be so hungover."

I close my eyes and nuzzle into Vida, willing the world to stop spinning. To be honest, I don't even know why we're sitting out here.

"Your dad is on his way," Angel declares, dropping into the spot on the other side of me.

I grumble without lifting my head. "This is so embarrassing. I'm nearly thirty and my dad is coming to get me. Ugh. Stupid Hannah. Stupid, stupid, stupid."

"Hey, don't be so hard on yourself. You're allowed to..."

But I don't hear anything else as my eyes flutter closed.

The room is spinning when I open my eyes. I'm not sure how I ended up back in my childhood bedroom, but here I am with my dog curled up beside me. My mouth feels like I ate a tablespoon of flour, and daggers pierce my skull when I try to move. Textbook hangover. The likes of which I have not felt for… ever.

I pick up my phone to check the time, noticing it's almost noon. I'm scheduled to work at two, which means I need to get myself in gear. This entire day is going to suck.

My mom is in the kitchen when I drag myself down the hallway to get some water. She doesn't speak at first; instead, choosing to greet me with a smirk, partially hidden behind her mug. Even the light of the refrigerator hurts my head, but the sweet relief brought by a tall glass of water is worth the pain.

"Have a nice time?" Mom finally asks.

"I have no idea. You'd have to ask Angel and Vida." I try to return her smirk, but my eyes are closed now, so I'm sure I look like a lunatic. Maybe I am. I'm definitely a sucker for punishment.

"Your dad told me you were talking about Caleb. Is that why you drank so much?"

Curse my stupid drunken rambling. Until now, I've managed to keep my new boss a secret from my parents, but I was fairly certain if my mom and Noa had spoken, she would have said something. Judging by my mother's raised brows and creased forehead, she isn't privy to the details yet.

"Caleb is my new boss. Apparently, he got back from France in January and landed his dream job at the same place that's supposed to be mine."

"Oh, honey. Why didn't you say something?"

I don't have a good answer for that, so I keep sipping my second glass of water.

"You know you can come to me, right? With whatever's on your mind. I might not know how you're feeling, but I can always listen."

I swallow down some more water… and a heaping mound of guilt. "Yeah, I know. Thanks, Mom. I really do have to get ready for work, though. Are you home to look after Akili, or do you need me to walk her before I leave?"

My mom strides across the floor and pulls me in for a tight, motherly hug. "I'll take care of your little diva. Your dad flies out early tomorrow morning, so we'll both be home."

"Oh, nice. I'll be home late, but I'll call later to thank him for being my DD last night."

She still doesn't let go. "There's nothing we wouldn't do for you. Even if I have to buy lye and a shovel, just say the word."

I chuckle. "That won't be necessary. Caleb and I are long over and we can both be mature adults about it."

"He's not who I was talking about." She releases me and turns to grab her tea from the counter. "Just don't think you need to handle everything yourself, okay? Dad and I are here for you and so are your friends. Don't let yourself be closed off again."

I swallow down more guilt without the side of water. "Okay."

With that, I head back to my bedroom to get ready to face the day. I can already tell it's going to be miserable.

I may have danced last night until my outfit was more sweat than cotton and drowned my sorrows in too much whisky, but none of that works to ease the same stab to my chest when I walk into *Hibiscus* and see Caleb instructing Ellen how to do something. They're standing close, and logically I know it's a teachable moment, but I can't stop the surge of jealousy I feel. He never takes the time to teach me like that.

That's probably for the best.

As the afternoon drags on, I'm lagging. My reaction time is slow. My pace in completing tasks is rivalling Ivan's. I'm dehydrated, tired, and grumpy. Each time Caleb shouts an order, my pounding head makes me want to bite back. My desire to keep this job stops me from doing so.

"Hannah, what *is* this?"

I look over at a plate I sent out about ten minutes ago, but it's returned almost full. That never happens to me. "What's wrong with it?"

"Look at it! This fish is so raw, it could join *The Little Mermaid* in a duet." He's never looked at me with that kind of anger before—or worse, disappointment.

"Sorry, Chef. I'll make a new one." I step around the corner from the stove, hiding for a second while I pull myself together. This isn't me. I don't screw up in the kitchen.

In order to help me focus, I rush across the room to my purse, down half a litre of water and a couple of acetaminophen tablets, hoping they'll kick in quickly.

When I return to the stove, ready to recreate the visual masterpiece I had already sent out, but this time in an edible version, Caleb's furrowed brows capture my attention. If he's worried I'm going to screw this up again, he can relax.

"I'll handle this, Chef. Watching over me won't make it cook faster." I start sauteing the flounder that should be the showpiece of the plate. "It was a onetime screwup." Every part of me is screaming not to look at him, but I do anyway. To prove to him that I will not cower in the corner or stare off into space again. And to myself that I'm not going to fold under pressure.

Caleb is the first to look away, which leaves me to get back to searing this fish to perfection and him to dish out some colourful insults to Ivan. I'm nearly done plating another meal—

pain medication doing its job so I can do mine—when I hear Caleb shouting from the other end of the centre island.

"I know how Russians love oil reserves, Ivan, but this is ridiculous. They're about to launch a takeover of your plate. There's enough oil under here, they've mistaken it for Venezuela."

Ivan doesn't seem bothered by the cultural dig or the critique of his plate. He sets it on the serving station, disregarding Caleb's assessment. My dish is ready and if it doesn't go out quickly, the customers are liable to riot, so I walk past both men to set the dish beside Ivan's. Caleb was right, and he knows it, because he takes the entire thing and throws it in the garbage—plate and all. The shattering glass in the steel trash can startles everyone. Collective gasping and curious gazes add to the uncomfortable situation.

Caleb catches my eyes for a second, but returns his focus to Ivan. "Do it again, and do it right. There won't be a third chance." His voice is so full of rage and frustration, that when he storms off, I fight the urge to follow him.

Why? I'm not sure.

So we can commiserate together over the disaster this day has been?

Because behind that abrasive chef personality, I know the Caleb who used to live underneath.

Or maybe it's because, without him, this kitchen doesn't operate. He runs it with a no-nonsense mentality, but it gets work done. He calls people out on their mistakes and makes them correct them. We're all learning under his command, and I, for one, am grateful for that. He pushes people to be their best.

I respect him as a chef, even when he's dishing out insults, because the *food* he's dishing out is world class. Everyone else here knows what he's capable of, so the pressure on his shoulders must be overwhelming.

This job comes with long hours and a lot of stress, and I know aside from his grandparents and sister, he doesn't have a huge support network. Or at least, he didn't ten years ago. A lot changes in that time.

But I don't try to comfort or encourage him because I learned my lesson on my first day here. Do the job I was hired for. Nothing more; nothing less.

van Antonov. Nephew of *Hibiscus'* owner, Sergei Antonov. Grandson of notorious Bratva associate, Mikhail Antonov. Familial connections are likely the only reason he's still employed. They're certainly the only reason he still has his front teeth.

After I walked in on Tuesday to find the entitled third-generation Russian playboy hitting on Hannah, and her telling him it was an *intriguing invitation*, I was surprised at the surge of jealousy I felt. Jealousy that I have no right to feel. I walked away from her, and she's free to date whoever she wants. But the thought of that being Ivan made me despise him for more reasons than his shortcomings in the kitchen.

So today, his unapologetic behaviour has depleted what little resolve I had left, and now I'm hiding in the walk-in fridge to cool down, literally. Not only did he not listen to anything I said, he laughed, and that just compounded my anger. People who feel they don't have to be held accountable for the behaviour are not people I have any use for.

Grow up. Stop hiding behind your grandfather's tired gangster reputation, or soon you'll be joining in his excitement over discounts on econo-boxes of Polydent at *Costco*.

All the effort I've made so far to keep Hannah from distracting me is proving pointless. And it's only been eight days since she started here. Ten days since the woman who has always been *the one who got away* returned to my life.

It's been ten years since I walked away, and it's taken her ten days to come back and derail my laser focus. She looks tired and almost like she's nursing a hangover, which also makes a surge of jealousy rush through me, wondering if she was out on a date. That may be why I was harder on Ivan than I should have been.

Breathe in. Breathe out. For ten minutes, I stand in the walk-in refrigerator, trying to ground myself again. I focus on the fresh produce and marbled cuts of meat, imagining what I can create with them. All is well and good until the door opens and Hannah walks in, making it feel as if all the oxygen is sucked out and the space shrinks by a factor of ten.

"Oh, sorry. I didn't know you were in here."

It's a weird place to hide out, but at my last job, I didn't have my own office. The cooler became the place I'd escape for a minute to collect myself when the barrage of culinary knowledge being thrown at me became too much.

I want to apologize, but I don't. "It's fine. I'm leaving." I walk toward the door, brushing past her in the narrow aisle, inhaling her scent. How can a woman who spent the last three hours sweating and cooking fish still smell like strawberries?

She freezes as I pass, and I don't get the impression it's because she's as captivated by me as I am by her. She looks... nervous. I exhale and step a few feet past her. Like Hannah does best, she gets back to the task at hand, searching through the produce area for whatever she's looking for. I don't wait around to find out.

My return to the kitchen has several of my staff eyeing me cautiously. I'm not going to set them at ease. This chef isn't going to be flashing any reassuring smiles or passing out compliments at random. If they want a kind word from me, they need to earn it. If they don't want harsh words, they better smarten up and get the job done they are paid for.

Since last week's disaster service, when I threw dishes in the trash and sought refuge in the fridge, things have been better. We had a seven-day stretch when each shift went reasonably well. Today, it feels like we're back where we started. Like everyone is here for their first day and can't even make a proper salad.

Just as the dinner rush is picking up, Maria walks into the kitchen. "Chef, there's someone here to see you. Sophie?" Her tone suggests she's not pleased about being an errand girl sent to deliver a message.

"Send her back, please." I'm in the midst of creating a pair of time-sensitive dishes and can't leave either. Nor can I entrust them to anyone else today.

Maria huffs and walks through the servers' swinging exit door. Less than a minute later, my sister enters, wearing one of her typical skirt suits. She must not have gone for "coffee" today. Regardless, the sight of my sister and, as cheesy as it may sound, my best friend, eases some of the tension that's been surrounding me since I walked in here today.

"Hey. Give me a couple minutes. You can wait in my office if you want." I don't glance up from the scallops I'm searing, not wanting to miss the sweet spot to cook them to perfection.

"No, it's fine. I'll stay out of the way over here." She stands against an empty prep station that is normally reserved for raw meat—but she doesn't need to know that. "I have a favour to ask."

I could count on one hand the number of favours my sister has asked me in my life. She doesn't ask favours of anyone, and

I have mad respect for her because of it. If she's coming here to ask me something and not just calling me, it must be serious.

"Okay. What is it?" I tilt the pan to slide the scallops onto each of the plates Ivan already prepared to a satisfactory standard. At least he can manage celery puree.

"I need you to come to a gala with me next week."

My dear sister seems to have forgotten a critical bit of information, but I don't want to shoot her down outright.

I gesture for her to follow me to my office. "My staff are not on their games today, so I only have a minute." I swing the door open and step back to hold it for Sophie to enter, but she doesn't budge from the doorway.

"Caleb. What the hell is this? You call this an office? This doesn't even qualify as a... dumpster."

"I know, but I haven't had time to sort through everything. I've got my necessary contacts, contracts, and purchase orders, so beyond that, I don't care right now."

She still doesn't move. "This is not okay. You need someone with good business sense to get this organized for you." Sophie gives me her best smile and puppy dog eyes.

"In exchange for?"

"Baby brother"—she scoffs—"I'm offended you think I would only offer help expecting something in return." She pushes some random equipment catalogues to the side with her foot.

"Soph, I can't take an evening off right now. We're booked every night, and none of the staff here are ready to handle it."

She sinks into the chair in front of my desk, still scanning the mess. "I was afraid you'd say that. I don't have anyone else to ask, as pathetic as that is, and Dad made it clear I need to bring someone. The big, bad, male-dominated world of international business is already bad enough. Showing up as the poor single girl is even worse."

This is not new information for me. My sister has confided in me many times about the difficulties in her job because a lot of our father's clients subscribe to the mentality that women are the lesser sex. That they're meant to stay at home, baking fresh bread, embodying June Cleaver. Still, when she mentions what it's like working in a boys' club, I can't help but think of Hannah's experience at her last job. Then she comes here and gets hit on by Ivan, resulting in whatever that blackout she had was. That thought makes my irritation with Ivan inch upward.

"What is happening to you? You just stared off in space and made the full range of emoji faces."

I blink a few times and shake my head, settling back on Sophie. "Why don't you ask the barista guy? You obviously have a thing for him. Just give it a go."

"I can't ask him! Could you imagine Dad's reaction?" She scrunches her face. "It would be worse than if I brought you!"

"Gee, thanks."

She stands from her chair, clutching her purse in front of her. "We both know it's true. I'll let you get back to work. Someday I hope you'll make me something spectacular to eat."

I wrap my sister in a hug, resting my chin on her head. "Once my staff is settled in, I'll make you something amazing. I promise. Love you, Soph."

"Love you too, little brother."

We exit my office into the flurry of activity happening in the kitchen. Immediately, I hear Ivan yelling something at one of the other line cooks, and I'm so close to relegating him to dishwasher. I start walking over when I hear my sister squeal, "Hannah? It's me, Sophie! How are you?"

10

HANNAH

Don't Let Me Stop You

My arms are full as I exit the walk-in cooler *again*, making it difficult to see over the amount of uncooked food I have perched precariously on my forearms. A feminine voice calls my name, startling me, and I struggle to keep hold of everything. A dainty hand reaches up and removes the two heads of cauliflower from the top of my stack and places them in a prep bin to my left. That would have been a smarter choice before I started gathering everything, but I ended up needing more than I realized.

"Do you remember me?" Sophie asks.

I stare at her, recognizing her as the grown-up version of the beautiful teenager who was a big part of my younger life. "Of course I do. I'm good, thanks. How have you been?"

"Good. I'm glad. Grandma was so excited to tell me you were working with Caleb. Apparently, Mom raved about your food."

"Oh, wow. That's really sweet of her." Even if I do suspect Noa had ulterior motives in doing so. "She was instrumental in getting me this job, so please, if you speak to her, let her know how much I appreciate that." Maybe I can kill her with kindness and everything in the past will be forgotten.

Sophie smiles and her vibe is quite the contrast to her grumpy brother. "I will."

"Are you staying for something to eat?"

"Not tonight. It seems a little tense in here and Caleb shot me down when I asked him to be my plus-one for an event next week. I don't want to add on more work for anyone."

It doesn't surprise me Caleb said no to anything that means time away from work. Still, Sophie is so sweet and always has been; I feel bad that Caleb thinks he can't take a night off to support her. He walks up behind his sister, eyeing the stack of ingredients in my arms.

"I'm sure we can hold down the fort if you want to go with your sister for a few hours." The words spill out before I think.

Caleb's narrowed eyes make me wish I could rein the whole sentence back in.

"I mean… Sorry, Chef. It's just…" My stammering is starting to irritate me. The last thing I need is to be reduced to a stuttering fool in front of my boss. "It's your call, but I'm sure we can handle things."

The narrowed eyes Caleb has been sporting for twenty seconds are now glaring at me. "I'll tell you when I think you're ready, Hannah. Leave the managerial decisions to me, yeah?"

I look at Sophie to gauge her reaction because I'm mortified by Caleb's response. I was trying to be nice, and he had to respond in his trademark arsehole-ian language that he seems to be the only native speaker of.

Sure, I should acknowledge his words, but I don't. I dump the ingredients I've been holding into the bin Sophie deposited the cauliflower into and march off toward a vacant prep table. This ninety second delay has held me up long enough and I'm not getting yelled at again. After Caleb's tirade last week, when I was nursing the world's worst hangover—or at least my worst hangover—I've tried to keep my head down and stay off his radar. Successfully until now.

Five minutes later, as I'm whipping together the next ordered entrée, Sophie marches out the door looking so defeated, I can see it from thirty feet away. She sends me a little wave, but my hands are busy plating food, so I nod. I wonder if her demeanour is thanks to Caleb's foul mood he chose to direct at her or if he made it clear he won't be joining her at her event. Maybe both. Regardless, he doesn't say anything when he returns to his position and gives Jorge instructions to return to his.

It's none of my business, anyway.

I'm learning that Caleb is more temperamental than a soufflé. One moment he's full of hot air, gorgeous, and ready to be the star of the show, then the next, he's deflated, dry, and disappointing. My curiosity about him has me daydreaming of ways to peel back his layers and figure out what it is that makes Chef Caleb McNamara tick. The reasons could be the same or vastly different from what mattered to teenage Caleb.

"Hannah, call it back to me."

I grimace at the sound of my name and realize I tuned out something important. "Sorry, Chef. I didn't hear you."

"Where's your head at, Hannah? Daydreaming about your latest hot date? Too hungover to do your job again? If you can't handle the heat, get out of my kitchen!" Caleb is fifteen feet away, but I can feel the heat from his gaze on top of the heat from the gas stove I'm standing in front of. He looks disproportionately angry over me missing one ticket call.

I promised I wouldn't cause drama. I *promised* I wouldn't be combative. But I learned the hard way that being a doormat isn't going to work for me. That instinct to apologize and try to get back in Caleb's good graces isn't here today. Neither are his good graces, if I'm being honest. Unfortunately, my courage has flown the coop.

"I can handle the heat just fine, Chef. If you give me a second, I'll do my job." It feels wrong not to add "please", but that's too much like begging. Like conceding to his abrasive demeanour and uncalled for comments about my personal life. It's my job to produce stellar food, so it's my fault for missing the order call, but what I did or did not do last night is none of his business. He made sure of that when he shattered my heart and fled the country without a second thought.

Instead of him looking angrier at my clap back, a flash of regret crosses his face. Almost like Akili when she's been caught chewing my mother's custom orthotic slipper. But "flash" may have been generous because a nanosecond later, he shouts through gritted teeth, "*Cassoulet de Toulouse* and two *coq au vin.*" Not going to lie. His French accent is on point and kind of dreamy.

"Yes, Chef." I glance to my left and see that two of the line cooks, Tyson and Adriano, have gotten all three dishes started. "Thanks, guys."

Adriano flashes me a killer smile. He's the friendliest of the longtime kitchen staff and the only one who doesn't treat me like I'm at the bottom of the pecking order. He also doesn't give off any of the creepy vibes Ivan or my former co-workers did, so I send him an appreciative smile in return.

Enough feeling sorry for myself today. The rest of my service is going to be flawless. Make good food, don't give anyone reason to take exception to my presence, and shrink back to the Hannah that I hate and swore I'd never become again.

This dream job is turning out to be more of a nightmare.

I made it. The rest of dinner service, prep for tomorrow, and cleanup all passed without incident. Caleb's prickly personality didn't soften the rest of the evening, but at least I didn't have to be a direct beneficiary of his creative snubs. Most notably telling one of the younger line cooks to go put his sirloin steak back in the field because it was closer to dropping some fertilizer than being eaten. As unorthodox as Caleb's methods may be, the rest of Tyson's steaks were cooked perfectly.

It makes sense for Caleb to take his job seriously when he has to consider profit margins and critics. People don't come back to a restaurant because of the atmosphere. They want good food. The success of *Hibiscus* lives and dies with the quality of the meals we're producing, and with thousands of restaurants to choose from in the city, people won't be inclined to give it a second chance if they don't love what they're served.

Still, I can't help but take some of his comments personally. I feel like he doesn't think I'm good enough.

But then I walk in the front door of my parents' home to the wagging curly tail of my fur baby, and suddenly whatever Caleb thinks of me doesn't matter. No matter what I screw up, or how many times I may fail at something, Akili still loves me just as much. So long as I provide her with her daily meals and regular walks.

"Hey, baby girl. Were you good for grandma?" I whisper, since all the lights in the house are off.

"I told you not to call me grandma." My mom's voice pierces the darkness, startling me.

I follow the sound of her chuckle and once my eyes adjust, see a faint shape of a human on the couch.

"Sorry, Mom. What are you doing up?"

She stands, then walks toward me, her long nightgown drifting around her feet with each step. "Call it mother's intuition. I had a feeling you'd have something you wanted to talk about when you got home. I couldn't sleep."

"No, I'm fine. I'm sorry if my schedule is keeping you up."

Mom comes into the faint light of the foyer where I'm clipping on Akili's leash. "Are you sure?"

No. "Yes."

My mother pulls me in for a hug, which never fails to offer a sense of comfort. I don't even have to earn it with walks or daily meals—she loves me despite my failings. And I've really tested that over the past few years.

I say good night, encouraging her to get to bed, then take Akili for a short neighbourhood jaunt. The entire time, I chastise myself for not opening up to my mom. This is how I ended up in a bad situation before—by failing to confide in people who cared. Instead, I gave everything to someone who didn't.

There is no way I will allow myself to lose who I am or what's important to me for someone who can't see my worth. I'm enough for Akili, my friends, and my parents, and that will sustain me until I can prove to Caleb I'm good enough for *Hibiscus* too.

11

CALEB

I Hate Myself for Losing You

I needed a good night's sleep, which didn't happen.

Instead, here I am attempting morning yoga. Never tried it before. So, could someone explain to me why I'm in boat pose, staring out the window onto my patio? Well, it's simple. I'm channeling some inner peace before I go into work today because sleep did little to quell my anger over yesterday's dinner service. Never mind. I'm still holding onto anger over Ivan's behaviour. I'm still angry because that blank look on Hannah's face scared me. For a minute, I thought she was going to throw down her apron and walk out.

Tortoise pose.

Instead of focusing on whatever *Ashtanga* is, I keep dreaming about pounding Ivan's stupid Russian face in. In between those thoughts, flashes of my hand caressing Hannah's soft skin pop in. Then I think about how lush her lips are and how silky her hair looks. Other primal urges overtake my need to defend her honour, and instead, have me thinking dishonourable things. So, really, I'm trying yoga to clear those images from my memory bank before I have to spend nine hours in a sweaty kitchen with her.

Failing miserably.

It would have been much more beneficial to join my cousin Oscar at his muay thai gym and let him pound the thoughts out of my head. Or at least pummel things myself until every ounce of anger drips from my pores. But I don't have time to drive across the city before I have to be back at the restaurant.

My yoga flow is as smooth as a sea urchin, and I'm not sure I get any benefit from it. It doesn't lower my blood pressure. Nor does my shower before I get dressed for another long day in the kitchen. Far too close to Hannah Parker.

I arrive at work at 11:30, a mere eleven hours after I left. Any dedicated chef will tell you their kitchen becomes their primary residence. When we're not in the kitchen, we're thinking about it. Restaurants are a dime a dozen and operate with a slim profit margin. Success isn't an accident.

A knock at my office door startles me, and I look up to see the silky hair and lush lips I spent my morning yoga session dreaming about.

"Sorry if I'm bothering you, Chef. I just have to drop something off."

Why is she in normal clothes? Why is she holding a single piece of paper that looks like a typed letter? A resignation letter. She can't quit. I won't let her throw away this opportunity.

I clear my throat before I can reply because I have to swallow the Brussels sprout-sized lump forming there. "What can I do for you?" I try to sound nonchalant, but my mind is reeling, coming up with different ways I can convince her to stay.

"Just dropping off this paper Mr. Antonov asked me to fill out."

So much tension rolls off of me, I slump into my chair. That realization slaps some sense into me, and I remember my initial plan. No distractions. "Put it there." I point to the drop tray on my desk. "I'll deal with it when I have a chance." Like the idiot that I am, I wave my hand to dismiss her before I can say anything I'll regret. Something like, *Can I taste your lips?* What I hate the most about the gesture is how much I've just reminded myself of my father.

She spins to leave, which I only notice from the corner of my eye because I'm trying not to look at her, but she turns back around, drawing my full attention. "I'm sorry about yesterday. It won't happen again." Then she walks away.

And it feels terrible.

It's obvious I need to keep my distance from Hannah because she elicits a primal reaction in me. The square footage of this restaurant kitchen does not provide enough real estate for that to be possible, though. Physical distance may not be an option, but if I revert to my initial plan, I can maintain a professional barrier. She'll hate me enough that I'll have no choice but to see her as my employee, and not as my teenage fantasies come to life. That's all she is. A familiar reminder of a simpler time.

With a fortifying exhale, I step out of my office door thirty minutes later to find eleven members of my staff bustling around, fulfilling lunch orders. The one person I don't see is Hannah.

She exits the cooler, walking toward the kitchen without sparing me a glance, stopping at a prep table covered in flour.

I march in behind her to see how my team is managing. Stepping back and allowing them to take control is a challenge for me, but the reality is, I can't work 100 hours every week for the rest of my life. If something isn't working in my absence, I need to know so I can fill the gap.

But something is bothering me.

"Hannah."

Without looking up from the pasta dough she's started for our *ravioli de erbette*, she replies, "Yes, Chef?"

"Why are you the only one I see restocking ingredients?"

She stops breaking the eggs into the well of her flour and sweeps some stray hair from her forehead. In the process, she leaves a streak of flour above her eyebrow. "Would you believe me if I said it's because I'm the only one who knows where anything is?"

"No." Not even a little. There's no way that's the reason, because when Hannah isn't here, they manage.

She huffs a sigh, turning back to her pasta dough in progress. "Pecking order."

Those two words get her point across, but I still need clarification. I can tell by her tense posture and lack of eye contact that she doesn't want to talk about it. I'm not giving her a choice.

"How has anyone decided on a pecking order when I haven't assigned official titles yet? Everyone is on a level playing field."

When I hired each person, I informed them and the former staff they'd be on three months' probation, after which time I'd assign official positions. I wasn't about to call someone my sous chef or head chef without knowing how they work. My brigade is going to be carefully crafted to create the best functioning team. I'm not blind to how unreceptive some of the other people in the kitchen have been to new staff, but I didn't realize Hannah viewed herself as the errand girl. She's far too skilled and valuable to be relegated to fetching green beans. Ivan can do that.

Hannah begins kneading the dough, leaning forward and pressing the ball with the heels of her hands. "It's fine, Chef. I only need to prove myself to you, so I'll do the work."

She has a point. This is *my* kitchen and every major decision is mine to make, but no one is going to treat an equal as inferior on my watch.

"I never thought I'd see the day when you became a doormat. Where's your fire? Your passion?"

She freezes in the middle of folding her dough over itself, making it slowly flop back to its initial position.

Silence. No words. No movement. Just the soundtrack of the kitchen chaos happening behind me.

Finally, after thirty painful seconds, she mutters, "I'm nobody's doormat."

"Could have fooled me. You said it first. I'm the only one you need to prove yourself to."

"I. Am. Nobody's. Doormat," she repeats. Her words sound convincing, but when I look closely, I see her eyes glassing over. She sniffles and juts out her jaw. "I'm doing my job."

Words fail me. I'm ill-equipped to handle Hannah standing in front of me with tears pooling in her eyes. My arm twitches, wanting to reach out to her. It's getting harder and harder to resist. "Hey. I'm sorry."

The surprise on her face matches mine. I shouldn't need to apologize for being honest. But that's not why I said it. She looks hurt, and knowing I caused it makes me feel truly sorry. This entire plan of making her hate me is so much harder than I ever thought it would be.

"If I didn't want to fetch ingredients, I wouldn't. I'm trying here. *Trying* to prove to you that I can do this job without creating drama. There's no reason for me to make an issue over a non-issue."

She thinks she can't stand up for herself because she's creating drama? Is that why she spaced out after I interrupted her with Ivan? Or why she froze when I walked past her in the cooler? Because she wants to say something but she's trying to stay silent?

This woman is becoming more complex with each interaction. The Hannah I once knew had a fierce intensity, and she didn't back down from anything. She never would have stayed silent. As much as I respect her not wanting to cause drama, I want to pull that Hannah back out.

"Standing up for yourself isn't an issue, Hannah. They'll treat you how you allow them to."

But those two sentences don't seem to relax her pained expression at all, and I can't figure out why.

I've never been great with puzzles. Never enjoyed them and never sought to solve them. So I can't explain why I keep obsessing over this one.

Beyond that, the pieces I thought I wanted making up the picture of my life are no longer the ones I'm trying to fit together.

12

HANNAH

Don't Waste Your Time

Can you get whiplash from someone else's mood swings? One minute Caleb is being kind and compassionate; the next he's making a scathing restaurant review from Pete Wells feel like a glowing recommendation. Teenage Caleb was never like this. He was measured, readable… dare I say, predictable. The man who just walked away from me isn't the same one I loved. He's changed a lot in his years away, so I can't even say I know him anymore.

I'm well aware how competitive and serious French culinary schools can be, but do they have an actual class on berating your brigade?

His hot and cold demeanour is both crushing and reassuring. On one hand, he's no longer the boy I loved, so it's easier to remain detached and focus on my work. On the other, I realize how much I miss what we once had. Not to mention, it's a constant reminder that I'll probably never find it again.

We limp our way through dinner service with a lot of shouting, sweating, and mistakes, all while my thoughts linger on Caleb. A record number of dishes don't even make it through his final inspection, and I don't think it's because he is being exceptionally tough. It results in thirty percent more work than we should be doing and a lot of food waste. No wonder the profit margins in this place are so slim.

I drag myself in my door at 9pm, grateful I was on an earlier shift today, and smile at Akili when she runs to greet me. There's something so honest and pure about the love of a dog that makes me feel so unworthy, yet so happy to be able to receive it and give it to her in return. If any human tried to lick their butt while lying on my pillow, I'd be unlikely to feel the same way.

"Hi, baby girl. Guess what."

She tilts her head at me as if she understands, and she's waiting for a reply.

"I have the whole day off tomorrow," I tell her as I scoop her into my arms.

"You're home early."

I look up to find my mom in the shadows of the living room again. It's not past her normal bedtime, but I can't figure out why she chooses to sit in the dark.

"Do you want me to pitch in for the hydro bill?" I ask, flicking on the lamp in the corner of the room. Immediately, I wish I hadn't.

My mother is seated on the sofa, wearing a silk negligee. A sight my eyes can never unsee.

"What are you wearing?" I panic and frantically look for the lamp switch to plunge us back into darkness.

"Oh, Hannah. Your father's flight landed about two hours ago, and I was trying to surprise him. I didn't think you'd be home so early."

Gag. I haven't eaten since lunch, but the thought of interrupting my parents' sex life has my appetite running far and fast. "Suddenly, I wish I could have put in for overtime."

My mom chuckles. "Don't be silly. How do you think you appeared? I certainly didn't use a turkey baster."

She knows I'm a chef. That I *use* a turkey baster on occasion for its intended purpose. And now she's gone and given me another mental image I'll never get rid of.

"Gee, thanks for that. I'm taking Akili for a walk. Just… hang a sock on the doorknob or something." I make an exaggerated gagging sound, because even at my age, the thought of my parents having a more active sex life than me is a little depressing.

Without waiting for another response that will leave me with a new level of trauma, I clip on Akili's leash with her still in my arms and walk back out the door.

My dad's job as a pilot has meant my mom and I were alone a lot. We were a lot closer until I started culinary school. Then I made some bad choices that drove a wedge between us we're still repairing. I haven't even talked to her much about Caleb being my new boss. Yes, she told me I could come to her even if she doesn't have answers, but I can't bring myself to voice my feelings when I haven't figured them out myself.

The problem is, she'll read more into it than she should. Caleb has changed, and so have I.

I want to talk to someone about it, and as much as I love Akili's uncanny ability to tell me what I need to hear, I need someone objective who isn't my own subconscious dishing out tough love. And clearly my mother has other plans for the night. So I decide to call my dear friend, Vida, in hopes she can talk some sense into me.

"Hey, working girl. I mean… No, that's not right. Sorry." Vida laughs, immediately putting me at ease.

"Hey. How were you feeling after our night out? I was in rough shape."

She laughs again. "I didn't drink as much as you did, so I was okay. I was meaning to call you, actually."

"Oh, yeah? How come?"

Silence. For far too many seconds. I pull my phone away from my ear to make sure we're still connected.

"You kept talking about seeing *him* again. How he broke your heart." She breathes a heavy sigh. "Please don't tell me Todd has returned."

"What? Oh, my gosh. No. Not Todd." Then I hold the silence, knowing this is the opening I need to talk to someone. "Caleb. My new job... My boss is Caleb."

"As in your one true love, Caleb? High school sweetheart, Caleb?"

"Mm-hmm." I tug at Akili's leash after she pauses to sniff a random mailbox for much longer than necessary.

"I thought he was in Europe somewhere. France?"

"He was. Turns out he got back earlier this year and his world-class education landed him a job as the top dog of one of the city's premiere restaurants." I cut across the street to enter into Blantyre Park, where I can let Akili sniff to her heart's content.

"No wonder you drank so much. How are things going so far?"

"Honestly, it's harder than I thought. He hasn't acknowledged anything about our past. Then he has moments where he reminds me of the boy I loved so much, and it makes it hard to hate him for how he left. He's my boss, so I need to be professional, but outside of work hours, I *want* to hate him, and I can't."

"So you don't think you guys can reignite the flame that once was? Is that totally out of the question?"

"Absolutely impossible," I reply without hesitation. "Too much has happened to even consider that. I guess it's just those lingering feelings of what could have been, you know? What if he hadn't run off, and we went according to our plan? How would things look now?"

"Well, if I'm being honest with you, dwelling on that won't change anything. You can't go back and stop him from leaving or get a complete do-over. So it's best to just focus on who you are now and what you want in the future. If it's too hard working with him, keep putting resumes out and see if something else comes up."

That's a reasonable suggestion. So why do I hate that idea so much? Then again, I hardly have a stellar track record for making logical decisions where men I've loved are concerned and tend to justify things for the sake of my comfort zone. That has never served me well before.

"Yeah, I'll think about it. I love the kitchen and the other staff are finally warming up to me, so it's a better environment than *Harvest*—"

"Anything would be," Vida interrupts.

"That's true. I just need to figure out where I see myself in a few years and whether it's worth the emotional roller coaster. If I keep focusing on my job and doing that well, I think I can handle it." There I go... justifying again.

"Well, keep me posted. My new job doesn't have a kitchen or I would ask you to come work with me again. But hey, if *Hibiscus* is hiring bartenders or waitstaff, holla at your girl, okay?"

"Deal." I pause for a second to watch Akili plop down in the grass, all but guaranteeing I'll have to carry her back home. "Tell Cosmo Akili says hi. And thanks... for letting me vent."

"I will. You know I'm here for you any time."

"Thank you. Likewise, even if I'm a disaster." I pause for several seconds, forcing my failures from my mind. "Tell me what's going on with you, since I have no memory from Tuesday night."

My friend and I chat while I pick up Akili and walk back toward my home. Vida talks about her new job, some new people she's met, and how much I embarrassed myself on our girls' night. As mortifying as the recounting of events is, it distracts me until I get to my front door.

My dad's car is in the driveway, so I'm hopeful he's been home long enough my parents have made it behind their closed bedroom door. Though, that's not much of a reprieve since the walls of our old house are thin. I'm not sure any walls are ever thick enough for this scenario.

Vida and I make a tentative plan to meet up with Angel on our next co-ordinating day off, then end our call as I walk inside. I place Akili on the ground and she goes tearing down the hallway toward our bedroom. Go figure, now she has excess energy. I slip off my shoes and follow her path, assuming she's gone to my room.

She has not. She's sitting in front of my parents' bedroom door, which, to my horror, has my father's airline-issued tie hanging from the knob.

If Akili could talk, she'd be telling me, *"Grow up, Hannah. They're in love. It's not their fault you have a history of choosing men who don't value you. Focus on your goals and my cute face, and one day, you'll find your ride or die who won't break your heart."*

I stand in the hallway, contemplating what Vida said and Akili's pointed advice, but that is short-lived. My mother's voice carries through the door and since I'd like to be able to make eye contact with my parents in the future, I high-tail it into my room to find my headphones.

This is definitely not the way I saw things working out ten years ago when I thought I had a clear direction for my life. But, much like people, plans change, and I just need to figure out what my plan is now.

13

CALEB

Because Of You

"Um, Chef?"

"What?" I snap at Maria, who is interrupting my efforts to fix another one of Ivan's mistakes. My frustration is obvious that he hasn't made the slightest effort to improve over the last month.

"There's a couple in the lobby without a reservation. They asked to see you."

Before I can reply, Maria says the words I've been dreading for the past two months.

"They said they're your parents, so you might want to—"

"Fine. Tell them I'll be out in a minute," I demand, while trying to finish this entrée, because I refuse to let Ivan screw up another one. Suddenly, all of my passion for creating a fantastic meal dissipates like a plume of smoke. Henry McNamara has a special way of doing that.

Worse yet, when I look up after plating the third attempt at this customer's meal, Hannah is looking at me like she understands the implications of my parents showing up. That's the problem when you have history with someone. Some secrets can't stay that way because you can't start with a clean slate. I don't acknowledge her concerned expression before I untie my apron and exit into the dining room.

Sure enough, there are Henry and Noa McNamara, both looking as sour as an unripe guava, but not nearly as good for my health.

I don't know how to greet them, if I'm being honest. I haven't called Henry "Dad" in over a decade. My mother hardly behaves like one to me or Sophie. Calling either of them by their first name will set off a tirade I'd rather avoid in my place of work. So I skip pleasantries and titles altogether.

"What are you doing here?"

"That's no way to greet your parents," Henry says with the same condescending tone that marked most of my childhood. "We came to see what you abandoned your family for."

The laugh that bursts out of me is not one of humour, and I can tell by the look on my mother's face, she understands that. "You seem to be mistaken. You're the one who abandoned me, remember?"

"That's not how I remember it at all. You were told there would be consequences for your actions." Henry steps forward, but I'm not the little kid he looked down on anymore. I'm taller than him by a few inches, broader, and, as much as I hate to say it, equally stubborn.

"Henry." My mother places a hand on my father's forearm, which he shrugs off. She doesn't say anything else, and I hate seeing her concede after one slight gesture.

I really don't want to get into this here. It's not the time, nor the place. "Next time you show up at a fully booked restaurant, make a reservation first." I turn back to Maria. "Find them a table in a corner somewhere." Then I walk away with a pit of dread looming in my stomach.

I return to the kitchen and immediately lock eyes with Hannah. The same expression she wore before I left the kitchen is still on her face. I don't need the rest of my staff to know about my family drama, though, so I look away and get back to the reason I'm here. Evidently, the reason I abandoned my family.

Orders continue to fly in and my staff perform their practiced movements through the kitchen. We're getting the hang of this. Everyone minus Ivan, who I think is more a case of not wanting to learn than not being able to—which is worse.

I want to be proud of the progress we've made in the short time since I took over. I still haven't assigned official roles, but I have a good idea of who will be responsible for each task. Even with the constant rotations and adjusting to each station, most of my employees are learning to pull their weight. Something about my parents' presence rips that pride away from me, and I hate that they still have that much power.

I'm driven and determined to prove that I made the right choice in abandoning my parents' plans for me—and everything else—to pursue my own goals. It's stupid, really, because I shouldn't care what they think. I could turn this place into a Michelin Star restaurant and Henry McNamara still wouldn't accept my choice. Nor would he grant his approval.

But running *McNamara Enterprises* was never my dream; it was his. Shipping and receiving goods from around the world doesn't excite me. It doesn't make me want to get up in the morning. It certainly doesn't push the limits of my creativity to new heights. I would have spent my life pushing papers and forcing a smile on my face through meetings I had no interest in. Sophie, on the other hand, thrives on closing business deals. She's far more capable of running that place than I'd ever be.

So why, after ten years, is my father still holding a grudge?

Because I went against him. He made an investment in me, in my education, and it didn't pay off for him. He doesn't make bad investments—ever. He refuses to accept that my fancy private schooling won't pay off for him like he thought it would, so he's set on making things as difficult as he can for me until I come groveling, admitting I made a mistake.

Not going to happen.

Our relationship is so strained, when I returned from France, I didn't even tell my parents I was home. I stayed with my grandparents in Muskoka until my grandmother finally encouraged me to reach out to my mother. She told me time heals, and my parents would love me no matter what. She was wrong.

I know this, because Maria is sulking back into the kitchen, carrying the two dishes that went out a few minutes ago. Dishes that I *know* were perfect.

"He said the beef is overcooked, and the escargot is so chewy, he might as well eat a used condom." Maria, who has a perpetual scowl around most people, now looks defeated. "I've had some rude customers in my day, but wow, he's something else." Her eyes pop wide, likely realizing she said that out loud and that she's talking about my parents. "I'm sorry, Chef. I didn't—"

"It's fine, Maria. That's a lot nicer than what I have to say." I take the plates from her hands and inspect them both.

Henry is wrong and I know he is, but he's the type of person who will complain just to feel as if he has some power. I'd hate to guess how many times over the years he's had someone spit or sneeze on his food or had it dropped on the floor and served to him anyway. It wouldn't surprise me if some chef scratched his butt crack with a spatula and used it to serve Henry's food. I wonder what it would do to his fragile ego if he realized he's been at the mercy of servers and cooks around the world, and some of them won't play nice. He's lucky that's not the kind of place I'm running here, and *my* pride won't allow me to screw up a meal over a longstanding grudge.

"Refire a Chateaubriand and an escargot," I call out.

"Yes, Chef," Hannah says the loudest.

The irony isn't lost on me. Hannah working away to prepare a meal for the main cause of our breakup. She doesn't know that, but I'm confident that she wouldn't send out sub-par food for any reason, even if she did.

"Ready, Chef." Hannah drops a plate of escargot on the service counter minutes later. The herb butter mousseline and garlic crème look flawless, and the snails are seared to perfection.

My instinct is to wink at her. A silent gesture to show I appreciate her skills and effort. But that's the opposite of what I told myself I'd do. "Where's my Chateaubriand?" I yell out without acknowledging Hannah's presence.

Jorge sets the entrée on the other side of me, and confirms, "Order up."

Maria returns, and based on her hopeless expression, I can only assume Henry has continued to victimize her, too.

I stop her before she picks up the freshly made dishes. "I'll deliver these. Don't worry about going back to their table. I'll ask Alec to sort them."

She finally relaxes with a small smile and exits the kitchen as fast as she entered.

"Hold down the fort for five minutes, Jorge. I'll be right back." This time, I leave my apron on so I can make my father squirm, seeing the son he invested so much money into is working in a service job, and gave up everything he knew to do it.

Sixty seconds later, I'm standing in front of my parents, noticing how irritated they both look.

I drop the plates in front of Henry, the ceramic dishes announcing their presence on the glass-top table. "Here are your fresh condoms, Sir. Enjoy."

If Henry lived in a cartoon world, he'd have steam coming from his nostrils and ears. He pushes his chair back to stand, but because they're in a cramped corner at a temporary table, there's a giant potted hibiscus behind him that stops the slide of his chair, keeping him seated. "Boy, don't disrespect me that way."

"You're the one who walked into my workplace, demanding to be served. This is me serving you for the one and only time you'll be welcome here. Eat your food and leave." I stare down at the man I lost respect for a long time ago.

But I respect myself enough to walk away.

14

HANNAH

Walking After Midnight

Henry and Noa McNamara's appearance here tonight derailed our entire dinner service. Caleb's reaction to their arrival made it pretty clear he wasn't expecting them. Once Caleb returned to his station after delivering their re-made meals, he was even crankier than normal. We limped through dinner and put out decent food, but the vibe of the room was sour.

Now the restaurant is closed, and it's just me and Alejandro left on clean-up duties. My mind is full of distractions; namely, a tall, broody, dark-haired man who prefers a black chef's coat to a traditional white one. A man I have great respect for in a professional capacity, but that's not who I really see when I look at him. A man who has been so motivated by his passion, he's created a barrier between him and his parents that obviously hasn't been demolished since my last interaction with them.

His relationship with both of his parents was tenuous back when we were teenagers. They were often gone on trips overseas for Henry's job, and there was a distinct contrast between when Caleb was staying with his beloved grandparents versus when his parents were home. That's clearly the same effect they have on him now—though his demeanour isn't particularly sunny on any other day.

I exit the prep area with a container full of vacuum-sealed portions for the *Magret de Canard* that is supposed to star as the special tomorrow, headed for the fridge, when I walk past Caleb's office door. It's open a crack with the light shining through. A quick glance, and I don't see anyone inside, so I'm assuming he forgot to turn the light off. Though, I never saw him leave.

Once I deposit the duck breasts in the cooler, I return to his office, reaching my hand inside and flicking the light off.

"Hey!"

Immediately, I switch the light back on and swing the door open. "Oh, sorry, Chef. I didn't think you were still here."

He's seated in the chair on the opposite side of his cluttered desk, now sitting upright, but judging by the condition of his hair, he was running his hands through it until a few seconds ago.

I could leave our conversation with my apology, but I don't see hardened, tough Caleb right now. He looks like the conflicted teenager I once loved who was so confident in his future plans, yet so wracked with fear over his father's reaction. So I step inside, stopping a metre away.

"Want to talk about it?" I ask, shrugging as if I'm indifferent to his feelings. I'm not, as much as I wish I was.

He shakes his head, blowing out a long exhale. "I'm fine. Nothing to talk about."

"Caleb," I say, uttering the two syllables with more affection than I should. "For five minutes, just pretend you're not Caleb McNamara, chef extraordinaire. You can be human sometimes. I promise I won't tell anyone."

For the first time since we were love-struck teenagers, I hear Caleb chuckle. I've seen him hint at a smile a few times since I started working here, but a real chuckle is an anomaly.

It's nice. The scary thing is, it floods my entire body with tingles like we just shared an intimate moment. My head starts flashing a *danger* warning, so I step back. I tell myself if he doesn't want to talk, I'll leave. Before I can reach the door, he stops me.

"He never hesitated to disown me. Made it clear that if I left, there would be no coming back. So I don't understand why he shows up in places he isn't welcome."

"Because people like him don't like to lose control. Even if they can cling to the tiniest amount, they will." I step farther into the office and lean on Caleb's desk. "It's hard for me to give you advice when it's been so long since I was around your father. And obviously that didn't go so well."

He chuckles again, which has the same effect on me as the last one. "'Didn't go so well,' is putting it mildly. Before you, I'd never seen anyone tell off Henry McNamara, so watching an eighteen-year-old girl do it was a highlight for me." He leans back in his chair, relaxing his legs so they fall open, and drops one arm against his inner thigh. Now, he's the epitome of relaxed, except his eyes still look troubled.

This is the first time Caleb has acknowledged our history. The first hint that he even remembers we were each other's best friend and first love.

"If I was the first one to confront him, it was long overdue." I pause for a moment, reflecting on that day and recalling the hatred that spewed from my mouth. "That doesn't mean I don't regret it, though. I don't regret what I said, because it was all true, but I regret—"

"Hannah…" Caleb interrupts. Now he takes his own pause, standing and stopping mere inches away from me.

I swallow down my irrational thoughts that are swirling with memories of the last time he was this close, willing myself to move away. But I can't. His imposing presence isn't the least bit intimidating. Until his eyes flash and the vulnerable Caleb standing here a second ago morphs back into boss Caleb in an instant.

"If you've clocked out, you should go." He steps back and turns around, pulling the door open wider.

The silence between us creates an awkwardness that's impossible to ignore. So too is his pointed stare, ordering me with his eyes. The dismissal hurts, even if it shouldn't.

I exit his office without casting him another glance. I'm a fool for thinking he'd actually want to talk about what happened between us like a rational adult. Like I ever mattered to him or hold any place in his life other than as a member of his kitchen staff. None of our years'-long relationship has any bearing on Caleb's life now, and I was an idiot to think otherwise. That's also why I need to stick to the job I'm paid to do. It's obvious anything above and beyond that—like treating him as a person with feelings instead of a boss with orders—isn't welcome.

With a few lingering tasks to finish, I rush through them, mutter a quick "good night" to Alejandro, and descend in the elevator to street level. The stupid weather seems intent on dishing out some sort of symbolic ambience, and it's now raining. I checked the forecast earlier today and there was no mention that I could be standing in the freezing cold November rain, waiting for a bus at midnight. Billions of dollars in equipment and they can't predict rainfall. I pull out my phone to look at the weather app, and it says *6°C, 4% chance of precipitation*. I roll my eyes as I duck into the bus shelter, at least grateful I can keep myself from getting soaked, but that doesn't stop the chill from seeping into my bones.

This time of night, buses run less often. On a dry, warm day, that's not an issue, but standing in this three-walled shelter, damp and freezing, it feels like an eternity. Fifteen minutes pass before I pull up the online schedule and see the bus I need will still be another ten minutes. I missed the last one by five minutes. If I hadn't stopped to talk to Caleb, I would have been almost home by now. Serves me right.

Like I really need another lesson to teach me to keep out of his way and stick to my work. He made it clear a long time ago how he really felt about me.

Maybe Vida has a point. If it's too hard to work with him, I should just keep putting my resume out to different places. It could be good to get out of the city and find somewhere new. Strike out on my own and prove to myself and everyone else that I can be a functioning adult.

I consider the logistics of leaving my friends, parents, and a job I do enjoy most aspects of while I wait. Right until a dark sporty sedan pulls up alongside the bus stop. I guarantee whoever it is isn't stopping to ask for directions.

The passenger window lowers and a shadowed face leans forward until I can see it from the light of the dashboard display screen. There's my boss, looking handsome and irritating and confusing, all at once. "Come on. I'll give you a ride."

That does sound appealing because I'm cold and I'm sure that car has heat, but the chill that radiates from Caleb would counteract that, making it pointless.

"No thanks. The bus will be here in a minute."

"Get in the car, Hannah."

15

CALEB

Just Missed the Train

Apparently, twenty minutes wasn't long enough to wait to ensure avoiding Hannah after she left my office. I mean, I could have kept going, but she's huddled in the corner of the bus stop after midnight, and I can't afford for one of my best employees to get sick. Not when we're finally gaining momentum. That's the reason I'm telling myself. Strictly professional.

"It's fine, Chef," she declines again.

I may have worked for the better part of two decades toward my role as an executive chef, but having Hannah call me *Chef* outside of work tells me I've done exactly what I was trying to do and put her squarely in the employee zone. I should be happy. Instead, it stings.

"Just get in. I'll drop you home. I'm going that way, any-way."

She raises an eyebrow and steps forward, still seeking shelter inside the bus stop. "You are?"

Right, she'd have no way of knowing where I live now. I have the upper hand there, because she handed me employee forms, and I know she still lives with her parents. "Yeah, I live in Fallingbrook."

Finally, she steps forward and pulls the handle on the passenger door. I rush to put up the window so the heat can work its magic, then I flick on the seat warmer.

"Thanks. I didn't know you… How do you know I live near Fallingbrook?"

I avoid her eyes by checking my blind spot and easing back into eastbound traffic. Once I adjust to the flow of vehicles around me—which, thankfully, aren't many—I reply, "You're still at your parents' place, yeah?"

For several seconds, the only sounds are the low mumble of the radio and the rain assaulting the undercarriage of my car, being sprayed upward from the tires.

"Yeah. Not still there. *Back* there."

In addition to her address, I also know that Hannah attended a nearby college for culinary school, so I don't think she moved away for that. All of her jobs have been nearby too.

Curiosity wins out. "Why'd you move back?"

"Uh… I got a dog."

I vividly remember Hannah's obsession with getting a dog, but with her dad's schedule and her mom working full time, they never allowed her to get one. Now, with demanding hours as a chef, it makes sense she'd move back home to divide the responsibilities of dog ownership.

"Let me guess. A pug?" I ask, knowing that was her favourite breed.

She huffs a laugh and finally relaxes into her seat. "Yeah. Her name's Akili."

"Akili. Interesting. How did you come up with that?"

"It means bright." She hesitates for a moment. "When I got her, she was a bright spot in my life I desperately needed, and she's exceptionally wise. So it seemed like a perfect name for her."

Two things about that pique my interest. First, I'm wondering why she sounds so sad when she says she needed a bright spot. Second is the point I choose to focus on. "She's exceptionally wise? What are you? Dr. Dolittle?"

This time she releases a full chuckle, which strikes me in the nostalgic part of my heart. "No, she just has soulful eyes that make me stop and look at situations rationally. It's stupid, but she's a great life coach."

"A life coach? Interesting." I merge onto Kingston Road, which I know means Hannah's house is only a few minutes away. The last time I dropped her off here, she was in tears, and I only held mine in long enough until she was inside. I drove back to my grandparents' house that night in a daze, unsure if I had made the right choice.

Now, as I pull up in front of her house, I'm still not sure. That uncertainty is scary.

"Thanks for the ride, Caleb."

Without a backward glance, Hannah opens the door and steps out of the car. In a weird episode of déjà vu, I watch her walk away again. It doesn't hurt this time, but it does remind me that I need to maintain a boss/employee relationship without rehashing old times. Without digging up the emotional baggage left in my wake.

Once she's safe inside, I accelerate away from the curb and loop back around to head home. I may have exaggerated my proximity, because I technically live in The Beaches neighbourhood, but I knew if I said I lived fifteen minutes nearer to work, she wouldn't accept a ride.

But she can't know that, because I want to have this opportunity again.

And that's a problem.

I agreed to meet Oscar at his muay thai gym at 7am on a Sunday morning. Don't ask me why, because I don't enjoy it nearly as much as he does. Maybe it will be a good opportunity to burn off some of the lingering frustration over my back-and-forth feelings. Experience tells me I'm just liable to get my butt kicked by my cousin, who is ten years younger.

"You look tired," Oscar greets.

"I am." I chuckle and pull him in for a one-armed hug so I can rustle his blond hair. "You'll have to take it easy on me today."

He pushes himself away from me and lifts his fists into a boxing stance. "Not gonna happen. Go get changed. We'll start with jumping rope to warm up."

I grumble and walk toward the change room, where I drop my bag on the bench. My athletic experience was limited to the cross-country team in high school, but when I returned from France, I needed some kind of outlet. Since Oscar was back at home for part of his summer break and I was still staying with our grandparents, he convinced me to join him. The difference is, he's been doing kickboxing and muay thai since he was nine. It shows.

In the three minutes it takes me to stuff my things in a locker and get ready, Oscar has already gotten a head start on his warmup. He takes me through my paces, jump rope, shadow boxing, running—all of which he calls the warmup. I call it a workout. Then he takes me through three rounds of sparring and heavy bag work.

By the time we're done, I can barely lift my arms.

"I don't know why I keep coming back for this. I might need you to wash my hair," I joke.

Oscar smiles, but doesn't laugh.

"What's going on with you?"

"Me? Nothing." He spins around, grabbing a towel to wipe the sweat dripping on his forehead. Somehow, his hair still looks to be intact, and he's not even breathing a little heavy.

I don't press him. For as wild and carefree as Oscar was as a kid, he couldn't be more opposite now. He's stoic, disciplined, and reserved. As far as nineteen-year-old kids go, he's got a good head on his shoulders, so if he doesn't want to talk, I won't push him. For now.

"Hollis said you hired Hannah," Oscar says as we walk toward the locker room.

Suddenly I'm regretting not pressing for details about whatever seems to be bothering him. "Yup," I reply, holding in a groan. Mostly because I have a twelve-hour shift to get through after this and need to save my energy.

"And? How is that going?"

I grab my towel and toiletry kit from my bag and head for the showers. "She's a great chef. Hard worker. I'm happy to have her on my staff."

"Mm-hmm." Oscar steps into a shower stall, pulling the curtain closed.

I walk into the one next to him, expecting the conversation to stop.

It doesn't. He shouts over the sound of rushing water, "So how does she look?"

My shoulders tense. "What does that have to do with any-thing?"

"Ah, come on, man. How does she look? I may have been a kid when I saw her last, but I wasn't blind."

Now my jaw joins my shoulders on the tension scale and clenches tight enough I stop myself from saying something unnecessary. Not to mention, I could threaten Oscar, but that's as far as I'd get because he could pound my face in, and I'm man enough to admit that. "She looks good. She looks the same and completely different, if that makes sense."

"Not really. You still have a thing for her?"

I reach my aching arms up to wash my hair, again delaying an answer. I could confess that I never got over her. Tell him that she's always been it for me. That would mean admitting something out loud that I'm trying to keep under control.

So I lie. "Nah, but I'm not blind, either."

Monday mornings are notoriously daunting. For people in a seven-day-a-week industry, they're just as exhausting as every other day. I've worked the last five days, but Adriano asked to switch shifts with me for later in the week, meaning I've got Wednesday and Thursday off. It will be nice to have a full forty-eight hour break. For now, that means dragging myself out of bed, disturbing my dog, and getting ready for day six of seven straight.

My dad is in his uniform, sitting at the kitchen table, watching the radar on his tablet. "Morning, Buttercup. Working again today?"

"Yeah. I switched shifts, but I have two days in a row off after this stretch." I reach into the cabinet to grab a coffee mug. "Where are you off to?"

"Nassau, Bahamas again, then Santiago, Chile. I'll be back Friday night. I have to leave in thirty minutes. If you want a ride, I'll drop you off on my way."

"Thanks, Dad. That'd be great. Did you eat?"

He waves off my leading question. "Don't go trying to fatten me up. I had some oatmeal."

I can't say I'm disappointed with that answer. After five days in a restaurant kitchen and a long upcoming shift, I don't really want to cook, anyway. "Ungrateful, I tell ya," I tease.

I rush to get ready, first by feeding Akili and letting her outside, then having a quick shower. My parents are in the front hall saying their farewells as I round the corner. Each time I see how much they love each other, it makes me grateful to have their example, but also discouraged I'll never find that with anyone else.

Except Akili. She looks at me with that same affection, and I'm confident I return it. I give her a pat on the head right before my dad and I walk out the door. We climb into his sedan and head west toward *Hibiscus*.

My dad and I make easy conversation the entire way, which only takes twenty-five minutes. He drops me off at the main entrance with a few parting words. "I'm proud of you, Buttercup."

"Thanks, Dad. I'll see you when you get back." I lean over to give him a seated hug before climbing out of the car. When I was little, I used to worry every time my dad left for a flight. I was young during the events of 9/11, but I still understood the days of airplane travel changed forever. Now, I still worry, but after each flight he's returned home safely from, that concern has lessened a little more.

My dad merges back into traffic, and I walk inside the ornate lobby. The one face I'm not expecting to see is staring at me with a thousand questions dancing in his eyes.

"Hi," I say as I approach Caleb near the elevator to the right of the entrance.

"Hey," he replies, now turning to press the up button, even though someone else has already pushed it.

The elevator doors open and we're corralled inside by other employees or clients from the other businesses in the building. Everyone else is wearing neat suits and expensive jewellery, which makes me feel like I should be riding in the service elevator like the help. I sneak a glance at Caleb, wanting an ally to relate to. He may have been raised by a man who runs a multi-million dollar company, but he's never acted like a spoiled rich kid. Probably because he never was a spoiled rich kid.

Most of the crowd exits on the ninth floor, leaving me, Caleb, and one other grey-haired woman to ride the next three floors in silence. Caleb and I exit, but he doesn't stop to continue our conversations beyond hello.

Ever since he drove me home on Friday, he's been weird. My standoffishness probably hasn't helped. If I'm being honest, I'm afraid to let my guard down around him, but his back and forth is both frustrating and exhausting.

Instead of dwelling on it, I try to throw myself into my work. I'm taking Adriano's spot on the fish and seafood station today, which makes me wonder if that's why he asked to switch. He's never kept his dislike for sea creatures a secret.

"Hannah."

My shoulders tense at the sound of Ivan's voice. He's given me a wide berth lately, but his random winking, waggling eyebrows, and creepy grins have not gone unnoticed.

"Yes, Ivan?"

"Did you know lobster is an aphrodisiac?" he asks, brushing himself up against me.

I try to ignore it, continuing to slice and skewer the lobster tails for dinner. "So is a strong work ethic, Ivan. You should try it sometime."

He chuckles and manoeuvres himself to stand beside me, resting his butt on the prep table. Gross.

Before I can open my mouth to tell him to move, a loud, angry voice booms behind me.

"Get back to work, Ivan. I'm sick of telling you. Start pulling your weight, or you'll be out of a job."

I don't turn to look at Caleb, but I lift my gaze to take in Ivan's condescending smirk.

"Yeah, good luck with that, *boss man*. You might think you have power in this kitchen, but it ends with me. The only reason I don't have your job is because I didn't want it." He pushes himself to stand and steps closer to Caleb.

It's one thing when he's attempting to flirt with me or flaking on his responsibilities, but it's another for him to insult what Caleb offers this restaurant. I drop the lobster tail in my hands and tug off my disposable gloves as I turn around. This time, I don't let Caleb speak before I do. "See, Ivan, that's where you're wrong. You don't have the job of executive chef because your uncle wants his business to succeed. Of the two men in front of me, only one is capable of making that happen. So how 'bout you listen to your *boss man* and do the job you actually have? Hmm?"

Both men stand side by side, staring at me. Neither speaks for about ten seconds until Caleb clears his throat.

"Try me, Ivan. Family loyalty only goes so far when your multi-million dollar investment is at stake. Get back to work."

This time, Ivan listens to the instructions. He gives me another unwanted wink before slinking away.

I avoid Caleb's eyes by turning back around and grabbing a new pair of gloves. He stands behind me for a few seconds before leaving without another word.

By the end of my shift, I've successfully avoided all interactions with Caleb and Ivan that were not work related. I wish some of the other women here were a little more approachable because having friends at my last job made all the difference. Granted, they were part of the reason I stuck around for so long, and why I quit, but it was nice having friendly faces there to see every day. Here, Caleb is the only person I've had any interaction with outside of work, and that can't happen again. It just... can't. Sitting in the front of his car, mere inches from him, felt too much like when we were younger and he'd drive to the city— usually in his grandmother's Volvo while his parents were out of the country. We'd lose entire days exploring The Scarborough Bluffs and talking about our future. A future that we always discussed as happening together. Until one day, he decided I wouldn't be a part of his anymore.

Just thinking about it breaks my heart all over again. How could I have been so naïve and foolish, thinking a nineteen-year-old guy was ready to commit his life to me? That started an ongoing trend of stupid decisions and foolish thinking on my part. But I'm not that naïve, idiotic girl anymore. I'm jaded. Cynical. More notably, I'm guarded and don't want to give anyone else the opportunity to break my heart again. Least of all Caleb, because our history gives him greater likelihood of crushing me beyond repair.

So I exit *Hibiscus* without looking back, counting down the hours until my day off so I can reset. I need a girls' night and some of Akili's sage advice. Tonight, though, I'll settle for some sleep.

17

CALEB

Bad Reputation

My phone ringing jolts me awake, and I'd be annoyed about it if it wasn't one person I am always happy to talk to.

"How did you know I was just going to call you?" I answer. Maybe not "just", but I did want to call Sophie today.

"Twin intuition. My ears were burning."

I laugh as I adjust myself in the bed to sit up and stretch.

"Caleb McNamara, are you still in bed? At 10:40?" My sister is perceptive if she figured that out from the minimal noise I just made.

"I got home late. Not all of us operate on banker's hours."

"Ooh, do tell. How are things with Hannah?" she sing-songs.

I blow out a breath, then crack my neck, buying myself some time to answer that. "I'm the executive chef of a popular restaurant, Soph. Long hours have nothing to do with Hannah. Boring work stuff."

"Well, that's anticlimactic." She pauses for a moment before launching into a summary of her latest failed first date, through which I question the deadbeat's motives and she defends him—as per usual. We also end up arguing about our father—as per usual.

Instead of a conversation with my sister giving me a modicum of peace, I feel on edge. Angry. Frustrated that she allows our father to control her life. But when I think back to his visit at the restaurant last week, it's clear he still has some control over me too, despite my efforts to put an ocean and a decade between us.

Our conversation is cut short by Sophie's assistant needing her for something, so we hang up with an empty promise to get together on my next day off. I might as well get ready for work now that I'm awake. And I'll keep telling myself that it's my commitment to my job that makes me want to show up early.

Another day, another dollar… or however that saying goes. It's also another day, another several hours in a cramped, sweaty kitchen with the woman I can't seem to stay away from. The one who was dropped off yesterday in a car I hope was a ride-share, but I have no business being upset if it wasn't. Just because I shouldn't be doesn't mean I'm not.

When I walked in a few hours ago, Hannah was hard at work. So much so, I don't think she has noticed my arrival, so I pretend like I need to check in on what she's doing. I bet her pug doesn't even beg for attention like this.

She doesn't allow my presence to distract her and continues working without acknowledging me.

Like I've been reminding myself all along, I settle into my role as executive chef and start directing traffic amongst my staff, ensuring we put out incredible food.

We knock out every order with very few hiccups for the rest of lunch service. The entire time, Hannah keeps her distance, and I'm not sure if it's just her responsibility at the meat station today or her desire to stay away from me that's the cause. I'd like to think she's a consummate professional and that's why she's so focused. Common sense tells me she's feeling weird about our last interaction. I shouldn't have been so dismissive after she defended me to Ivan. The fact she stood up for me after how things ended between us tells me the same fierce Hannah is still lurking under the surface. And I so desperately want to see more of that fire.

While everyone carries on preparations for dinner service, I duck into my office to sit for a moment. My thoughts are more complicated than an ancient *mole poblano* recipe and far more time consuming. At least if I spent a few days trying to craft the perfect Mexican sauce, I'd have something to show for it. In this case, I'm just wasting time and energy I don't have to spare.

Get a grip.

Maybe I need to get my hands dirty and create something. If I can direct my passion there, less will be available to aim at Hannah.

I exit my office and walk into the cooler to grab a few ingredients I know we need for tonight. For the next thirty minutes, I work silently alongside my staff to prepare for another great night.

But even once I finish crafting the perfect sauces to complement our menu, my passion still isn't where it should be. Hopefully that will change when diners start to appear in twenty minutes.

"The lady who ordered the special was taking notes and pictures," Maria reports.

Hannah and I exchange a glance. Chances are that means we have a food critic or blogger in the dining room who isn't very good at keeping herself covert. That means it could be my first opportunity to prove myself since taking over.

I stand tall and address all the staff who heard Maria's observation. "That changes nothing. We keep putting out food and deliver the same quality we send out to every customer in here. Just carry on, business as normal. Got it?"

"Yes, Chef," everyone replies.

Something about the potential for having their work critiqued by someone other than me or regular customers has all of my staff on their games. Not just the possible critic's food, but everyone else's goes out without a hitch. The waitstaff flow in and out of the kitchen seamlessly, and only one dish is returned because the customer forgot to disclose an allergy.

Hannah really stepped up tonight. I was feeling torn between her and Jorge as my head chef, but if I'm being honest, Hannah is head and shoulders above Jorge in terms of skill. The only reason I'd choose him over her is because she's more talented with food and he's better at directing people. Regardless of her job title, though, she'll still be around, and my priority needs to be this restaurant's success.

So when she's done her shift, I do something out of character.

"Hannah?" I call as she hangs her apron by the service elevator.

"Yes, Chef?" She brushes her hair from her face and straightens to look at me.

"Good job tonight. Thank you for... well, for working hard."

She flashes a brief smile that looks a lot like the one she used to give me before she ducked around a corner and wanted me to follow her. Like she did at her parents' anniversary party, which was the day we transitioned from acquaintances whose mothers were friends to a whirlwind teenage romance.

But that's not why she's smiling at me today.

"Thanks, Chef. See you Friday, I guess."

I freeze for a second until a dish clanking in the background startles me into action again. I forgot she traded shifts, so she has the next two days off. Now I wish I had scheduled her later today so I could have driven her home again.

No. I can't. A few days apart will be good. That's what I need to get my head back on straight.

If I had any doubts about Hannah's impact on my kitchen, they were put to rest over her two days off. I put in three times as much effort to keep everyone in line when she wasn't here, and by Thursday night, I had run out of patience. I thought the two days apart would help me refocus and find my love for creating amazing food again, but I'm so bogged down by the business side of things, without Hannah around, I struggled to find anything to enjoy about it.

Watching her walk in now, looking refreshed and gorgeous, I'm questioning where my real inspiration lies. One other thing I notice as she hangs her purse and tugs out a newspaper is the wide smile she's wearing.

With a confidence she hasn't shown aside from when she's cooking, she saunters over to me and slaps down the newspaper on the counter. "Look."

I'm curious what she's trying to show me, but every decision-making component of my brain wants to look at her.

"Look," she prompts again.

I tear my eyes away from her smile and comply. The newspaper is open to the lifestyle section with a title *New Chef, New Era for Troubled Restaurant, Hibiscus*. I grab the paper and start reading.

Hibiscus *isn't a new feature in the city, with its iconic waterfront location, high-end furnishings, and marketing promises that have fallen short in recent years. My first experience in the twelfth-floor dining room was underwhelming.*

My stomach is in knots as I read that far. The reputation that preceded me isn't a surprise by any means, but it sucks that people are still dwelling on it. I continue skim reading with the paper scrunched in both hands until I get to the actual critique.

Under the direction of Chef Caleb McNamara, Hibiscus *has ushered itself into a new era. One that is marked by fresh takes on comforting classics.*

She goes on to detail all three courses, naming each herb and spice in her meal with impressive accuracy. She doesn't mention a single flaw and finishes off the article by stating *A lobster hasn't excited me this much since Sebastian burst into song with Ariel at my fourth-grade sleepover. Chef McNamara really has me believing everything from under the sea is, in fact, better once he's brought it onto dry land and cooked it to perfection.*

I stare at the words for a few more seconds, blinking and refocusing, trying to confirm I just read what I think I did. When I tear my eyes away to look at Hannah, her broad smile confirms that this is a glowing review.

"It... it's good."

"Did you ever have any doubt? It's amazing. And to top it off, we know how much you love a *Little Mermaid* reference."

I cringe, recalling my jab at Hannah about her undercooked flounder. In an effort to make up for that jab, I add, "Sophie always loved that movie because Ariel defied her father. I'm not ashamed to admit I know the lyrics to every song."

An awkward pause lingers between us instead of the laugh I expected.

"The fact you've turned this place around so quickly is astonishing. Now everyone in the city will know *Hibiscus* isn't a one-hit wonder anymore."

In what I'd think is an out-of-body experience, Hannah wraps her arms around me in a tight hug. It takes my brain a few seconds to catch up to what's happening before I drop the newspaper and reciprocate. It's the closest we've been in ten years, and it feels equal parts right and wrong. Right for my personal life. Wrong for my professional one.

When she looks up at me with her gleaming eyes, I don't care about my professional life right now. My only goal is to taste her lips. To discover if that electric spark still exists between us. If the way she affects me is familiarity or an undeniable chemistry I've never found elsewhere.

But she loosens her grip and pulls away, taking the flicker of hope with it. She clears her throat and smooths down her shirt.

The fact she's so excited when she did so much of the work and I'm on the receiving end of the praise feels unfair, and I want to acknowledge that. She should know how much I appreciate her talent and hard work in rebuilding this restaurant. But she seems intent on stopping *my* intentions short, because she walks away before I can. And I can't be upset with her for that, since I was the one who walked away first.

18

HANNAH

Catch My Breath

Two days away from *Hibiscus* left me bored out of my mind, other than the few hours I met up with Angel and Vida for dinner. Talking things out with them made me come home more confused than ever. What should have been a relaxing and restful two days off was exhausting and frustrating. Every meal I ate, I analyzed its marketability. Every message I received, I wondered if it was Caleb needing a favour or a co-worker asking me to cover their shift. Important to note, Caleb has never once asked me for a favour.

Beyond that, I spent countless hours searching every local food blogger's website, all the Lifestyle sections of the newspapers, and set up a Google alert on *Hibiscus*, so I'd be notified if any news stories popped up. Call me a girl obsessed. Though, I'm not sure it's anything to do with the restaurant... or the food.

Being back in the kitchen today felt a lot more like coming home than being at home did. Despite Akili's stern warnings to protect my heart at all costs, I can't seem to stop my figurative brick wall from crumbling.

Caleb's success is important to me. It shouldn't be, because he walked out of my life and didn't give a second thought to mine. Not until I submitted my resume and my skills could benefit him. So why do I care so much?

Because he's seeped under my skin like herbed butter on a Thanksgiving turkey.

So now, as I wait in the lobby for my dad to pick me up after returning from Chile, all I can think about is how it felt to be back in Caleb's arms. I didn't mean to hug him, but excitement took over, and reason fled.

"Hannah?" That recognizable deep voice calls from behind me.

I spin around to find Caleb. "Yes, Chef?" I ask, wondering if I missed a task when closing up the kitchen.

"What are you doing?"

"Uh… waiting for my dad. He was supposed to pick me up on his way home. His flight should have landed a few hours ago." Now, saying the words out loud, some of that childhood worry trickles back in.

"Oh. Have you tried calling him?" Caleb's eyebrows collapse together as he steps forward.

That would have been a reasonable step fifteen minutes ago, but I didn't want to interrupt him if he was driving. "Maybe I should." I flash him an awkward smile, feeling a little foolish. I'm claiming my brain is as fried as the scallops I spent the day searing.

The phone rings four times before my dad answers, breathing heavily. "Sorry, Buttercup."

"Sorry for what? What's wrong?"

Again, Caleb steps closer until he's inches away.

"My car was stolen from the parking garage. I had to contact security, then file a police report. It's been a headache. Now I tried to get a rental so I could come pick you up, but nothing is available. That's what I get for having my car stolen on a Friday night."

"Oh no. Don't worry about me. I can take the bus. Can you call a ride-share?"

Caleb places his hand on my forearm and mouths *what happened?*

"One second, Dad." I place my hand over the mouthpiece and relay the update to Caleb, hoping that will ease his curiosity and he'll stop looming over me with his delicious cologne and irresistible brown eyes.

Instead, he says, "Let's go pick him up. It's not that far out of the way and it's late." He doesn't wait for me to reply before he's pulling his keys from his pocket and moving toward the elevator.

Meanwhile, I'm frozen. It's been an unspoken topic in our house ever since my parents first found out I was working for Caleb. Allowing him to pick my dad up from the airport is a task so far beyond duties a boss should perform, I'm afraid my dad will think we've blurred lines. Or that he'll think more of the situation than it is.

But with another head nod, gesturing for me to join him at the elevator, it's hard to say no. Impossible, really.

"Just wait there, Dad. Caleb is going to give me a ride and we'll come pick you up."

He tries to argue, but Caleb waves off the suggestion Dad find an alternative mode of transportation. So, without further argument, I hang up the phone and join Caleb in the elevator to head down to the parking garage.

"Why did you stop in the lobby?" I ask, not ready to acknowledge what's happening.

"Normally, the dishwasher is the last person out, but Alejandro left five minutes before me. I had to stop to let security know the floor is empty."

"Oh." Good thing I've never been the last person to leave, because I would have neglected that step.

The elevator door dings and we step out into the parking garage. Caleb has a designated parking spot to the left of the elevators. Perks of the job, you could say. I climb into the front seat, wondering how to explain to my father why Caleb offered in the first place.

Instead of mulling it over for the ten-minute drive to the airport, I blurt, "My parents loved you, too." Now is the time to open the passenger door and do a Charlie's Angel roll onto the pavement just to escape my own stupidity.

Caleb says nothing as he turns westbound on Lakeshore Boulevard. Then he utters the two syllables I hate to love when they spill from his mouth: "Hannah."

"Sorry. I didn't mean anything by that. It just… came out." Did I really just liken my words to an accidental fart? It just came out? Really, Hannah?

"It's fine." He's quiet for the rest of the drive, which thankfully isn't long.

I could elaborate on what I said and explain that I just meant my dad will be happy to see him again, but I think the damage is done.

When we pull up to the curb in front of my dad, I jump out and disguise my escape as a welcome home hug.

"Did you get everything sorted with security and the police report?" I ask after he lets me go.

"For tonight. I'll have to deal with insurance in the—" My dad's words halt and his eyes redirect from me to something else.

I know what that something is the second he stops speaking.

"Caleb. Well, would you look at you? All grown up and making me feel old. Thanks for coming to an old man's rescue."

They greet each other with a handshake, then Caleb replies, "No problem, Sir. I'm happy to help. I'm headed your way, anyway."

"Really? Well, isn't that a funny coincidence?" My father smirks at me. Actually smirks. Like he's just been let in on a scandalous secret.

Meanwhile, Caleb's address probably has more to do with affordability and what was available when he accepted his job at *Hibiscus* than proximity to my childhood home. He had no way of knowing I still lived there before he moved in. Or maybe he did. His mother likes to spread news around like it's her job.

In an effort to ease the awkwardness, I tell my dad to get in the front seat and I hop in the back. Caleb tucks Dad's carry-on into the trunk, and we're off.

The men make conversation for the full thirty-minute drive with little input from me. Not that they exclude me, but I feel it's safer to stay silent so I don't have another word-fart episode. They discuss the hassle of dealing with insurance, the downfall of society as a whole, and the potential for new car shopping. I never pictured Caleb as a car guy, as evidenced by his modest Camry he probably drove right off the lot—practical and reliable; not flashy. He seems to enjoy discussing the topic with my dad, though.

He pulls into our driveway, where my dad's sedan would normally park, and my father asks, "Do you want to come in for a minute, son? Catherine would love to see you."

Caleb eyes me in the rear-view mirror. I resist the urge to express my feelings on the matter with a throat-cutting gesture. Instead, I smile.

"Sure, yeah. I'll come in to say hi. It's late, so I won't keep you. I'm sure you're tired."

"Oh, none of that. Just because I'm old doesn't mean I need a siesta after a day of work. Let me just go in to make sure she's decent."

Just when I thought I couldn't embarrass myself more, my dad comes in clutch. He climbs out of the car as Caleb insists he'll grab Dad's bag.

I exit onto the light dusting of snow in the driveway and walk around to the trunk. Finally, I'm able to say the words I was too cowardly to say before. "I just meant he'd be excited to see you again. Not anything else. The past is in the past, and that's where it belongs." Okay, that was more than I needed or wanted to say. I really need to stop talking.

Caleb's shoulders slump as the trunk pops open. "Yeah. I hear you loud and clear." He hoists the suitcase out and closes the trunk with his free hand. "Maybe just tell your parents I had to—"

"Well, if it isn't Caleb McNamara, as I live and breathe?" My mom is standing on the front porch in a robe. A red satin robe, to be specific. "Get over here and give me a hug, young man."

I send Caleb an apologetic smile, but it's so dark out, now that the car lights have turned off, I'm not sure how well he can see it. He places his empty hand on my lower back to let me walk in front of him and lead the way.

The short distance feels so much like it did back in the day when Caleb would drop me home. He'd come in to say goodbye to my parents each time, and they'd be almost as sad as I was to see him leave, knowing it would be at least a week before I saw him again.

And now that I see him five days a week, I miss him more than I ever have.

19

CALEB

Heat

I t was surreal dropping Hannah off last week. That gets eclipsed by the intimidating feeling of approaching her parents on the front porch. I might be nearing thirty, but there's just something about the situation that makes me feel like a kid again. Part of me wishes we were back there, but as Hannah confirmed, *"The past is in the past, and that's where it belongs."*

Clearly, I'm the only one of us who is having memories of the past.

"Mrs. Parker, nice to see you," I greet, striding up the three steps, passing Warren his bag, and giving Catherine a hug.

"So good to see you, Caleb," Catherine replies, leaning back out of our brief hug, still holding onto both of my arms. "Come in. I'm freezing my fanny off out here." She doesn't wait for me to agree or argue.

After Hannah's pointed words moments ago, I would prefer to go home to sulk, but Catherine and Warren have always been good to me. I follow Catherine into the house that doesn't look like it has changed at all. There's something comforting about that. My mother doesn't have much else to do with herself beyond spending Henry's money and redecorating, so their home never looks the same two visits in a row. Granted, those visits are few and far between. Even after ten years, aside from a new sofa and some updated photos, the Parkers' living room looks just as I remember it.

With one major difference. A small dog lifts its head from the chair, then, with an exaggerated stretch, saunters over to the crowd in the foyer.

I bend down to let her sniff my hand when she comes to investigate me. "You must be Akili. I'm Caleb."

She licks the side of my palm, making me laugh at her wrinkled face. I give her a pat on the head before I stand to face the three other humans in the room. Akili jumps up at my leg and stares at me with her big, expressive eyes. Almost like she's trying to tell me something.

"She likes you," Hannah declares. She gives me a tight smile as she bends down to pick up her beloved pet.

"Doesn't seem like she's too hard to please," I reply, watching as she kisses Hannah's chin.

"Oh, you're wrong there. She follows me around all day, every day, like a micromanaging Karen, and I can never do anything right. Pleased is not something she comes by easily," Catherine adds. There's a long, awkward pause for several seconds before she continues, "Congratulations on your glowing review. Hannah was pretty excited this morning." She glances at her daughter, who is now blushing.

Mention of the review gives me the chance to say what I wanted to earlier. "She deserves all the credit. She's been a great asset to the kitchen."

Instead of looking proud or excited about my praise, Catherine and Warren's shoulders drop, along with the smiles on their faces.

Another awkward silence.

"Well, I should—"

"We'll let you two catch up for a bit." Catherine turns away, wearing a scheming smile. "Come on, Stud. Let me welcome you home." Then she drags Warren down the hallway of their bungalow as he shouts back his appreciation for picking him up.

More awkward silence resumes as I watch their retreating backs, wondering if that just happened. Doesn't seem like the type of thing I'd dream up. I blink and refocus on Hannah's face, which is a new shade of pink.

"I really need to find my own place," she says after a few more seconds. "I'm not sure you ever reach an age where your parents acting like newlyweds isn't just…"

Her scrunched-up face and full body shudder make me laugh.

"You're probably right. Can't say I've ever had to deal with that." I decide to change the subject, because any mention of the elder McNamaras always dampens my mood. "I'm glad you finally got your dog. Did I tell you Sophie has a labradoodle?"

Hannah's eyes widen along with her smile. "No, you didn't. We both used to talk about getting a dog someday. I know how obsessed she was with your cousin's German shepherd."

"Bond, yeah. Soph's dog, Wilson, is a big goof. Just lopes around making friends with everyone. Sophie loves him."

"I can attest to the dog-mom love. Akili is the only living thing who loves me, other than my parents, but they're basically forced to by biology."

"Not necessarily." I grimace. Love is not something my parents have ever expressed toward me or Sophie. I don't think either of them are even capable of feeling it.

Again, we stand in silence. This is getting painful and repetitive.

"Caleb, I'm sorry. I didn't mean—"

"It's fine. Well, I should get going. Another long day tomorrow."

"Yeah. Okay." Hannah's smile has disappeared, and now the corners of her lips are tilted downward. "Thanks for the ride and for picking up my dad."

"You're welcome. Gotta keep my staff operating in peak form, and that means getting some rest." I step forward and pat Akili on the head.

Her curly little tail starts wagging as she wiggles in Hannah's arms.

"Bye, Akili." Then I look her beautiful owner in the eyes and utter, "Bye, Hannah."

I exit the house that holds more positive memories than my childhood home ever did, walk to my car, and drive home through the falling snow.

I couldn't sleep last night, so getting through today's shift was torture. My mind was reeling over Hannah's words that our past needs to stay in the past. I feel equal parts stupid, disappointed, and relieved. It's tough to navigate. All I've wanted for years was to run my own restaurant and prove to myself and everyone else that I have what it takes. But Hannah walked back into my life and all of a sudden, my one-track mind had two trains heading in opposite directions. Whether they're diverging or converging remains to be seen.

A knock at my office door startles me, because I thought everyone else had left.

"Mr. McNamara?" Sergei walks inside, eyeing the remaining mess I still haven't dealt with.

"Yes, Mr. Antonov? I didn't realize you were here so late," I reply, standing to greet him.

"Sit, sit." He drops into the chair opposite my desk. "I've been talking with our marketing team and we've decided to run a promotion featuring locally sourced ingredients for two weeks. Drive in some new traffic and generate some buzz heading into the holiday season. People are reluctant to spend money on extra things unless they have a reason to."

I stare at him for a moment, trying to wrap my head around this information. "Right. Where exactly do you think we're getting local ingredients from in November? In Ontario. At best, we'd get things grown in greenhouses, which lack the colour and flavour of superior ingredients grown elsewhere. Proteins are a different story, but we won't be able to offer any fish or seafood."

This is a terrible idea, and I wish he had come to me for my input before deciding this with the marketing experts. They may understand how to promote a restaurant, but running one is a different skill set.

"Whatever needs to be done, I trust you'll figure it out. I'm running the campaign for two weeks, starting Monday, and I expect an all new menu by the twenty-first, so we can get them printed."

"Sir, I—"

"I hired you because of your tenacity, determination, and talent, Mr. McNamara. You assured me you'd do what it takes for this restaurant to succeed. I expect nothing less than perfection." With that, he walks out the door and doesn't give me a chance to argue.

Well, now what? Like I didn't have enough work already, I have to source local ingredients and reconfigure our entire menu in a week? That barely gives me time to work out different meals and see how practical they are in a restaurant setting. It's not just a matter of creating food that tastes good.

I anticipate another sleepless night.

Instead of staying in my office well past midnight again, I decide to head home. I exit my office and round the corner into the main part of the kitchen to find Hannah dancing and humming, facing the opposite direction. I stand for a moment, watching her hips sway and try to recognize the tune she's singing.

She puts any questions to rest when she blurts out the chorus of Miss Independent by Kelly Clarkson. She stops before the second line when she turns around and her eyes lock on mine.

What makes the scene even more entertaining is the filet knife in her hand.

She uses the back of her empty hand to sweep the side of her face and an ear bud drops, dangling over her chest. "Oh. I thought you left."

I step toward her, unable to stop myself, even though she's still wielding what could be an effective murder weapon. "You mean that little performance wasn't for me?"

Her cheeks blaze scarlet. "I... Um... Since I'm off tomorrow, I figured I'd prep the protein and make the day a little easier."

"I'd expect nothing less from Miss Independent." I step forward again, taking the filet knife from her right hand. "You don't have to do that, Hannah. Everyone else can handle it."

"Yeah, I know they can. I just... wanted to."

"You're a very dedicated employee, Hannah Parker." I'm close enough to her now, I can smell her strawberry scent. I'm not sure if it's perfume or shampoo, but the fact she still smells so amazing after ten hours in the kitchen is entrancing. "Let's finish up and I'll drive you home, yeah?"

"No. It's fine. You don't have to stay just because I insisted on it. I'll finish up and take the bus."

"You're not taking the bus home at midnight. It's freezing cold and... Saturday."

"I've always managed before." She takes a step back so she's leaning against the prep table. "It's just... I can't."

"Can't what?"

"You driving me home? It's not a good idea."

I pause for several seconds, trying to analyze what she means by that. Why would me driving her home be a problem? Did her parents say something? "You're going to have to elaborate on that for me. Why is it a better idea for you to take the bus than for me to drive you?"

"Caleb." She exhales, avoiding eye contact with me. "It's just better this way, okay? It feels too much like old times."

She's wrong about that. It never felt awkward before. Back then, if I wanted to kiss her, she read my mind before I could make a move. There was never a moment when I didn't feel like we were on the same team. Now, it still feels like we're on different continents. I want to tell her I wish I could go back in time and change things, but that won't fix anything.

"Can you let me drive you home this one time? I need your help with something and there's no one else whose input I value more."

She sighs, delaying a reply for several seconds. "Fine. Just let me finish this."

I roll up my sleeves beside her and we work in silence for ten minutes to finish her task, then we head home. There really is no one whose input I would consider, but more than that, there's no one else I'd rather spend time with.

20

HANNAH

Park Side

Other people my age are living on their own, getting married, having kids, or otherwise moving forward with their lives. When I moved out of my parents' house at twenty-three, I never thought I'd end up going back. Not only did I end up moving back in, but I begged, ashamed of the situation I found myself in. That was hard enough to handle, and in the two years since, I've been picking up the pieces. Gluing them back together in hopes this time they'll stick. Hopeful that I can line up the seams well enough, no one looking at me can see how damaged I am.

Caleb's presence outside of work often shines a magnifying glass on my cracks. There's no way he doesn't notice. Any moments of kindness are just Caleb's decency shining through and have nothing to do with any unresolved feelings toward me. They've been resolved just fine. I'm also pretty sure this little trip to find local ingredients is a pity invite.

"Sergei chose the worst time to do this promo. Who schedules a local menu promotion in November in Canada?" I huff as I yank open the door of one vendor at *Henderson Market*.

"It would be nice if he ran menu ideas past his executive chef before he paid a fortune on marketing, yeah. Now we have no choice but to make this amazing. If anyone—"

"Hannah, Babe. I've missed you."

That voice—the nasally, irritating sound that haunted my dreams for the better part of the last five years—makes every hair on my body stand on end. I look up to find my ex-boyfriend standing in front of me and my *other* ex-boyfriend-slash-boss, leering at me with his infuriating smirk. My body tenses automatically.

"You look good."

My skin crawls hearing his voice, but the confidence I've worked to build over the last twenty-eight months disappears in his presence. Words fail me, and instead of acting unbothered by Todd—the man who tried to destroy my life and me as a person—his presence still very much affects me.

"Uh... I'm Caleb. You are?"

This is an actual nightmare. My mouth goes dry. My heart beats in an unsteady rhythm. My eyes are stuck open, staring at Todd's face, but it's as if my mind is vacant. Again.

"Todd. Hannah's my girl." Todd reaches a hand out to shake Caleb's with a smug smile spread across his deceitful face.

Those words are enough to jolt my vacant brain into action.

"Ex, Todd." I clear my throat and straighten my posture, relaxing my shoulders from around my ears. "Ex. How's... what's her name? Selby?"

Caleb's eyes bounce between me and Todd. Each glance in my direction makes my face warm even more. "Should I, uh"—he waves his hand between us—"give you two a minute?"

"No—"

"Yes—"

Todd and I speak over each other, disagreeing, much in the same way we did for the entirety of our relationship.

I focus on Caleb, needing him to understand that he cannot leave right now. "No. Todd and I have nothing to say to each other." I scowl at the jerk who I'm so over, but not yet recovered from. If I had it my way, I'd run him out of the city and never have to worry about this situation again. "Everything has been said already."

Actually, there's a lot I have dreamed about saying over the past two years, but now is not the time, nor the place, to voice any of it.

I grab Caleb's arm and pull him down the aisle to our left, leaving the blond man with the innocent baby face and the wretched heart behind. Something I took way too long to do last time.

"Hannah, wait." Caleb stiffens and stops walking before we reach the doors. What for? I don't know because I refuse to stop.

Not until I'm back on the sidewalk, signalling a cab.

"Hannah. Stop for a second," Caleb pleads as he walks up behind me. "We didn't get what we came for. Are you forgetting I drove here?"

You've got to be kidding me. I spin around to face Caleb, abandoning my attempt to hail a cab. "I can't go back in there. Please don't ask me to do that. Things with him... they're complicated." But I'm too embarrassed to explain what those complications entail.

"The promotion starts today. You know if we don't hand select our ingredients, they'll send us the worst stuff. Are you forgetting the small fortune the restaurant spent on marketing?"

No, I haven't forgotten. In fact, it's been on the radio every five minutes for the past two weeks and I'm getting sick of hearing about it. That's not my biggest problem right now. "I can't."

Caleb steps closer, but stays far enough away, he's out of reach. Which is ideal, because I don't want anyone touching me right now. Not even accidentally.

"I get that he's your ex," Caleb starts, clearing his throat to continue, "but you need to get over whatever the problem is and do your job. Let's go get what we came for. I brought you because I value your input and could use your help. Please? For me?"

Guilt tripping. Perfect. If it were easy to just *get over it*, I would have by now. However, as upset as I am about Caleb's dismissive words, he has a point. Todd's presence may have rattled me, but he already derailed my life once. I can't let that happen again. This job is important to me.

I've stood up to other men over the past several months. I've prided myself on defending my friends when needed. Imposing men don't make me shrink back anymore. Most of the time.

"Let's go then." I don't spare Caleb a glance before walking back to the door I exited through two minutes earlier. We head back inside the meat market in search of some amazing proteins to make for dinner service. The clock is running out, so we need to get what we came for and back to *Hibiscus* before the lunch rush.

We speak with the butcher and, together, we request everything we need for our week of local food. Caleb's mood is improving; mine is stagnant. Of all the weeks that Caleb has been hot and cold, going from blast chiller to gas stove every time I turn around, now I can't help but feel an overwhelming sense of disappointment coming from him since we ran into Todd.

What's worse than running into my ex? Running into my ex, who I'm still recovering from, with my other ex in tow, who I also have conflicting feelings around. I'm not about to dive into that chapter of my life and try to justify how I reacted. If my boss were any other person, my past relationships would have no bearing on my job. That shouldn't be any different with Caleb.

With our order placed and deliveries scheduled for meat, we're off to the produce markets to gather what we need for our sides and appetizers. This entire week, we'll be featuring a *du jour* menu, meaning no two days will be the same. It's ambitious, but the goal is to generate a buzz with curiosity, and hope people will want to come back for new things.

Though, I'm feeling off-kilter since our run-in with Todd, and can't seem to focus on what needs to be done. The professional facade I've tried to maintain crumbled the instant he appeared.

"What do you think?" Caleb is holding up a pair of russet potatoes with a label stating they were grown just north of the city.

"Potatoes? What's your plan?"

"You weren't listening, were you? I asked if you have ever made a *Tartiflette au Reblochon.*" The way he effortlessly says that with a dreamy French accent makes me pause. Sometimes I forget he lived in France for so long.

"No, never. I'm not sure I'd—"

"Don't worry. I'll handle it." His expression changes from neutral to disappointed.

As if I didn't feel like enough of a failure today, not being able to create something he wants sinks my emotional state deeper into its pit of despair. "I think it's a great idea. Something less predictable than a ratatouille or French onion soup."

The right side of Caleb's mouth raises an infinitesimal amount. One could almost call it an attempted smile. "I'll teach you."

Those words turn my mood around. I've worked hard to get to where I am, and my drive to keep learning will keep me climbing. "Thanks, Chef."

The look on his face in response to mine looks stoic. Unsure. Maybe a little hesitant. Like there's something on his mind that's hanging between us, but he won't ask. I have a feeling I know what he is curious about and that's not a conversation I'll go into willingly.

Instead, I force us to stay on task. "Let's see what else we can find, hmm? Do you want to stick with a French theme? Local foods with a French flair?"

Caleb clears his throat and slides into step behind me as I peruse the offerings. "Yeah. French foods suit what's available."

We walk past the other options, inspecting and smelling produce that looks appealing. We settle on a few other sides to round out our menu. Creamed leeks, glazed carrots, broccoli *au gratin*, and *hericots vert amandine*, which Caleb makes sound more exciting than the almond green beans they really are.

The second we turn to place our order, I'm stopped dead in my tracks.

21

CALEB

I Dare You

When Hannah slinks back, looking like a timid child, I don't even need to be told what happened between these two to be set on edge. Our initial encounter made me angry, but we came here for a purpose and have things to accomplish. Logic told me that *Henderson Market* was big enough we wouldn't run into him twice. I was wrong.

Since Hannah isn't speaking, I do. "Uh, Todd. If you don't mind, Hannah and I have work to do. So if you'll excuse us."

Todd raises his index finger and pokes me in the chest. That's bad enough, but Hannah cowers behind me and every toxic alpha male quality known to man roars to the surface of my personality because whatever this guy did to her, it wasn't good.

"Listen here, pretty boy. I don't care who you are. I've been trying to talk to Hannah for over two years. No pansy is going to stand in my way."

I step forward, hoping we can resolve this without a fistfight because I don't have time to clean this guy's blood off of my knuckles, but I'm not a coward. He'll leave here today knowing I'm not a pansy, either.

"Did it occur to you that she doesn't want to speak to you? Does it look like she wants to talk to you now?"

He pokes me again and steps closer. His nose is almost touching my chin. "No one asked your opinion."

A gentle hand grabs my arm and Hannah whispers, "Please, can we just go?"

This Todd douchebag isn't going to derail this promotional week. Not for Hannah, and not for me. More than that, I will not stand here and let Hannah think this guy is going to win. He will not belittle her or make her lose her focus. Not when I've seen how hard she has worked.

I turn my head just enough to catch Hannah's pleading eyes without turning my back on Todd. "Do you want to talk to this guy, Hannah?"

Her grip on my arm tightens. Something about that touch shifts my mentality from *man with an unrelenting attachment to his teenage girlfriend turned employee*, to *man who cares about this woman's well-being and won't stand for anyone making her feel scared.*

"Please. Can we go?" Her voice cracks, and that does it for me.

I level my gaze on Todd, looking down at him. "We haven't placed our order yet. Todd, here, isn't going to get in the—"

Another poke at my chest halts my words.

"Go play Suzy-Homemaker and buy your vegetables. I'll talk to Hannah."

Over my dead body. The small hand squeezing my arm now is only serving to ground me so I don't knock this guy's teeth out.

I won't make this more of an issue for her. "No, you won't. Have some dignity. She doesn't want to talk to you. Tuck your tail between your legs and run off." I wave my hand to shoo him away. "Go."

Before I can react, Todd's fist flies at my face and I hear a piercing shriek from Hannah as it connects with my left cheek. I have to give him credit. As far as sucker punches go, it's a decent one, but it doesn't knock me down. I've taken worse from Oscar in a warmup. I'm stunned for a second, and in that time, Hannah jumps in front of me, trying to act as a shield. Two workers from the market rush around the counter to restrain Todd and force him onto a bench in the corner.

Hannah's eyes peer into mine and her delicate hand reaches up to inspect the damage on my throbbing face. I suspect I'll have a black eye, but he missed my nose, so all in all, it's not so bad.

"I'm so sorry. This should have never happened. I should have told you he..." Her breathing becomes really rapid and shallow, and she gets that same blank look on her face she's had twice now.

It freaked me out then, and it's freaking me out more now. "Hannah, look at me."

Her eyes don't budge. She doesn't even blink. Seeing her shut down like this hurts as much as filleting my pinky finger.

"I'm fine, okay?" I lift my hand, desperate to touch her, but I stop myself short. Until I get a good look at the scar on her cheek and a terrifying thought occurs to me. "Did he do this to you?"

She still doesn't blink, but her breaths are starting to slow. All she does is give me a vacant nod that's barely noticeable.

My eyes close involuntarily. I was hoping her fear of him was just because he was a domineering jerk. That little nod confirms that's not the case.

Logic has left the building. I stride across the room and manoeuvre through the employees trying to keep Todd seated. His cocky smile would have tipped the scale on whether or not I keep my cool, but it's already way out of balance.

"You piece of trash," I growl, grabbing his shirt collar. "You think you're tough, huh?"

Todd's entire body goes limp like a cooked fettuccine noodle, making it impossible to force him to stand. A couple of hands attempt to pull me back, but I resist. Only until I hear Hannah's quiet, cracking voice say my name and ask me to stop. That's the only reason I drop the lame noodle back on the bench.

He immediately jumps up, now with his renewed tough-guy act. "So that's what it is? You want to defend your lady's honour? Well, you should know, I had her first."

Todd takes another swing at me, but this time, I'm ready. I duck my head out of the way as I feel the breeze from his failed punch blow by my ear. I return his failure with a success of my own, landing a wicked right hook on his nose. The snap would concern me if it came from anyone else. The blood gushing from Todd's face feels like sweet retribution, though. Not even a fraction of what I'd like to do, but hopefully enough to tell him to stay away from Hannah. Forever.

The staff members pull me back, and this time I don't resist. I come to a stop beside Hannah, who is blinking rapidly now.

I pull her into my arms and rest my chin on her head, protecting her from every angle possible. "Shh. It's okay. I'm sorry he hurt you, Hannah. I'm so sorry."

What hurts even more is that she pushes me away and utters, "Don't touch me." When her eyes finally land on me, she looks scared. And I don't think it's a reaction to Todd.

She's scared of *me*?

This day has gone completely off the rails. We were supposed to come for one reason, and instead of leaving here with protein and produce, I'm left with a heaping load of guilt.

So I just repeat, "I'm so sorry," hoping she'll understand.

She doesn't reply for several minutes. Finally, two police constables walk through the front door and an employee directs them to the offending parties. The taller of the two men stops in front of Todd, while the other makes his way to me.

"I'm Constable Leon. Can you come with me?" He looks down at my throbbing red knuckles.

"Yeah," I reply before turning to face Hannah. "Can you finish sorting our order?" I ask, hoping the task will keep her distracted.

She nods, then the officer leads me outside. We stand beside a patrol car as I relay the sequence of events. I don't hide the fact I provoked Todd once I found out he had hit Hannah. Constable Leon asks about the history of abuse, but I admit I don't know much. I'm not sure if I want to.

Far too many minutes later, I'm stress-sweating under my coat—which never happens outside of my kitchen—until the constable informs me he'll be in touch if he has any further questions. Leon hands me his card, then I give him mine, thank him for his diligence on the matter, and pull out my phone to check the time.

"Hey." Hannah sneaks up on me while I'm looking at the screen. "Everything okay?" Her face looks raw, her eyes are puffy, and her cheeks are red. She must have been crying inside.

That realization feels like a belt cinching around my heart and lungs simultaneously.

I step toward her, worried I'll get too close and she'll push me away again. "I'm fine. Are you okay?"

She shrugs, turning her gaze away from me. "Really, I just feel bad for all of this. If I had known—"

"You didn't. You didn't know he'd be here and didn't know he'd haul off and punch me."

She looks down at the ground. "No, I knew that part. That's how he's settled every confrontation with people who question him." The pain in her voice just about brings me to my knees.

I regret not taking my opportunity to practice everything I've learned from the muay thai gym on Todd's face. I genuinely hope I run into him in a dark alley somewhere. But the way I'm feeling right now, I could run into him on the steps of Constable Leon's fifty-second division, and I'd still make sure he was bloody before anyone could rip me off of him. I'd do my prison time with a smile on my face, to be honest. Though, that likely wouldn't do me any favours with Hannah.

"I shouldn't have let him get to me like that. You know I'm not like him, right? I'd never—"

"Don't do that. Don't stand here and pretend like you solving an issue with your fists is different. You might have thought it was justified, but he always did, too."

An unexpected surge of anger rushes through me again. This time it's because she seems to think Todd and I are anything alike.

"Hannah, don't lump me together with that guy. I wasn't going to hit him. The only reason I did was because he swung at me, and the only way to make someone like that stop is by teaching them a lesson."

"The only reason he swung at you is because you went back over there. It was handled, Caleb."

She's right.

"I'm sorry. I'm sorry I made a bad situation worse, okay? It was immature." I'm not going to admit out loud it's because I care about her and the thought of someone hurting her made me unable to think straight.

That realization, once again, makes it clear how much of a liability having Hannah around is. If the employees hadn't corroborated my story of Todd swinging at me first, I could have derailed my career with an assault charge.

Now, seeing the look of disappointment on Hannah's face is all I need to get my head on straight.

"Let's go do what we came for. We've got a job to do."

Never Again

The last thing I wanted was for Caleb to find out about my past with Todd. Not just as someone else I once loved, but as my boss and someone whom I respect on a professional level. Ever since our run-in with Todd last week, Caleb has treated me differently. He's short and dismissive. Like the cold fronts that kept coming in for the first two months I worked here are now as consistent as the looming winter temperatures outside.

I can't survive this frigid weather until spring. And I don't mean the outdoors.

As a result, every day for the past ten days, I've been drowning in anxiety over going to work. My passion for cooking great food has dwindled to nothing, and I'm questioning if this is the right path for me after all.

But as I lie in bed, snuggling my cuddly pug, I can't imagine doing anything else. The last time I felt this beat down about my job, it was a direct result of Todd. I can't allow him to do that to me again.

Akili paws my shoulder, serving as a reliable alarm clock, forcing me to start adulting for the day.

"Okay, okay." I kiss the top of her head before throwing the blankets back and climbing out of my warm cocoon. "I know. Time to grow up and be an adult. You've told me before," I tell her as I lift her off the bed.

We go through our normal routine for a day when my mom is home, and by the time I'm ready, my excitement over spending the next nine hours at *Hibiscus* is at zero.

The only thing I can do is show up to work and hope my inspiration finds me again.

Caleb scheduled me on an earlier shift today, and since it has become a regular thing, I'm going to assume it was intentional, so we don't leave at the same time. But I hate how things have become between us. I wish he'd offer to drive me home so we can talk and I can convince him to go back to normal. At least the hot and cold version of Caleb expressed some emotion around me. Now I'm on the verge of getting frostbite.

I can't take it anymore.

Even though my shift is technically over, the kitchen is still busy, so I clock out and continue to help with random tasks until the backlog of orders has been cleared. I fade into the background, listening to the orders called out and retrieving necessary ingredients from the fridge.

Why am I retrieving items like an errand girl and not getting paid for it? Is it because I care about the success of this kitchen or I care about the success of Caleb?

They're one and the same right now, so I don't need to differentiate.

On my next trip to grab items from the cooler, I'm stopped on my way out.

"Hannah."

I meet Caleb's eyes, which portray as little as his tone does. "Yes, Chef?"

"What are you still doing here? Your shift ended at nine."

How do I tell him I'm here because I wanted to talk to him without sounding like a needy puppy?

"I already clocked out, but I saw a few others who could use some help, so I stuck around."

"This isn't a volunteer position. The people on the schedule can handle whatever they need to. I'm pretty sure I've told you before to leave the managerial decisions to me."

I should have known better than to do anything outside of my job description. He can swoop in and insist on driving me home, and that's fine. He can break my ex-boyfriend's nose, supposedly defending me, and that's well within his rights as my boss. Me giving a little extra time to help my co-workers is a problem. Got it. As much as I want to point all that out, I don't want to step outside the lines again.

"Fine. I'll leave." At least if I go home, my dog will give me a warm welcome.

Caleb exhales with his eyes closed. When he opens them, showing his remarkable dark irises, they express the pity I've been so afraid to find. "Don't let people take advantage of you."

I stiffen at his assumption. "Nobody *asked* me to stay. I *wanted* to stay and help. Nobody is taking advantage of me."

"Really? Because that's not how it looks from here. What happened to the tough-as-nails Hannah who told off Henry McNamara without flinching?"

Is he waiting for me to stand up for myself and tell him off so he can fire me with just cause? Does he think I'm such a fragile human being, I can't tolerate life in his restaurant? Or maybe he just wants to bring up our complicated past to rub it in that he's thrived without me, while I so clearly did not without him. Whatever the reason, any of the above makes me angry.

"She disappeared when her heart was shattered into a million pieces."

Then, after witnessing Caleb's expression fall, I leave like I should have thirty minutes ago.

Akili is waiting at the door when I arrive, and while it's more likely she just really has to pee, I'm going to pretend it's because she knows I'm upset and sensed it from miles away. I'm disappointed in myself for throwing our past back in Caleb's face. That was an immature response to his challenge, but the irrational, petty part of me wanted to strike back at him. Not to hurt him; just to let him know how much it hurt me when he left.

My mom has gone with a friend on a spa getaway north of the city for a night, so instead of relying on my little life coach for some solid—yet harsh—advice, I pull out my phone to call one person I can always count on for the truth.

"Hey, stranger. I've been meaning to call you," Angel answers.

"Sorry, I've wanted to call for a few days too, but work has been so crazy," I reply, opening the back door for Akili to stick her nose up at the snow and refuse to go out.

"Good crazy?"

I close the door and shake my head at my diva dog. "Not really, no. Emotionally crazy."

"Oh? How so?"

"Working with Caleb is hard." I sigh as I sink down into the couch and let Akili jump up onto my lap. "We ran into Todd while we were out sourcing ingredients for this promo, and they exchanged fists."

"What? Like they punched each other?"

"Yeah. Todd gave Caleb a black eye, and Caleb broke Todd's nose. Ever since, it's felt like Caleb is mad at me over it. I'm just... exhausted."

Angel stays silent for a few seconds before replying. "I'm sorry. That's... You know what? I'm lost for words, actually. What happened that resulted in a fistfight?"

I explain to her how the situation played out, right up to my confrontation with Caleb.

"That doesn't make sense," she replies. "Why would he get so worked up like he was trying to defend you, then be so cold ever since?"

"I know. Exhausting."

"Well, I once had a very wise friend tell me that hearing out other people's truth is important. Have you tried talking to him?"

"He's scheduled me on earlier shifts, so we never leave at the same time, and we're never in the kitchen alone. I tried to stay late today, off the clock, and he basically kicked me out." It's embarrassing to admit that. First, that I stuck around just to talk to Caleb. Second, because he dismissed me the way he did.

Angel mutters something to her dog in the background before continuing. "Honestly, I think his reaction speaks more to him feeling guilty than a problem with you."

"Why would he feel guilty? For punching Todd?"

"Possibly, but from what you've told me about your relationship with Caleb and how he left, learning about what you went through with Todd probably bothers him. I never got the impression from how you talked about Caleb that he was a heartless jerk, so I really don't think he's mad about the fistfight or mad at you."

I take a solid sixty seconds to wrap my head around that possibility. "He'd have to still care to feel guilty, though."

"Mm-hmm."

"That's not possible, Angel. He's… I don't know. What we had is long gone."

"He punched the guy who hurt you. People don't do that when they don't care."

I don't believe that. Not that I don't; I can't. The false hope that I still matter to Caleb after all this time will only end up hurting me again. If the third time's the charm, my heart won't handle another break. That would be the final crushing blow to obliterate it into irreparable pieces.

But she has a point. Why would he have gone back over to confront Todd just for the fun of it? He has always been passionate, but he's not an idiot.

"Now I don't know what to think," I say, looking into Akili's eyes, hoping for some clarification. All I get is a reminder she needs her eye drops before bed.

"Just don't go into work every day assuming he's mad at you. Try talking to him. Remember, your own version of truth only counts for so much. You need to see the other person's too."

"That is a brilliant piece of wisdom." I snort a laugh. "Whoever told you that is a keeper."

"She is. And she also deserves some peace. Don't let your fear of the truth keep that from you."

I hate how right she is. One way or another, I need to set things straight with Caleb.

Happier Than Ever

"Chef," Maria calls as she walks into the kitchen.

I hesitate to look up because I'm afraid she's returning a dish. Each returned meal is wasted time and money that I was hired to resolve. But when I focus my eyes on her, her hands are empty. "Yes?"

"You have company again." The way those words come out of her mouth makes the hairs on my arms stand up.

If Henry thinks he's going to walk back in here and I'll just roll over, he's mistaken. I don't bother asking who is here before I storm out of the kitchen and into the lobby. If I had, I wouldn't be coming face to face with my grandparents and cousins with the intensity of a raging bull. The tension rolls off of me as soon as I see my grandmother's smiling face.

"Hey, what are you guys doing here?" My greeting is a stark contrast to how I welcomed my parents.

"We wanted to surprise you. It had been a while since we saw our grandkids, so we made a day trip," Grandma replies.

I try not to let the worry seep into my voice at the thought of them driving so far in unpredictable weather, but as far as I know, the roads are clear today. Not to mention, my grandfather is a retired firefighter and is perfectly capable of handling anything, even as he approaches his eighties. Instead, I focus on their presence, greeting them all with a hug. My grandmother, Alanna, holds me the tightest, refusing to let go.

When she finally does, I ask, "Do you guys have a reservation?" Again, a contrast to my parents' arrival, because I'll roll out the red carpet for my other family members.

"We do. Hollis booked one for us a few weeks ago. It's tough to get a reservation here." Grandma beams at me, and the note of pride in her voice is yet another major difference.

"Good marketing, I guess. I can't take any credit for that."

"Since when did you get so modest? I saw that critic's review." Grandma chokes up a little, and her eyes start to water. "We're so proud of you, Caleb. I know this journey hasn't been easy for you, but we're so, so proud."

I pull my grandmother in for another hug with one arm and pat my grandfather on the shoulder with the other. "None of this would have been possible without you both. None of it. I owe everything to you guys." And I'm not just saying that. Our grandparents acted more like parental figures than our parents ever did. Not to mention, they cashed in my grandmother's life insurance policy to send me to France. Something I'll never take for granted, even though I paid it back years ago. "Whatever you want tonight is on me. Maria will take you to your table and take good care of you."

With a few parting words, they get ushered off to their table by the window and I go back into the kitchen. Things seem to be moving along well in my absence, which feels like a major win. It's also helpful that Ivan has the day off.

I slide back into directing orders and inspecting everything as it goes out. I'd like to say I put extra care into every plate I serve, but when the order belonging to my grandparents and cousins comes in, I go the extra mile to ensure they're perfect. Even more than I did when the food critic was here. For her, I said business as usual. For my grandparents, nothing could ever be enough to show them the depth of my appreciation.

When the servers come to take out their food, I decide to deliver them personally. Maria helps with two plates and I grab the others, because I am not a skilled server and lack the talent to balance four dishes.

The smiles on everyone's faces cause one on mine as I walk toward their table. I set down Hollis' and Oscar's meals while Maria delivers my grandparents'.

Oscar swats my stomach. "You've been slacking on your workouts. Getting round here, old man."

I rustle his hair, like I've done since he was a kid, and retort, "Says the guy about to eat lamb shanks in cream sauce."

He leans back and pats his stomach. "I can afford it. *I* didn't skip my workout today."

"I'll be there on Tuesday. These past few weeks have been insane. Trust me, I put what you've taught me to use."

Oscar's playful expression disappears, and his wide eyes flash a hundred questions.

I grip his shoulder and answer them with, "Tuesday." Then I listen to my grandparents and Hollis gush over their food for a few seconds before I realize my staff is stuck doing their own work and mine in my absence, so I bend down to kiss my grandmother's head and tell them to enjoy.

Before I make it two steps away, Grandma calls my name.

I spin around to face her, hoping there's nothing wrong with her food. "Yeah?"

"Is Hannah working today?"

"Yeah, she is." I can't make eye contact with my grandmother because I know what she's thinking.

"If she has a minute, could she come out to say hi? We'd love to see her."

"Yeah, we would," Oscar jokes. At least, he better be joking. Based on his chuckle when I glare at him, I'd say he was just trying to get the exact reaction I gave him.

"Uh, I'll see if she's got a second to come say hi." I turn to walk back to the kitchen, but pause once again. "Don't leave without letting me say goodbye, okay?" Who knows when I'll get to see three out of four of them again.

Grandma smiles and nods, then picks up her fork to dig into her dinner that's now been sitting here for several minutes. Hopefully, she enjoys it anyway.

As I walk back into the kitchen, I feel a little nervous about asking Hannah to go say hi. I don't want to say no to my grandparents. They're the only people who know the full reason why I left for France, and I don't want them getting their hopes up that this is some reunion for us. Not even Sophie knows the full truth, because I didn't want her feeling like she had to choose between me and our parents. Hannah definitely doesn't know the full truth, and I hope she never does.

Instead of taking more time to speak to Hannah when I return to the kitchen, I slide back into my job and pick up the slack I left in my absence. Walking away during the dinner rush is irresponsible, but I've been so consumed by this job for the past couple of months, I needed that feeling of home for a few minutes. It helps to restore my focus and allows me to keep a firm handle on my staff.

After about fifteen minutes, we have a lull in orders, so I ask Hannah if I can speak with her. Things between us are awkward, which is evident in her expression. One that appears nervous.

"My grandparents are here… Oscar and Hollis are with them, too. They asked if you'd come out to say hi."

Her dark brows raise several centimetres up her forehead. "Really? Why? I mean, I don't mind going to say hi, but I just don't understand why they'd care. I'm… me."

She has no idea how much my time with her shaped the entire course of my life. Not just in young love and finding the courage to pursue my dream. I never would have ended up in France without her, either.

"My grandparents loved you, too." I repeat the same words she said to me when we went to pick up her dad.

"Oh." She opens her mouth to speak three times, closing it without a word. Finally, she spits out, "Okay, I'll go say hi." Then, after untying her apron, she disappears into the dining room.

This is so weird. I adored Alanna and Fred Levy when Caleb and I were dating. There was such a contrast in his demeanour when he was around them versus when his parents were home. Even on the phone. They loved him and Sophie, and judging by the difference between how Caleb reacted to his parents showing up and his grandparents, the feeling is mutual.

He never asked me to go say hi to Noa and Henry, and no surprise, they didn't ask to see me, either. But I'd rather scrub my eyeballs with a barbeque brush than spend time around Henry McNamara. Thankfully, I don't have the same hatred toward the elderly couple I'm now approaching.

Alanna still looks as sweet as ever, but I can't get over how much Oscar and Hollis have changed. All four pairs of eyes light up as they see me drawing near, and I'm greeted with warm smiles.

Both grandparents stand and pull me in for a joint hug. Alanna squeezes me tight as Fred wraps his arms around us both. I'm surprised by how emotional the reunion is. I didn't realize how much I missed them, too. My grandparents all passed away before I started kindergarten, so I never had the loving relationship Caleb has with his. And by extension, I guess I had with them many years ago.

"Look at you!" Alanna states, leaning away from me. "You look beautiful."

I drop my eyes to take in my chef coat and can only imagine what my hair is doing. "You are too kind."

The adorable couple sits back down so we can stay out of the way of the waitstaff.

I turn to Oscar and shake my head in disbelief. "Last time I saw you, you were nine years old and obsessed with karate."

"Ah, well, I've moved on from that." He flashes me a brilliant smile, looking every bit the young man he now is. "How have you been?"

That's a loaded question, so I redirect it to answer it in a way suitable for a family dinner. "Good. I'm really enjoying working here." Most of the time. Okay, about forty percent of the time. "I can't believe my eyes right now. You guys have grown up so much."

"Not for lack of trying not to," Hollis retorts, smirking at her brother. "Some of us more than others."

The two siblings bicker back and forth for a moment, making me laugh with their snappy comebacks and good-natured pestering. If I remember correctly, Hollis is four years older, so when I last saw the Luna family, their bickering was even worse. I can't help but laugh, realizing some things never change.

I've been out here for several minutes and know I should be getting back to my job before I get in trouble. The last thing I need is for Caleb to find another reason to be upset with me. As I open my mouth to tell the diners I need to leave, I feel a palpable presence behind me.

"How is everything?" Caleb asks, coming to a stop beside me, wearing a wide smile.

"Amazing. Everything tastes good and looks even better," Oscar answers, sending Caleb a wink.

I'm a little confused by that because as chefs, we want our food to look *and* taste amazing. It's disappointing if it looks great but doesn't live up to expectations. Before I can question his answer, Caleb lifts a hand and places it on my lower back. The immediate rush of butterflies is surprising, but not.

A decade ago, I had the same surge of excitement in my belly every time Caleb so much as flashed a tight-lipped smile at me. I was so painfully in love with him, when he touched me—even something as innocent as holding my hand—I lost all sense. The same thing is happening now.

"Hannah?" Alanna calls, redirecting my attention.

I shake my head and focus on the sweet grey-haired woman. "Yes?"

"I hope my Caleb is being a good boss." Her smiling eyes stare up at her beloved grandson, then focus on me.

"Oh, uh… Yeah. He's uh… way better than my last boss." I laugh awkwardly, prompting Caleb to drop his hand. I'm not sure if he remembers our conversations about my old boss, but if he does, he probably won't see that as much of a compliment.

Judging by his narrowed eyes, I'd say he remembers.

"Well, the boss says it's time for you to get back to work," he demands. He's not harsh about it, but it feels that way. Like he's chastising me for not singing his praises.

Maybe if his moods weren't so unpredictable, I'd have given him a glowing review. But his family all know our history and I don't want to give anyone the impression we're anything other than boss and employee.

So I listen to my *boss*, saying goodbye to everyone and turning to walk back to the kitchen. I sneak one last glance before walking through the doorway and see Caleb smiling wide, laughing with the rest of them. A surge of heartbreak rushes through me with an intensity I haven't felt since he left.

The sudden realization that the love he had for everyone else withstood the great distance and lapse in time. I am the only person he stopped loving when he left. Everyone else still has a place in his life and a piece of his heart. The width and depth of the Atlantic was only too vast for us.

I struggle to ease back into my work, but thankfully the dinner rush is slowing, and the pace of the kitchen is more manageable. Today is my first closing shift since before the Todd fiasco, so it will be several hours before I can escape the whirlwind of emotions trapped within these walls. I'm in desperate need of a snuggle with Akili and some distance from this place.

That's especially true when Caleb returns fifteen minutes later, carrying four empty dishes. He shouts to Adriano, who is manning the dessert station tonight, requesting four different options from the menu. Caleb slips back into his position at the service station without looking my way. If I put enough effort into ignoring the cataclysmic hole burning through my heart, I can survive the rest of this day.

Three hours later, the entire kitchen staff, minus Alejandro, has cleared out. Most of the time, I love the hustle and bustle of the kitchen, but there's a feeling of calm and peace at this time of the night that you can't find at any other time. The mornings are marked with anticipation and the rush to prepare for the day. Open hours are a flurry of chaos, trying to align each of your own tasks with multiple other people and theirs. The pressure to be perfect is consuming. Exhausting. But now, with the lights dimmed and the only sound is the clanging of cookware being washed, it's relaxing.

I continue to scrub down the last of the surfaces after I've prepped what I needed to for tomorrow.

The footsteps I've come to recognize start getting closer. Smooth, confident strides. They come to a stop at the other side of the prep table I'm disinfecting, but I don't look up.

"I can drive you home when you're done."

With a final swipe of the gleaming stainless steel surface, I blow out a breath and allow my gaze to land on Caleb. We need to talk. I know that. I *want* to talk to him, but I'm also dealing with the lingering sting of realizing I was the only person he claimed to love that he walked away from.

I am torn between protecting my heart and protecting my job.

But I can always find another job.

"It's fine. I've still got another twenty minutes of work to do, so you might as well head home."

The deep brown eyes I used to get lost in focus on me. The bottom half of his face is relaxed, but his lower eyelids are raised and his brows pulled tight. "If we divide and conquer, we can be done in ten," he says, his voice low and husky.

He doesn't give me a chance to argue before he snatches the prep container to take it back to the fridge.

I guess today it's my heart that's going to be put on the line.

Sure enough, ten minutes later, I'm grabbing my coat and saying good night to Alejandro. Caleb and I descend in the elevator to the parking garage in complete silence. Neither of us speak until we're several minutes away from work.

"Are you mad at me for what happened with Todd?" I blurt.

Caleb's head turns toward me so quickly, he swerves slightly. "What? Mad at you? Are you kidding?"

"Well, if I was texting that question, I probably would have added an emotional support LOL at the end, but no, I'm not kidding."

"An emotional support LOL?" He smirks, which is barely visible in the streetlights as we whip past.

"You know? When you have to say something serious, but you don't want the other person to feel like it's a big deal, so you just add LOL at the end to soften the blow?" I mimic texting as I try to explain.

"Does that help?"

"Probably not, but it makes me feel better. Hence the emo—"

"Emotional support LOL. Gotcha." He signals to pass a slow-moving car in the right lane. "To answer your question. No. Not even a little mad at you, Hannah."

I hesitate to ask the next question, but I know we need to sort this out. "Then why have you been avoiding me ever since the market?"

Not Today

I should have been more prepared for that question. Ever since Hannah started at *Hibiscus*, I've scheduled her on a variety of shifts. I need to see how everyone operates in different situations so I know who to assign where. Since my confrontation with Todd, I've put her on earlier shifts to minimize our time together. Though not for the reason she thinks.

So I lie. "I haven't been avoiding you."

She scoffs and turns her head to look out the passenger window. "Yeah, okay."

"Would I have insisted on driving you home if I was avoiding you?" I challenge, knowing full well I offered because I care about her more than I'll admit. Knowing I stayed in my office, organizing that cesspool until I thought Hannah would be ready to go.

She doesn't have a response for that. I just feel her eyes burning into the side of my head.

I don't want to confess the real reason I've been keeping her at a distance. It's not fair for me to show her special treatment because of our past, but trying to stay objective around her is impossible. That became more obvious the day I committed assault. And by the realization I'd punch anyone else to protect her too.

Instead of focusing on our personal quandary, I shift back to work. "Thank you for all the work you've done for this promotion. It wouldn't have been half as successful without you."

She scoffs again. "You know me. Just doing my job."

I turn onto Hannah's street, then pull up along the curb in front of her parents' house. "I really mean that. You've been a great asset to my kitchen." Even I wince as I say those words, because that simple statement doesn't encompass everything she is to me. It's just all she *can* be to me.

"Sure. You're welcome, I guess. Thanks for the ride." Without waiting for a response, she hops out of the car and walks through the snow across the yard, into her home.

Watching her walk away floods me with disappointment all over again.

As teenagers, I never would have let her walk to her door alone, because I wanted to spend every possible minute with her. Sometimes we'd freeze on the doorstep, trying to keep each other warm, refusing to say goodbye. Because I lived two hours north and my school schedule kept me busy all week, we'd only get to see each other one day on the weekends. We made the distance work then—with a lot of miles on Grandma's Volvo—which is probably part of the reason Hannah was so confused when I said we couldn't make it work between here and France.

I drive home, dwelling on my mistakes, and wishing I could fix things. If I could turn back time and spare her from the pain she went through with Todd, I would in a heartbeat. I'd take on all of it myself.

But it's too late for that.

Few things irritate me more than running late. Especially when it's no fault of my own. If people didn't drive like complete idiots, it wouldn't have taken me fifty minutes for a seventeen minute commute.

By the time I reach my office, I'm already in a sour mood. Running late only compounded the issue since I stayed up all night dwelling on what could have been with Hannah. Like a pathetic fool.

"I said back off. Okay?" Hannah shouts.

Either that was really loud, or my ears are finely tuned to her voice. Whatever the reason, I exit my office and speed walk to the fridge, resisting the impulse to jog. When I round the corner past the open stainless steel shelving holding our prep equipment, I find Hannah with her arms full of produce and Ivan pinning her to the open cooler door with an arm on either side of her.

Rage. I feel pure rage, and my career is no longer my primary concern. After what happened with Todd, I'm not going to allow anyone to intimidate her or not take no for an answer—not that I would have tolerated that before I knew what she had dealt with.

My anger appears to only be a fraction of Hannah's because before I can react, she handles the situation. With her arms full of produce, she steps forward, shoving Ivan away from her, making him crash into a temporary prep table full of stainless steel mixing bowls. The clanging of the metal makes the encounter sound more dramatic.

I want to cheer or high five her, but as soon as she notices me, her face drops.

She steps forward to drop the potatoes and green beans into a prep bin as Ivan glowers at her back.

"Is there a problem here?" I ask, directing my words at Ivan.

Hannah answers, "You don't have to say it, Chef. I know the deal." Then she walks past me, toward the hooks by the service elevator.

What? I'm focused on processing her words as I stare at Ivan, who's muttering profanities with a look of hatred on his face. Hannah is twenty feet away, hanging her apron, by the time I clue in and stop daydreaming about delivering a clearer message to Ivan.

"Hannah, wait." I jog after her and stop a couple of metres away.

She won't lift her head to meet my eyes. Her expression isn't upset, though; it's indignant. "I know drama isn't acceptable, and that was one of the terms of my employment, so you don't need to say anything. It is what it is. Give me a minute to gather my things and I'll be gone."

"You're not leaving over this." No way am I allowing this situation to derail her life again. "I heard you tell him to back off."

"Maybe so, but I overreacted, and I know you can't fire him. I can't work with him, Caleb. I'm sorry, but I can't."

Her using my first name inside the kitchen tells me she's resigning herself as well as her position. In this situation, the right thing to do is not the easy thing. Firing Ivan won't be an easy sell, and technically, he's not even under my authority *to* fire. Letting Hannah quit isn't a suitable option, either. She deserves this job, and she's worked harder than anyone in the short time she's been here. She's the type of worker who I can leave in charge when I need a day off, or at the very least, operate as my right hand. I don't have to micromanage her, and that frees up my time to do other important tasks to ensure this kitchen runs smoothly. I need her here. I want her here. Just as much personally as professionally.

Even though I shouldn't.

Can't.

Her walking out on her own could be the answer to this dilemma I've found myself in, but I won't allow her to give up this chance because it's the easy out for me. If I were the type to take the easy way out, I never would have defied my father and pursued my dreams. I certainly wouldn't have hired my ex-girlfriend that I never got over.

"Hannah, I'm not mad. Not at you, anyway. I told Ivan to keep his distance. You told him to back off. It's not your fault." I resist the pull I feel drawing me closer to her. As much as I want to offer a bit of comfort, I have to be pragmatic here. "You can get back to work. Ivan is going home for the day."

"We'll be short staffed."

A surprising laugh flies out of me. "You think we'll be in a better spot if you leave?" I hold her gaze, studying her hazel eyes flashing a hundred unspoken things. "If the choice is between you or him, I'll choose you every time." That's all I say before I turn around to go find Ivan.

He's still standing where I left him, which is no surprise.

"Ivan, clock out. You're taking the rest of the day off and won't be returning until I write up an incident report."

"Good. She should be fired. If my uncle hears about this—"

"Your uncle *will* hear about this. I'll make sure he knows every detail. He can even pull the security cameras so we can get a full picture."

Ivan's jaw goes slack for an instant before tensing. He mutters through gritted teeth, "Cameras?"

"Yeah. Your uncle was worried about people stealing, so he had a few hidden cameras installed."

He didn't, but it's fun to watch Ivan squirm.

Apparently, it angers him a little more because he gets in my face. "I'm not coming back to work until she's fired." Ivan standing mere inches away, attempting to intimidate me, gives me flashbacks of Todd.

I only ever agreed to workout with Oscar because I needed something other than long shifts to keep me active. I never dreamed I'd turn into Hannah's personal vigilante. Yet here I am, fighting the growing desire to give Ivan a broken nose, too. The scarier realization is how my inherent need to defend Hannah is becoming a major liability.

I wasn't lying when I told her I'd choose her every time. Not just as a talented chef, but as someone I want—need—in my life, for a whole host of reasons.

"Talk to your uncle, Ivan. I'll be sure Hannah speaks with him, too."

"Why? He's not going to take anyone else's word over mine."

I clench my teeth, using Herculean effort to bite my tongue. "Take the day off and we'll get the situation dealt with. I promise." Too bad it won't be the resolution he's expecting.

never thought I'd see the day when you became a doormat. Caleb's words repeated through my head while Ivan had me pinned against the cooler door. But I also kept hearing him tell me *I have zero tolerance for drama.* In the end, my refusal to be a doormat won out. I don't feel bad about it.

What concerns me, though, is how infuriated Caleb looked at Ivan. He had the same expression he had when we encountered Todd. I never knew Caleb to be the type to communicate with his fists, but that could just be another thing that has changed. His father is hardly a shining example of how to deal with people you disagree with.

My next greatest concern is that I'll be fired.

It would almost be a blessing in disguise if I did. If I didn't have a say in the matter, it would put an end to my indecisiveness. Alas, I live to work another day. Now, if I could just focus on my work again, that would be great.

"Fire a *fricassee*, Hannah," Adriano whispers from beside me.

I blink a few times and look over at him, realizing he's trying to save my hide so I don't get caught slacking again. "Thanks, Adriano. Got it."

"You okay?" He flips the scallops he's searing, then sets the pan back on the heat to look at me. "I heard what happened earlier."

That's embarrassing. "Yeah, I'm good. Nothing happened."

Adriano gives me a one-sided smile. He's one of those people who are so ridiculously good looking, you want to hate them because the superior genes have been so unfairly distributed, but you can't because he's so nice. Not only that, he's so insanely in love with his girlfriend, who is a kindergarten teacher for special-needs children, yet looks like she's just stepped off the New York Fashion Week runway. Talk about unfair genetics.

"Hannah? How's my *fricassee* coming?" Caleb calls from the service station.

"Three minutes, Chef."

He continues to shout out directions to Tyson, who is in charge of side dishes tonight, leaving me to my task without another word.

I'm seventy-nine days into my ninety-day probation period, and I'm anxious to find out what our final job assignments will be. Everyone here, minus Ivan, is a capable chef, and Caleb would be fortunate to have any of them as his head chef. The lingering doubt in my mind about our past playing a role in my assignment is getting to me. Will he give me a better position because of our history, or will he relegate me to chopping broccoli and stirring soups? It's a mystery I'm eager to solve. Rather, have solved for me, since it's not my decision.

I approach the service station with my chicken dish right as Caleb spins around with his arms out. Before I can react, he knocks the dish from my hand, flinging the contents several feet, and the plate shatters on the floor.

"Don't sneak up on people like that. What if that was an iron skillet? One of us would be on our way to the hospital. You know better than that, Hannah," Caleb shouts. He makes no effort to hide his frustration, yet still has that familiar note of concern in his voice.

I can't even look at him. The longer I stay in this job, the more I feel myself reverting back to the doormat I swore I'd never be again. But only around Caleb. Is it because he's my boss, or because he's Caleb? Whatever the reason, this time, it fills me with an overwhelming sense of fear. "Sorry, Chef," I mutter.

Instead of cleaning up the mess of chicken and broken ceramic on the floor or returning to my station to cook a replacement, I walk out. Not out of the restaurant, but out of the flurry of activity. I seek refuge in the quiet corner by the service elevator, tempted to get in it and escape for real.

Several minutes pass with me crouched down in the farthest corner, resting my face in my hands. My head is a mess. My emotions are all over the place. And for the second time in one day, I've jeopardized my job.

"Hannah," Caleb calls from somewhere I can't see.

I stand, smoothing down my chef's coat. "Here."

Seconds later, he pokes his head around the corner. "It's not like you to abandon a job and leave it for someone else. What happened?"

He's right. These types of screw-ups never happened at my old job because I didn't have the consuming distraction of pleasing my ex-boyfriend I clearly wasn't enough for. I never had to worry about mood swings or where I stood with someone I so desperately wanted a clear picture from.

"I don't know. Fight or flight, I guess. I chose flight."

Caleb tilts his head and raises his eyebrows. "What are you afraid of?"

Shouting. Failing. Disappointing him. A lot of things. Mostly, becoming that shell of a woman I promised I wouldn't turn into again. None of which I can express right now, so I stay silent.

"Me?" he asks, stepping forward. "Hannah, did *I* scare you?" He stares at me, waiting for a response, with twin vertical lines appearing between his brows.

"It's fine, Caleb. I'm not that sensitive, but I guess after what happened with Ivan earlier, and... Todd... I just needed a minute."

He sighs, stepping back and turning around. He raises his arms to run his hands through his hair, tugging at the short strands.

"I'll get back to work and skip my break later." My attempt to glance over this entire conversation fails.

"I didn't mean to scare you, Hannah," he states, still facing the other way. "I was just trying to defend you."

Angel's words replay in my head. But I can't allow myself to think Caleb still cares. I need him to stop coming to my rescue before I read more into it than I should or he ends up in trouble over a situation he had nothing to do with. Either way, one or both of us will get hurt.

So I say something I regret as soon as it leaves my mouth: "Yeah, Todd always had justification for his outbursts, too." Then I walk away to get back to work while I still have a job.

As far as Saturday nights go, tonight was slower than normal. Or maybe it was because Ivan wasn't around to screw everything up and we have been able to execute a flawless dinner service after my *fricassee* disaster. Now my shift is done, and I am eager to get out of here.

Before I go, I look for Caleb to let him know I'm leaving because he's not at his regular spot at the service counter. I walk toward his office and stop outside the door, but I hear his voice inside.

"Sometimes I think it would be easier if she just quit..."

My heart falters. Probably cracks; reopening fissures I've spent a lot of years trying to heal. I don't stick around to listen to whatever he's saying or to learn who he's speaking to. The only thing I know is that he's talking about me.

I'm a combination of heartbroken and furious as I grab my jacket, then descend in the elevator. By the time I reach outside, the anger has subsided and the only remaining emotion is devastation.

My parents spilled in the door after midnight, giggling and stumbling over things. Based on the fact they got dropped off by a taxi, I'm assuming they had a date night involving alcohol. There goes my plan to confide in either of them and try to get some advice from a sensible adult. Now, if I leave the safety of my bedroom, who knows what I'll walk in on.

So instead of finding the listening ear I was hoping for, I stay wrapped in my Powerpuff Girls blanket that has officially reached vintage status, snuggling my loyal companion.

Desperate times call for desperate measures as I whisper in the dark, "I don't know what to do, Akili. All I've wanted for years was to move forward. Forget about the mistakes of my past and love my job." I pause, rubbing the short hair on her belly as she wriggles around to find a new, comfortable spot. "But I've never loved this job as much as I loved him."

That realization prompts me to make a decision without consulting my furry life coach further. I just won't make the same mistake twice.

27

CALEB

Nostalgic

My doorbell rings, jolting me awake. It's 7:30 in the morning and I feel like I just fell asleep. Yesterday was a rough day and sleep was evasive.

I swing the door open to find my sunshine sister smiling, holding a tray of four cups from her new favourite café. The coffee is good, but I don't think that's why she loves it.

"I brought coffee." She smiles wide, making it impossible to be annoyed with her for disrupting my sleep.

Still, I do what any good brother would do and make her sweat a little. "Soph. I just got home five hours ago and have to be back at the restaurant at eleven." My efforts fall short, though, when she steps inside and I pull her in for a hug.

She claims she has missed me, which I sympathize with, so I interrupt her when she offers to let me go back to bed.

"Want something to eat? I'll whip up breakfast."

The excitement on her face makes me laugh as she practically shouts, "Yes!"

I dig in my fridge while we talk about what's going on in her life. Again, her decisions for her future boil down to what Henry deems acceptable. It's easy for me to say just tell him off and do what she wants, but the truth of the matter is, he steered my life in a direction I didn't want it to go either. As much as I claim my decision to move to France was motivated entirely by my own goals and desire to stick it to our father, in reality, I was too much of a coward to defy him and stay in the same country. It was easier to be disowned by him than to face him.

That makes me a major hypocrite for telling Sophie to forge her own path and forget what Henry has to say. I can't blame her for not accepting my advice, like it's a simple decision to make. But just because I made the same mistake doesn't mean she should.

I slide our food in the oven and invite Sophie into the living room while it bakes.

She wastes no time in asking, "So, what's going on with you and Hannah?"

I blow out a breath, allowing myself to really sink into my sofa. "Grandma called last night and asked the same thing."

"And?"

"I said sometimes I think it would be easier if Hannah just quit. As soon as I said that, I realized that's not what I want at all."

"What *do* you want?" Sophie asks, fiddling with her second coffee.

"The one thing I've feared the most is ending up anything like Henry. Not just how he treats you, but how he's so dismissive with Mom, treating her like an inconvenience, and she just accepts it. Yet, here I am, doing the same thing to Hannah."

"What do you mean?"

"We have these moments, right? When it feels like it used to; before everything went sideways. But so much has happened between then and now, it's also so different. And…" I trail off, hesitant to tell Sophie about Todd, because I don't want to betray Hannah by sharing that. Even though I trust my sister with my life, she and Hannah used to be so close, there's no sense upsetting her with that information. "You remember how she used to be so fierce and unstoppable? Like there was nothing that could stand in Hannah Parker's way?"

"I do. She was my best friend, Caleb."

Our family has never been great at talking about feelings. Largely due to our father's inability to express anything other than anger or indifference. It makes my stomach churn, hearing Sophie's voice crack with a brief mention of her former friendship.

"I'm sorry, Soph. I never meant to blow up your friendship with Hannah. If I could go back and change how I did things, I would. I wish I had the guts then that I have now and I could just tell Henry off ten years ago." My eyes bulge wide when I say that, because I know she's going to have questions.

Ones I never wanted to answer.

Sure enough. "What did telling Henry off have to do with you leaving? I thought you going to *Ecole de Cuisine* was your way of telling him off."

"It was." I pause, fiddling with the biodegradable lid on my coffee cup. This is the longest secret I've ever kept from my sister, and it's done nothing but eat away at me. "After Hannah confronted him, he started taking it out on me. Which I was fine with for a while. You know how he was. The endless barrage of insults were nothing new; he just took them up several notches. But I had pretty thick skin by then, so it wasn't unbearable."

Sophie continues hugging her beloved flat white, listening intently as I tell her things she already knows. Her demeanour changes when I tell her what she doesn't.

"When that wasn't enough to satisfy his injured ego, he told me he'd go after Hannah. That if he ever saw her again, he'd ruin her life. He hatched this entire plan to frame her for drug possession, Soph. It was so ridiculous, but having that on her record, it would have destroyed her life. So my choice was to take the chance that he'd follow through and her life would be over because of me, or cut ties and let her move on."

My sister's coffee tips as her hand drops and goes slack, along with her jaw. She gapes at me for several seconds. "Why didn't you tell me this back then?"

"I knew you had your heart set on working at *McNamara Enterprises*, Soph. I wasn't going to blow up your dream because of his issue with me. But now, looking back, I wish I had so I could have saved you from years of working under his command."

She knows I hate that she still works for him. It's nothing to do with him as a boss—which is also not great—but everything to do with him as a father. Or failure as one.

"At the time, I just didn't see a way out. I had no way to combat Henry McNamara and the reach his money gave him. Especially with the business moving to Toronto, because I knew he'd build ties with people who could make his plan happen."

Now Sophie blows out a breath as she sets her coffee cup on the table, then slumps back on the sofa. "Does Hannah know any of this?"

I shake my head. "She would have felt bad for telling Henry off, and she shouldn't. She was right about everything she said. I didn't want her spending the rest of her life looking over her shoulder or feeling like she had to shrink back."

Even though, based on our interactions with Todd and Ivan, that's exactly what has happened to her.

"So I guess my question again is, what *do* you want now?"

For all these years, I thought focusing on my career would make my decision to leave worth it. If I found success on my own, it would justify giving up on me and Hannah. I thought I'd mature and move on, so it was just a stereotypical teenage love story gone wrong. A blip on the storyline of my life.

But having her back in my life again has made me question everything. And what I thought mattered for all those years isn't so important.

There's a major problem with my new realization, though.

"She isn't interested in rehashing the past."

Sophie stares at me with her intense big sister glower. "She told you that?"

"Everything that happened back then, good or bad, needs to stay there," I answer without actually answering.

"That's stupid, Caleb. Hannah will always be your person. I don't care what happened; never in the history of time have there been two people better suited for each other."

We were great together. Even as young as we were, my relationship with Hannah marks the happiest time of my life. Not even learning under the direction of world-class chefs compared. But too much has happened to go back to that.

"I left so she could move on. I need to let her."

"Are you honestly okay with that? If Hannah starts dating someone else? Gets engaged? Shows up to work, telling you she is going on maternity leave because some other guy is giving her the family she always wanted? You'll throw her a baby shower and be fine with it?"

My teeth clench when I picture that scenario. "What am I supposed to do, Soph?"

"You can start by admitting to yourself how you feel about her. You can't expect her to know if you don't."

"She doesn't need to know. If she had any interest in rehashing the past or trying to get back what we once had, wouldn't she have said something by now?"

"Ugh. Why are you so stubborn?"

"You're one to talk."

"Hush. Not my point. You haven't said anything, so why would you expect her to? You're her boss, *and* you were the one who walked away. Which, I'll remind you, she doesn't even know why!"

Way to spare my feelings. That is a possibility, though. The question is, do I want to risk derailing either of our careers to find out?

Sophie leaves me with a final question as the oven buzzes with our breakfast. "My point is, ask yourself if you'd be okay with disappearing from her life again. Now that she's here, could you walk away a second time?"

28

CALEB

Mr. Know It All

Today is the first time Sergei has been back at the restaurant since Hannah's encounter with Ivan. I'm not going to lie; it's been nice not having Ivan here. His absence has made it abundantly clear that he's dead weight, only dragging my kitchen down. That gives me plenty of talking points to plead my case as I walk into Sergei's office.

He's taken up a spot on the eleventh floor, away from the hustle and bustle of the restaurant activity. His office has the same south-facing view as the prime seats in our restaurant, but the sight of the water is not my focus when I walk in his door.

The elder Russian with the bad hair piece and nicotine-stained teeth looks up as I enter. "Ah, Mr. McNamara, how can I help you?" He gestures for me to sit in the chair by the window that is an awkward distance from his desk.

Instead of beating around the bush, I get straight to the point. "I need to fire Ivan. If not fire, relocate him out of the kitchen. He's become a liability, and he's destroying your profit margins with his refusal to learn."

Sergei's scowl deepens. "No."

"You're not hearing me, Mr. Antonov. He doesn't have what it takes to work in my kitchen. My other staff are constantly questioning how a man who makes no effort can keep his job, when the rest of them are expected to pick up his slack. If anyone else had as many failed dishes, I'd fire them on the spot."

"I *heard* you just fine." Sergei stands to loom over me, but because this chair is fifteen feet across the room, it's not the least bit intimidating. "The answer is no."

I wasn't going to go this route, but he leaves me no choice. "He's been harassing a female employee. He cornered her the other day, and she was pretty shaken up. If you keep him here, he's bound to be an HR nightmare."

Sergei drops into his seat and flicks his hand at me, turning his focus back to his paperwork. "Then fire the girl. My nephew will not go anywhere."

The incomparable rage I feel when it comes to matters involving Hannah is becoming more familiar. Also, more intense. Sergei's suggestion is not on the same level as giving her a three-inch long scar on her face, but it messes with her livelihood and I won't stand for that. Besides, even if it weren't Hannah, in no world am I okay with the victim being punished and a perpetrator facing no consequences.

"No," I reply as I stand. "She did nothing wrong. Your nephew is the problem, and I won't pretend like his behaviour is okay. So you can find a new role for him, or you can find a new executive chef."

There is no way I will ever let anyone bully me into choosing my career over Hannah again. Even if she never knows that.

Sergei stands to his full height, which is about seven inches less than me. He's no taller than Sophie, even with his fluffed up toupee. He opens his mouth, but closes it before any words escape. It appears he's weighing his options. Finally, he concludes, "Fine. Speak to Alec about finding him a different position."

"Thank you, Sir." I offer my hand to shake, but he refuses it. "I'll let you know what Alec decides. And I'll call Ivan myself to inform him."

He grunts in response as I turn to leave the office. That's fine with me, because I am over this conversation. Firing Ivan would have been ideal, but given the circumstances, I'm happy with the outcome. I hope Hannah will be, too.

Alec and I discuss the finer details of Ivan's new role after our lunch service is finished. The entire time, I'm glancing over my shoulder and checking my watch, waiting for Hannah to appear. She walks into work thirteen minutes after her shift was supposed to start. It's so unlike her, but what's more concerning is how exhausted she looks. It's not the same look as the day she came in, appearing hungover. This is a soul-consuming level of tired.

"Thanks, Alec. I'll give him a call to let him know, yeah?" I don't wait for his response before I jog back into the kitchen behind Hannah. Much like her dog would, I imagine. "Hey. Can I talk to you for a minute?" I ask as she hangs her coat.

Again, that downcast flicker of fear washes across her face. "Fine."

Her fearful expression, paired with that snappy response, throws me for a loop.

"Are you okay?"

Now she scoffs. Again. Like she seems to do so often around me. "Yeah, just say what you need to say."

Well, that doesn't seem okay at all.

"Can you come into my office?" I want a moment away from prying eyes to tell her about Ivan. Everything about this interaction says there's a lot more to discuss.

She doesn't say a word before she's marching her way to my closed office door. She doesn't even wait for me to open it; instead, barging right into the chaos. "Just say it. I'm late because Akili took herself for a walk, so you're firing me. Ivan's job takes priority, so you're firing me. I cause too much drama, so you're firing me. Take your pick."

"No. What do you mean Akili took herself for a walk?"

"She's fine. My mom forgot her out front, so I'm pretty sure she was trying to find somewhere else to live." Her shoulders drop as she deflates, like she's finally releasing the stress from her day. That relief quickly disappears. "What do you have to tell me, then?"

I round my desk to face Hannah, who has zero traces of the fear she had before. I'm happy about that, because I don't want her to be afraid I'm some unhinged meathead with a violent streak, but her flared nostrils and narrowed eyes are now leaving me fearful. "I wanted to tell you I spoke with Mr. Antonov, and Ivan is being reassigned to the dining room. He won't be an issue anymore."

Her scowl recedes, and a second later, she looks relaxed again. "Thank you. Can I get to work now?"

There's so much more I want to say, but it doesn't look like she wants to hear it.

"Yeah, sure."

She exits my office, leaving me to drop into my chair. I lean back, scrubbing my hands over my face. This added dynamic of a past relationship that went down in flames and trying to maintain professional boundaries is making everything I want to tell her impossible. I sit at my desk for a while, wondering if we never knew each other—if our mothers hadn't befriended each other in college, and Hannah and I hadn't been having playdates since before we lost our first teeth—would things be different now? But there's no point in going down that road because this is where we're at now.

And if I want her to know what she means to me, I need to prove it by more than just managerial decisions that benefit the entire staff.

For now, I've got a phone call to make.

Needless to say, Ivan is not thrilled about his demotion from line cook to busboy, but the risk of having him interact with customers is not one Alec nor I are willing to take. I tried encouraging him, telling him he can prove himself in that role and maybe he'll be reassigned, but honestly, that was more kindness than he deserved. Plus, I said that, but I know his work ethic is not leaving a lot of room for a promotion. If he keeps on his current trajectory, soon he'll be doing nothing more than taking out the garbage.

I enter the kitchen amongst the activity and find Hannah preparing the *potimarrons* for tonight's special. She's lined up alongside Adriano and Tyson, who are busy with their tasks too. Her demeanour with them is totally different. She's laughing, friendly, and relaxed. I'm not sure if it's them or the fact she's in her element preparing food that has her feeling that way, but I can't stop the surge of jealousy I feel over it.

So I carry on past the trio and check in with everyone else to make sure things are on track for when we open back up in an hour. It floods me with pride when I realize everything is in order. Because in three months of running this place, I've completely turned the kitchen around.

But the pride that I was so looking forward to when I took this job no longer matters.

All that matters is her.

HANNAH

Hear Me

Hopefully Caleb got the hint last night when I refused a ride home with him. If he thinks he's going to say he wishes I'd quit behind my back and then come in like a hero by getting Ivan reassigned, he's mistaken. I'm not the only one who wanted him out of the kitchen. Adriano and Tyson were both pretty thrilled when I told them yesterday, because everyone was tired of fixing Ivan's messes.

But the thought of going back to work tomorrow, knowing Ivan is in his new role and will probably blame me, has my nerves on edge. Beyond that, my job search hasn't turned up anything in the city, so I applied to a few in British Columbia, which would mean a major change. If he wants me gone, so be it, because I promised myself I'd never stay around someone who doesn't value me again. I just need another job in place this time, so I'm not spending weeks unemployed.

Akili starts barking like a madwoman at the front door, abandoning her perch on the kitchen chair where I was feeding her pieces of raw bacon. Whatever has drawn her attention must be good.

When I round the wall from the kitchen, I lock eyes with one person I'm not expecting to see through the door's window. Someone who has apparently *not* gotten the hint.

Akili has also abandoned her guard dog status and is now wagging her curly little tail, waiting for me to let him inside.

"Traitor," I mutter. I pull the door open, knowing there's no point in trying to hide after I've made direct eye contact. The most frustrating thing is that I know I wouldn't hide from him anyway, because I want to know why he's here. As mad as I am, I still *want* to be around him.

What's wrong with me?

"Hi," Caleb greets before bending down to pet my Benedict Arnold. "Sorry to just show up, but I don't have your number."

"Pretty sure it's on my contract." I glare at him as he stands upright. "Can I help you with something?"

He rubs a hand on the back of his neck, grimacing. "I was hoping you'd give me a few minutes to talk. Outside of work."

I try to soften my expression, but it won't budge. He's still my boss, and at the very least, I could use his reference, so I let him inside.

"I'm just making some breakfast before I take Akili to the vet. Come into the kitchen."

"Vet? Is something wrong with her?" he asks, toeing off his shoes in the front hall.

"Aside from her loyalty issues, no. Just her annual checkup and teeth cleaning."

"Oh." He follows me around the corner into the kitchen and watches as Akili tries and fails to jump back up into her chair. "Shoot." He rushes over to her toppled body and picks her up.

She seems happier in his arms than she was here eating bacon. I will not admit to anyone how jealous of her I am. I'm supposed to be mad at him, not thinking about being in his arms. But that's exactly what I'm doing, and it's *exactly* why I slice the tip of my index finger while I was meaning to slice this stupid bacon.

"Ow!" I drop the knife and clutch my wrist, not wanting to touch the oozing finger with my bacon hands.

Before I can spin around, Caleb sets Akili on her chair and rushes to the sink. He turns on the water and tests the temperature. "Here, wash your hand with soap, then we'll take a look at it."

I do as he instructs, wincing as the soap stings the cut. "Eek, that's a bad one."

The sink fills with splatters of diluted blood as I try to rinse the last of the raw bacon from my hands.

Once I'm finished, Caleb steps behind me, reaching forward to wrap a paper towel around my finger.

"You okay?" he asks, blowing his breath across my cheek as he leans closer.

Suddenly, having his body pressed against mine, the pain doesn't feel so bad. Then a realization hits me and I struggle to suppress a laugh. I bend over the sink, trying to contain it, but it's useless. Caleb follows suit, bending over me so he can hold on to the paper towel. My shoulders are shaking as I laugh silently into the sink.

"Hannah? What's wrong?" Caleb's concerned voice helps me get control of myself.

I stand, forcing him to straighten behind me, then shift my hand out of his to spin around. No way am I going to tell him that I sliced my hand because I was jealous of my dog being in his arms, and that's exactly where I ended up. I'd say it worked like a charm, but that wasn't my plan. Nor was clenching a paper towel around my throbbing finger for the morning.

"I thought you were crying." Relief washes over his face the second my eyes meet his. His shoulders drop, but his arms don't, still resting on either side of me on the counter.

Our faces are close—inches apart. I bite my lip and watch as his chest rises and falls faster than normal. He doesn't make a move. A sound. Nothing but our breaths and unwavering eye contact.

Until he breaks the spell. "Are your parents home?"

The way he asks reminds me of us as teenagers, trying to sneak in another make-out session before my parents entered the room or came back home from wherever they were. The husky whispered words meant only for me.

"Yes," I whisper back.

That response forces him to take a step back. Like somehow at twenty-eight years old, I'd get in trouble for being too close to a boy in our kitchen. He doesn't know my mother at all, because she'd probably be so excited about it, she'd park herself in Akili's chair and cheer us on.

Speaking of... I lean to the left to peek around Caleb and find Akili sitting patiently on her chair. Then I glance at the counter. "Akili, where's the bacon?"

Her expressive eyes say more than words ever could. She lifts her gaze to Caleb in her effective *poor me* manner. He glances at me, shrugs, and lifts my dog back up in a way that's so tender, I consider cutting off a whole finger so I can experience it too.

"Did she really just eat all that bacon?"

I shake my head to clear the overwhelming thoughts about what would have happened if Caleb hadn't brought up my parents. "She's a scavenger. It was only a few pieces, but... ugh. Akili. What am I going to do with you? And what do I have for breakfast now?"

Caleb sets Akili down, then steps toward me, stopping inches away. "One sec." He turns to the sink and washes his hands, drying them on the hand towel hanging from the dishwasher. "Let me look at your finger."

"Did you take first aid in France or something?"

"Caleb? So nice to see you. What brings you here so early?" My mother enters the room, thankfully wearing a securely closed robe, and pulls Caleb in for a hug.

He doesn't resist. And there's yet another woman in his arms in this kitchen. Seriously, what's a girl gotta do to get in on this?

"Good morning, Mrs. Parker. I hope I didn't wake you." Caleb looks down at his watch, then at me.

It's almost 10am.

"No, not at all. We were just… resting."

Kill. Me. Now.

"Mom—"

"What happened? Why is your hand bleeding?" She practically bulldozes Caleb to reach me and pull the paper towel gently off of my finger. "Oh, that's a good one. Let me get the first aid kit."

She disappears down the hallway toward her bedroom just as my dad enters the kitchen.

"Caleb, good to see you, Son." He claps Caleb on the shoulder with a huge smile on his face. Completely ignoring the fact I'm bleeding out.

"You too, Sir. Have you gotten your car situation sorted?"

"Oh, you know how insurance companies are. Still waiting for a cheque so I can get a replacement."

"I wondered when I didn't see a car outside." Caleb looks at me, down at my hand, then back at my face. Like he's asking with his eyes if I'm okay.

Mom returns with a white plastic container before I can wipe the scowl from my face to nod a response.

Caleb and my dad continue to talk while Mom cleans and wraps my finger. It hurts, but it's nothing serious. Except now I'm running late for Akili's appointment and I still have no idea why Caleb actually showed up at my door.

My parents clear out of the room with their coffee, leaving me and Caleb standing in awkward silence.

"I… uh… Akili's appointment is in twenty minutes. Can we talk later?"

He steps forward. "Let me take you. Please? I've got the morning off, and we still haven't talked."

Again, I have to remind myself that I'm supposed to be mad at him. But when I look into his dark eyes, I can't be. "Okay. Akili hates the snow anyway."

Like I'm actually accepting for her sake.

30

HANNAH

All I Ever Wanted

"Will she be okay after eating that bacon?" Caleb asks as he closes the passenger door for me.

I wait until he climbs into the driver's seat before I reply. "I'll ask, but I'm sure she'll be fine. At least *someone* got to enjoy it."

My gluttonous pooch settles in on my lap—her happy place—and Caleb reverses toward the street.

"Which way are we going?" He pauses the car at the end of the driveway, looking at me for instructions.

I direct him to the vet office that's less than three kilometres from home, happy we didn't have to walk. It's too cold and too far for Akili's little legs, so no doubt she would have been riding most of the way inside my coat.

When we enter the one-storey brick building, the receptionist asks us to wait. She's about our age, gorgeous, and clearly likes what she sees beside me. Though, in her defence, the vision that is Caleb holding my dog, gushing over her, oblivious to everyone else in the room, is hard to resist.

Again, I remind myself I'm supposed to be mad. But with each minute that passes, I can't rationalize his kindness and making this effort to talk to me with someone who wants me to quit. I guess that's exactly *why* we need to talk. This back and forth isn't getting us anywhere.

We sit and wait in the lobby, with Akili cuddled into Caleb like he's the one who's loved and pampered her for the last two years. Honestly, I should have gotten a chihuahua. At least they're loyal.

"Akili?" the vet tech asks, standing under the arched hallway entrance.

Caleb stands and steps forward. "Here."

"You don't have to stay. We can walk home," I offer. "You already saved me from walking here." If I'm being honest, I like having him here for this. Which is dangerous, because that means he's taken up space in my life as something more than my boss again.

"Do you want me to leave?" he asks, his brows furrowed, still clutching Akili.

I consider sparing myself the inevitable heartache; lying to say I don't want him here. But I let him leave before when I wanted him to stay... and it almost killed me. "No. I don't."

His eyes relax, and a smile transforms his face. Seeing him here—smiling at me, holding my dog—is alarmingly heart-warming. It also grips at the nostalgia of our broken relationship. He walks forward to follow the middle-aged vet tech down the sterile hallway, and I trail behind, thinking about what once was and what could have been.

Once upon a time, I envisioned him holding our children, smiling at me. And more than I wanted to be a chef, I wanted to be a mom. A *wife* and a mom. One who prioritized her family, but also had a thriving career. A woman who balanced it all flawlessly because she was so full of love and passion, none of it felt like work. Goes to show how naïve I was at eighteen, thinking my high school boyfriend was going to be my forever.

My reality looks nothing like I imagined it would.

We get Akili settled in the exam room after she has her weight checked. The tech notes she's gained a little weight, but I inform her of the bacon incident. It's not winter weight; it's pork fat. She does her cursory exam and asks me questions, which I happily answer. A few minutes later, she leaves the room.

Caleb stands over Akili like a protective father—I really need to stop thinking about that. "What does she need eye drops for?" he asks once we're alone.

"It's not that she *needs* them, but because pugs have such big eyes, they're prone to eye issues. So I give her drops to hopefully prevent them."

"Oh." He continues stroking her back, prompting her to lie on the table without a care in the world.

Belly full of bacon and a hot guy catering to her every whim? What more could a girl ask for?

"You're a good mom," he adds.

Four words that stun me silent. Four words I thought I'd lost the chance to hear him say. And certainly not about me caring for a dog.

The dentist enters the room, interrupting our silence. Mercifully. "I hear this little trouble maker had a treat this morning," Dr. Denise says.

"She did." I hold up my hand to show my bandaged finger. "She capitalized on a little kitchen mishap."

The woman laughs, lifting Akili's lip to look in her mouth.

Caleb doesn't budge, standing over her, and all I can think about is how he would make such a good dad. Moody, perhaps. A little cocky. Incredibly stubborn. But also caring. Protective. Gentle. If how he treats his grandmother and sister is any indication, it's obvious he has an unexpected soft side if you only saw him at work.

Unfortunately for me, in this moment, I've experienced the soft side of Caleb too many times to brush this encounter off as a onetime deal. *This* is the real version of him that only a few lucky people get to see.

Henry McNamara can take credit for that. For his son being conditioned to think showing emotion or a sensitive side makes him weak. For making him feel like he has to be harsh to be heard. For making him feel unworthy until he's proven himself.

"Hannah?"

I shake my head to clear that train of thought. "Yes, sorry. Totally spaced out there," I reply to the dentist.

"Are you okay?" Caleb asks, reaching out to place his hand on my bicep. He's looking at me with knitted brows and soft eyes. A look betraying the person he really is, and not his workplace persona.

"Yeah." I smile at him, hoping to relax his concerned expression. "I'm not suffering from catastrophic blood loss or anything. Just daydreaming."

Mission accomplished. He gifts me a devilish smirk, lifting one whiskered cheek and creasing around his eye. "Now I'm curious."

A throat clears beside us seconds later, and I look over to spot Dr. Denise, accompanied by Akili, who is panting and wagging her curly tail. She appears blissfully unaware that the newest object of her affection is a heartbreaker. As does Dr. Denise, if her conspiratorial smile means what I think it does.

Instead of clarifying to Caleb that I was thinking about his father's flawed parenting, I leave the possibility it was something more interesting hanging in the air between us.

The rest of Akili's appointment flies by, and an hour later, we walk out with her teeth sparkling and a clean bill of health.

"You really have to clean her skin folds?" Caleb asks as we approach his car.

I scrunch my face at him. "Uh… Every girl needs a good skincare routine. Of course I do."

"You really love her," he points out as he opens the passenger door for me.

"I do," I reply, dropping into the cold leather seat.

"Me too." He closes the door, leaving me with that strange response.

Is he asking *me too?* Like he wants to know if I love him too? Or is he saying *me too* as a statement because he loves my dog? He's met her two times. That seems like quite the jump from strangers to *love*. Even if she is totally loveable.

The driver's side door opens and Caleb slips into the seat with a shiver. "I like Wilson and all, but I feel like Akili is more discerning. Like winning her over means something. Wilson loves everyone."

"Wilson?"

He glances at me as he turns over the ignition. "Sophie's dog. Sorry, *labradoodle*."

"Oh, right. You should tell her my friends and I get together with our dogs sometimes. It would be nice to see her again." I don't realize the truth in that statement until I say it.

To be honest, after Caleb left and my friendship with Sophie dissolved overnight, losing her hurt almost as much as losing him. To keep myself from drowning in the heartache, I hadn't thought about her much until I ran into her at *Hibiscus*.

"I miss her—" Thankfully, I stop myself before I say *too*.

"She'd like that. I'll let her know."

I'm so busy watching his profile—the tensing and releasing of his jaw; the tilt of his lips; the glimmer in his eye at the mention of his sister—I don't realize we're headed in the opposite direction of my house until we pull into a parking lot. "Fast food?"

"Home of the breakfast sandwich. I figured you could use something to eat."

That's actually really sweet. "But fast food?"

"The salt content and trans fats mask the lack of flavour. Unlike some places that put kale in a bowl and call it a meal. At least here you know to manage expectations." He navigates his car into the drive-thru line, stopping behind a pickup truck. "What are you having?"

I duck so I can look up at the menu board. "BLT bagel, I guess."

"And Akili? For being a good girl at the dentist?" He faces me with the most ridiculous puppy-dog eyes, rivalling my pug.

"Seriously?"

"Yeah, seriously. Breakfast burrito? Donut?" He eases forward and stops at the speaker, then turns to face me with one raised brow.

I open my mouth to speak, but close it, because I can see how excited he is to treat Akili. Under normal circumstances—especially after eating raw bacon—I'd say no, but I let him have this. Even if it means she'll love him more than me.

Once we grab our food from the second window, Caleb pulls into a parking spot in a quiet corner of the lot.

"You have to be at work soon," I note, grabbing my bagel sandwich.

Akili can't be bothered with my sandwich—probably turning her nose up at the vegetables—and jumps over the centre console into Caleb's lap. It's almost like she knows he's planning to spoil her.

"I know." His words come out with zero enthusiasm. Whether that's because he's feeling burnt out after no days off or for some other reason, he doesn't elaborate.

But I don't allow myself to read into it, either.

His enthusiasm for Akili betraying me and settling in his lap is another matter entirely.

I force myself to keep my smile in check by biting my cheek more often than my breakfast sandwich. The pair of them are thick as thieves by the time Akili has eaten a quarter of Caleb's sandwich and a plain mini donut. It's a good thing she stepped on the scale before this stop, or the vet would have been concerned.

Once we've eaten, Akili hops back into my lap with some urging. She's not happy about leaving her new BFF.

Caleb sighs and slips his car into reverse. "Do you need to stop anywhere else?"

It's nearing noon, so if he detours any more than driving me home, he'll be late for his usual start time. "No, I'm good. We can walk—"

"Just let me drive you home."

I nod. Without giving it any thought, I rest my unoccupied hand on the centre console. It startles me when Caleb's arm soon rests beside mine. The proximity of our hands would make it so easy to reach over and link them together. Just like we used to when he drove me home.

Back when he loved me... or at least said he did.

We pull onto my street in silence, then into my driveway.

I know he's in a hurry, so I grab onto Akili and reach for the door. "Thank you for today." Before I climb out, I hand him a wrinkled piece of paper.

"What's this?"

"My number. We never got to talk. Now you don't have to show up at my door."

Because as much as these past two hours have made my stomach flutter with each accidental contact or slight smile, I can't get his words out of my head. I want answers, even if I can't be angry with him right now.

"You still have the same number," he states, looking at the paper.

Finally, I step out, clutching Akili in one arm as I bend down to reply, "That's probably the only thing that hasn't changed."

31

CALEB

How I feel

We never even got to talk. I wanted to hash out whatever was bothering her that explained why she had been acting so short with me. Instead, I showed up at her house and it looked like she wanted to kiss me rather than ream me out. Even while she was gushing blood. If her parents weren't home, I would have. No question.

Now that's all I can think about as I try to navigate the rest of my shift. I've never been this much off my game. Ever. Not even when my world was caving in around me in France. The kitchen has always held my focus and been the main source of my passion. At least, it was for the ten years I was on the other side of the Atlantic.

Now, my head is elsewhere.

"Chef, why don't you go home early tonight?" Jorge asks, interrupting me staring off into space.

If anyone else had suggested that on any other day, I would have pointed out that I'm the boss around here. The same way I've done to Hannah multiple times for making similar suggestions. But today, that idea sounds really appealing. I may have taken the morning off, but this place is functioning well enough in my absence, I think I can cut out an hour early again.

"Thanks. I'm overtired. I think I've hit the burnout stage."

The concession seems to surprise Jorge. "No problem, Boss. Working every day will do that. Go get some sleep."

I clap Jorge on the shoulder and nod. "Thanks, man. I appreciate it."

He responds with a tight smile. One that says he doesn't quite buy my tired excuse, but he doesn't call me on it.

Before he changes his mind, I unbutton my jacket and walk into my office. It's still a disaster, but it's better. Another task on my list that I've failed to find the time for. Trying to organize my office requires me being here outside of the normal hours I already am, and as much as I eat, sleep, and breathe this place, it's just not practical to spend more time here than I do.

For the first time in three months, I'm going home before 11pm, and all I get from the free time is more opportunity to question how I'm supposed to go forward.

Oscar has been harassing me to get back to the gym with him. Honestly, after the past few weeks, I could use an outlet for my pent-up frustration. Plus, I can pretend the speed bag is Todd's face. Or Ivan.

The second I walk through the change room doors and Oscar spots me, he says, "What happened to Tuesday?"

"I... uh... something came up. Sorry, man."

"Excuses, excuses." He smirks, finishing up his hand wraps. "Are you going to tell me what you meant last week?"

I drop my bag on the bench, then grip my temples with my thumb and middle finger. The mere thought of the situation I was referring to angers me all over again. I tell Oscar about running into Hannah's ex, the verbal exchange that preceded the initial physical one, and how I went after Todd once I found out he was the reason for the scar on Hannah's face. I don't tell him how I laid awake that night, wondering how many other scars she has hidden. How many bruises she suffered that have since healed. Nor how I daydreamed about repaying Todd for each one. But Oscar's not an idiot.

"Shoot. He's not pressing charges, though?"

"No, not as far as I know. He swung at me first, and I only hit him once, so they called it self-defence. But man, I tell you, I wanted to pound his face in. I can't get past…" My words trail off because my voice is cracking. The surge of emotion surprises me. "If I hadn't left—"

"Don't do that to yourself. I know it sucks, but you can't take on the blame for what happened. You might think you're Superman, but you're not."

I look up at my wise-beyond-his-years nineteen-year-old cousin and smile. "Nah, I don't think I'm Superman. I think you are."

He takes an easy swipe at my head, but I duck out of the way.

"You know I've always said what we learn here should stay here, but I'm glad you stood up for her."

Me too. But I don't say that, either. "All right, time to torture me to make up for missing the past few weeks. You've got an hour to have me begging for mercy."

He responds with a slightly maniacal laugh. "I only need fifteen minutes."

Sixty minutes later, I'm lying on a mat beside a heavy bag, with my chest heaving and my clothes drenched in sweat. Oscar was right. I was in a world of hurt after fifteen minutes, but I won't give him the satisfaction of knowing that.

"You okay, old man?"

"Shut up before I get Grandpa to come teach you a lesson, youngster."

He reaches his hand down to pull me up. "I have no doubt that he could."

We both chuckle. Well, Oscar chuckles; I wheeze, standing with my hands on my knees.

"So, where do you stand with Hannah now?"

That question makes it even harder to breathe. I settle for the obvious answer. "I'm her boss."

"Guy, I saw the way you put your hand on her back last week, like you were staking your claim."

"I did not!" Did I? If I did, it wasn't a conscious move, because I don't remember doing that.

"So, you missing Tuesday's session had nothing to do with her?"

This kid is too perceptive for his own good... or, rather, for mine.

Finally, I answer, "I miss when you used to run around trying to wipe boogers on everyone. You were far less annoying."

He swipes at me again, but this time, because I'm still hunched over, makes contact with my ear. "You wouldn't say that if you knew how many times I spied on you and Hannah." Then he jumps out of my reach and starts jogging to the locker room like the last sixty minutes of intense exercise were no more than a single flight of stairs. He sings loud enough for the entire gym to hear, "Caleb and Hannah, sittin' in a tree..."

All eyes are on me as I find my last bit of energy and dart after him. I chase him into the locker room, but he's nowhere to be found when I enter.

"Boo!" Oscar pops out from behind a locker door, scaring the little breath I had left out of me.

It might have escaped in a high-pitch squeal.

"Geeze, man. What the hell?"

He starts laughing the same irritating cackle he tormented us with as a kid. "You said I was less annoying when I was younger, so I was proving a point." He quirks an eyebrow at me. "Want me to wipe a booger on you for old time's sake?"

"I'm good, thanks. You win."

He claps me on the back, then walks into the middle of the near-empty locker room. "So, what's the deal with you and Hannah?"

I stare at the ground as I amble to my locker, not wanting to answer his question the second time, either. "I don't know, man. It's hard to separate work and personal feelings, you know? It's not like I'm a mensch in the kitchen."

"You don't say?"

"Har, har. You and Sophie should take your little act on the road. You're both hi-larious." I shake my head, putting the last of my gear away, with a clear reminder it all needs to be washed… or burned. "Anyway, then on Tuesday—"

"Called it."

"Job well done, Sherlock." I roll my eyes at him. "She'd been snappy with me at work the night before, so I went to talk to her on my way here. Then I just got… sidetracked."

"Listen, I know my opinion doesn't mean much, but what's the harm in giving it another go?"

I contemplate his question for a full minute, but it's too complex to articulate in a locker room. Maybe anywhere. "You're wrong."

This time, he raises both eyebrows as he tucks his shin guards into his bag. "About?"

"Your opinion means everything."

He barks a laugh—his normal, nineteen-year-old laugh. "Don't tell Grandma or Sophie that."

"Wouldn't dream of it. Then they'd know where the answers to all life's questions are, and I'd lose my guru."

"You're an idiot." Now he rolls his eyes and stuffs the last of his gear into his bag, then hoists it onto his shoulder. "All I'm saying is that if you want to make it work, make it work. If you're not interested, maybe you can give her my number."

I know he's goading me. Just like he did at *Hibiscus* last week. Just like he's done ever since he was old enough to ride a two-wheeler. Don't react. Stay cool. "Over my dead body."

Yep, that fit the brief. Calm, cool, and collected. Just like I told myself I would be.

"See. If you don't want your Superman Guru, ultra-good-looking younger cousin to take her out, maybe you should consider doing it yourself."

32

HANNAH

Honestly

"I'll get it," my mother calls as I exit my bedroom, rubbing my eyes.

Good thing she plans on answering the door, because I'm not dressed or even halfway decent. I slept in, and now I'm going to be in a rush to get ready for work and make it on time.

"Hannah, Caleb's here to see you… again," Mom says just when I reach the end of the hallway. Conveniently. Like she couldn't have said it five seconds sooner, so I wasn't standing here completely exposed.

Yep, that's Caleb. My boss. Looking at me in my Powerpuff Girls T-shirt and shorts—a pair of pyjamas that have seen better days, considering they're thirteen years old and way too tight.

Akili tears past me with an enthusiasm she only has for me when she's been alone all day. The little traitor.

"Hey," he greets.

I don't know what he's looking at because I can't focus on his face. I'm watching Akili jump at his legs. He bends down to scratch her ears. Oh, he was probably talking to her.

"Hi," I finally reply, in case he was addressing me. "Um… you could have called."

My mom's eyebrows inch upward, likely on account of the snark in my tone directed at my boss.

Caleb doesn't seem surprised, though. "I know. I... uh... I wasn't sure if you'd answer."

I step forward, not wanting to be rude, but also not wanting to get too close. "So you decided to stop in... again?"

"Just thought it would be good for the environment if we carpooled. Yeah?"

"That's not necess—"

"Let me get out of your way, kids. Caleb, can I get you anything? I won't embarrass myself by offering to cook something, but coffee? Tea?" My mother slowly backs away toward the kitchen.

"No, thank you, Mrs. Parker. I'm fine."

Without another word, our buffer leaves the room. I wish Akili wasn't so obsessed with Caleb so I could hold her over my braless chest like a shield. Instead, I cross my arms. "You don't have to drive me to work. Aren't you supposed to be there earlier?"

"Nah, Adriano and Tyson are there and I'm sure they have things covered. Want to stop for a breakfast sandwich on the way?"

I swear, Akili's ears perk up when he asks that. "You've spoiled her."

"Wow. You're a smart little thing, aren't you?" He nuzzles his nose into her neck, making baby sounds.

What is happening right now? I know he said that he loved her the other day, but I thought it was just... conversation. Like, *yeah, I love cheesecake*. But the way he's gushing over her, and she's lapping it up, I'm beginning to think he meant it in more than a platonic way.

And that does a number on my confused heart.

I need space. "Come in. You can sit in the living room while I shower and get ready."

Caleb's eyes widen, and for the first time, it appears he's taking in my outfit. Though, instead of the laugh I'm expecting, he bites his bottom lip and trails his eyes down my body. His gaze alone gives me goosebumps. "Right, yep. Okay. Akili and I will wait in there." He takes a deep swallow, slipping off his shoes without putting my dog down.

I don't wait around to make sure he gets settled. My timeframe to get ready just increased by thirty minutes, but the sooner I get Caleb out of here, the better it will be for my frazzled emotions.

The entire time I'm in the shower, I replay the extremes our encounters have wavered between. Cold, distant Caleb who first greeted me at *Hibiscus*. Angry, micro-managing Caleb who insulted my flounder. Caveman Caleb who beat up my ex to defend my honour. Or the one who used the sole morning off he takes each week to drive me and my dog to the vet.

He must be walking around with eight different personalities, because each day, I get a new one. Even if the cranky, harsh Caleb is appearing less frequently, that still doesn't mean anything. Not when I overheard him saying he wishes I'd quit.

A conversation we still haven't spoken about.

And now, enough time has passed, I'm not sure it's any of my business. It's possible he wasn't even talking about me. He could have been talking about his sister, because I know she works for Henry. Why didn't that occur to me before?

I run my round brush through my hair, blow drying my long locks, with Kelly Clarkson encouraging me with one of her many incredible pop ballads. Instead of singing the lyrics, I find my mind drifting to how Caleb would react to new extreme hairstyles. What if I got a perm? Dyed it blonde? Cut it all off? Why is this even crossing my mind?

I pause the song, then stare in the mirror for several seconds, willing my reflection to reply.

The answer is clear: because I care about his opinion of me. And not just the quality of food I'm creating.

Maybe that's why my passion for creating food has disappeared.

Maybe that's why I can't tell up from down in his presence.

Regardless, it's the reason I need answers to that burning question. Does he want me to quit?

Fifteen minutes later, I walk into the living room to find my mother chatting with Caleb. She finishes explaining to him that my dad left for his usual flight to Nassau. I can tell by her words that she misses him when he's away. Even after all these years of their routine, his leaving never seems to get easier.

"Ready?" Caleb asks, looking up at me from the sofa.

My little furry Brutus is still in his arms, tongue lolled to one side and a contented look glazed over her eyes. The only thing she's expressing is, *He's mine now.*

"Yes."

We both say goodbye to Akili and my mom, grabbing our coats and exiting into the cool winter air. Technically, we have a few days until it's officially winter, but the minus six temperature isn't waiting on a technicality.

As soon as Caleb's door closes and he's got the ignition on, I blurt, "Do you want me to quit?"

His hand freezes over the gearshift, and his eyes stay focused straight ahead at our lopsided oak tree. He opens his mouth. Closes it. Blinks four times.

"Are you having a stroke? Lift your arms. Try to smile." I know he's not having a stroke, but I just got a clear answer to my question. "Whatever. That was the only answer I needed."

He does lift his arm, but only to shift the car into reverse. "Hannah."

"No, don't bother, Caleb. I knew this was a bad idea from the start. I thought we could be adults and focus on our job, but I guess there's too much bag—"

"It's not that."

"Then what is it?" I swallow hard and close my eyes, refusing to shed a tear.

"I don't know about you, but given our past, sometimes the lines between employee and someone I once cared a lot about get blurred."

Wow. He couldn't be more clear about where he now stands. He doesn't *still* care about me. He *once* cared about me. As in *past*. I'm surprised by how much that confirmation hurts.

"You can count on me to focus on my job. There won't be any more blurring, Chef." I intentionally use his title instead of his name, trying to fake indifference. "If I've done anything to make you think I'm not capable—"

"You haven't. That's not what I'm saying."

"I heard you in your office." I don't mean for it to come out so confrontational, but I think we're beyond decorum. And apparently beyond caring whether he's upset I was eavesdropping.

If he is, he doesn't show it. "That's part of the reason I wanted to talk. So I could tell you how much I appreciate you— your skills. You're an asset in the kitchen, and I don't want our past to bleed into work. But that doesn't mean—"

"Heard. Loud and clear, Chef."

He huffs a loud sigh. I turn to look out the window. Together, we don't utter another word for the rest of the drive.

I should have listened to my instincts a week ago.

33

Impossible

"**C**an I speak to Caleb McNamara, please?" an unfamiliar man's voice asks when I answer my phone.

"Speaking."

"I'm calling to inquire about an employee of yours; Hannah Parker?"

I freeze the second he mentions her name. "Can I ask what this is about?"

"She's used you as a reference."

Again, I take a pause, running through different scenarios in my head. She did mention getting her own place some time ago. That could be it. Or maybe a credit application? A car loan? Then again, it's hard to know when she's barely spoken to me for the past two weeks. Ever since I choked in my car and couldn't explain what I wanted to.

Finally, I just ask, "A reference for what?"

"You're listed on her resume as her current boss. I just need to ask about her performance at work."

She listed me as a work reference? For another job? Why would she…? My arm goes slack, so the phone falls away from my ear. There's no way she applied for this job months ago and they're only calling her now. All this time, I kept wavering between wanting her to stay or leave, but now the answer is crystal clear.

I lift the phone back to my ear to reply. "Now isn't a good time for me. Can I call you back at this number when I have a minute?"

"Oh, sure. The sooner the better. We have some positions we need filled, and she mentioned on her application she'll have to relocate."

Relocate? "Where are you located?"

"Vancouver."

That's clear across the country. It's not as far as France, but it's far enough it would put an end to us before we even start again. I can't blame her for that though, when I keep screwing everything up.

I mutter a few final words to the man on the phone before hanging up.

Is this some karmic joke? After how I walked away from her, now she's planning to do the same? Granted, the situation is different. We're not a couple, and she doesn't owe me any professional loyalty. But the reality is, I don't want her to leave, and it has nothing to do with her job.

Now, not only do I have to make it through the day without letting this eat away at me, I have to make up a reason to talk to her so I can figure out what her intentions are. Obviously, she didn't care about me finding out, or she wouldn't have listed me as a reference.

I rush to get ready so I can go to *Hibiscus* and drown my racing thoughts in something more productive.

My shoulders are tense for my entire drive. I utter more than a few expletives at other idiot drivers who don't know how to work a turn signal. Oscar has been on my case about discipline and controlling emotions so I can harness them properly, or some other mumbo jumbo. Harnessing emotions has never been a real strong suit of mine. I'd rather pound them into a heavy bag or pour them out in the form of sweat. That's been working a lot better than yoga.

Lucky for the long line-up of people at the elevator, I've unloaded most of my frustration on the Gardiner Expressway.

Unlucky for me, I walk into my kitchen to find Hannah and Adriano working side by side, laughing and smiling. I like Adriano most of the time. I hate him right now.

"Morning, Chef," he greets me with a wide grin.

The smile falls right off of Hannah's face as she glances up at me, then returns to her work with her lips in a tight line.

I need to fix this.

But now is not the time.

"Morning, Adriano. Hannah." I give them both a cursory nod as I walk past into my office. The chaos in here is nothing compared to my head. I've systematically sorted through some of the rogue paperwork and product catalogues, but there's still a lot to go. Miguel must have been really upset about his termination, because he did a number on this room.

I hide out in my office for ten minutes, hoping that when I re-emerge, Hannah and Adriano will be on to new tasks—farther apart.

Sophie's question about whether I'd be okay if Hannah started dating someone else, got engaged, or announced she was pregnant with another man's child replays in my head. I knew the answer then. But that was when it was hypothetical. Watching her interact with Adriano, contrasting it with how she's been around me for the past fourteen days, it's more probable than possible.

And I'm secure enough to say, she could do a lot worse than Adriano Lombardi.

But I can't be upset with her because I'm sitting here, brooding, refusing to man up and admit how I feel.

She's standing in front of the fish prep station, filleting the salmon serving as our lunch special when I return. Adriano is across the kitchen, talking to Alejandro about something.

I watch Hannah for a few seconds, thinking I am being covert.

"Can I help you with something, Chef?" she deadpans.

"How's Akili?" I'm such an idiot.

Hannah raises a thick, dark brow and sets down the fillet knife. "Really?"

"I... uh... Maybe I can drive you home later?"

"So you can see my dog?"

"No. Yes." I run a hand through my hair, feeling more frazzled in Hannah's presence than I ever have before. Even as an awkward teen who was so in love with her long before she knew. I'm sensing a pattern. "No. I want to talk. For real this time. Not a half-hearted conversation with other distractions."

She picks up the knife again, resuming her task without answering for several seconds. "Fine. Now if you'll leave me alone before I cut another finger off..."

If I'm not mistaken, the corner of her lips tilt in a subtle smile, gifting me a glimmer of hope.

"Let me know when you're ready to go."

"You're the boss."

I waste no time after we get in the car before I blurt, "Where can we go to talk? Because these car chats aren't..."

"My parents are spending New Years in the Bahamas. They're not home."

That statement gives me pause. Ten years ago, if Hannah uttered those words, I'd have been looking forward to an epic make-out session that somehow felt more thrilling. Like it was a forbidden act that I'd been conditioned to find more exciting after years of trying to do things behind Henry's back.

But today, after the phone call I had this morning, I know things couldn't be more different.

"Okay. Should we stop to grab Akili a snack?"

Hannah shoots me a glare I catch from the corner of my eye. "No."

I can't help but chuckle. "I'm pretty sure she'll still love me, even if I show up empty-handed."

"Trust me; I know." Hannah scoffs and turns to look out the window, like she so often does.

The rest of our trip is relatively silent. I'm not sure what's on her mind, but I'm wrestling with the right words to ask her about her career plans. Beyond that, I need to come up with the right way to be honest and convince her to stay.

We enter her house as Akili comes tearing to the door like she's about to burst. She doesn't even stop to say hi before she rushes out the door to go relieve herself in front of the porch steps. Watching her walk in the snow is hilarious, because she refuses to place down more than two paws at a time.

"She's been home alone all day. Usually, Mom is here to cater to every demand."

Akili saunters back inside, looking much more comfortable, but still unenthused about the frozen ground.

As soon as she reaches the door, I pick her up. "Do you have a towel or something to dry her feet?"

Hannah stands in front of us, lips parted like she wants to speak, but can't. She lifts her right arm to flick the light switch, and now I can see her face much better than I could in the residual light from the porch.

"Oh, never mind." I reach into my back pocket, remembering I tucked a clean rag in there earlier. Carefully, I dry off Akili's feet while she licks my neck. "That tickles." I tilt my head, trying to shield my neck from the tongue assault, because if I don't, I'm bound to giggle like an idiot.

"Should I give you two some privacy, or…" Hannah asks, spinning around to exit the foyer.

That does make me giggle. It cracks me up how bent out of shape she gets over how much Akili loves me. Though, I'm sure it's just because I shared my breakfast sandwich. She's an easy girl to please. Her owner, on the other hand…

I set the dog down with a gentle scratch behind her ear, then follow Hannah's footsteps into the kitchen, where I toss the rag in the trash. "I got a call from someone about an employment reference for you."

She spins around to face me, only illuminated by the foyer light. She tilts her head and scrunches her forehead, much like Akili does when she's confused. But if Hannah applied for this job, she can't be too surprised they followed through.

"Why didn't you tell me you were looking for other jobs? I felt blindsided." As soon as the words leave my mouth, I know they were a mistake.

Her nostrils flare and her eyes open, immediately looking like a fire-breathing dragon. "Oh, so you're saying it hurts your feelings that I was looking for work somewhere else and didn't tell you? That I could possibly have plans for my life that I'm not involving you in? You said it would be easier if I quit. I'm giving you exactly what you wanted."

Yep, I knew that was coming. And I deserve it.

"That's not… No, that's not what I'm saying. If you leave, I have to replace you…" I decide to stop talking. I'll just dig myself a deeper hole.

Hannah huffs a laugh, but doesn't reply. She just opens the fridge, removing a filter jug of water. She slams it on the counter, then yanks open a cupboard to take out two glasses, and slams those down too.

I step closer, wanting to spin her to face me so she can see the sincerity in my eyes, but she's occupied pouring water.

"I wish I could make what happened right, but is finding another job what you really want?"

She turns toward me and slides me a glass of water. "No. But I don't know what I want anymore. Three months ago, I just wanted a decent job. Then you showed back up and now my passion for cooking isn't enough to drag me to work every day."

That admission hurts. My throat goes dry, making that water more essential. I can tell by the tension in her shoulders, she means those words, and feeling responsible for her losing her passion makes me feel like scum.

So I need to let her pursue her passion now. I can't tell her I don't want her to go. I will not be responsible for holding her back from her dreams.

34

HANNAH

The Day we fell Apart

When I was unemployed, I sent out dozens of resumes and went to countless restaurants looking for work. Not one place reached out to me. No one was interested. So when I sent out resumes ten days ago, in a moment of frustration over the confusing feelings between me and Caleb, I didn't expect anyone to show any interest.

Imagine my surprise as Caleb confronts me about it. But his justification for asking me doesn't make the decision any easier. He wants me to stay so he doesn't need to replace me, which should make me happy. That makes his motives clear. Instead, it leaves me feeling even more crushed than my dog abandoning me for him.

He picks up his glass of water, and I gesture for him to go into the living room. I follow behind him, not turning on any more lights, because I don't want him to read the disappointment on my face.

How pathetic can I be? Upset over a guy who left me without a second thought. Like it's a big surprise he doesn't care about me as much as I do about him. Just because he's given me a ride a few times doesn't mean he's anything more than my boss. Bosses drive people places... Right?

Certainly, Mr. Harrington never did, but I wouldn't have even gotten on a city bus with him.

We drop onto opposite sides of the sofa and Akili jumps into the middle, quickly showing where her loyalties lie. She turns to the left, planting herself in Caleb's lap.

"How do we reignite your passion?" he asks, settling his eyes on Akili.

I blow out a long breath because that's not a simple answer. "At my last job, I thrived on making the best out of a crappy menu and poor management. But at *Hibiscus*, things are different."

"So… you want a crappy menu and poor management so you can thrive again?"

Okay, in hindsight, that clarified nothing.

"No. But there, I wasn't afraid to call people out and stand my ground. I felt empowered, finally standing up for myself again. In your kitchen, though, I'm afraid to do that. I don't want you to have a reason to fire me, so I keep my head down and do my work."

"And that's a problem because…?"

I grumble at myself for dancing around the point. "I won't be the source of more drama."

In the dim light from the foyer, Caleb's shadowed face turns to me. "It doesn't count as drama because you stand up for yourself or push people to do better. Drama is making up issues or petty grievances."

"It's not just that, Caleb." I pause, turning my eyes to the coffee table so I don't lose my nerve. "It's you. Working for you. It's so much harder than I thought it would be. I thought I could leave the past in the past and we could just be professionals, but it's not that easy."

"And moving across the country will make it easier?"

I swallow to moisten my dry throat, hoping my words come out with the right level of conviction. "I love… *Hibiscus*. The menu. The location. I love what we create there, and now that the rest of the staff have become a cohesive unit, it's a dream."

He exhales a loud sigh. "But you don't want to work for me."

Those words, coming from his mouth, force tears to sting my eyes. "It's not that I don't want to. It's just..."

"Too hard," he finishes, with an obvious note of understanding.

"Yeah. I just don't like who I'm becoming again, and more than anything, I need to *not* be that girl."

Caleb drops his head to focus on Akili again. She's fast asleep curled up on his lap, but we both sit here, watching her for several minutes.

I'm so conflicted. On one hand, I want to find a new job and become more myself again; a woman I can be proud of. But on the other, I'm making every feminist's head hurt by silently begging Caleb to ask me to stay.

But for the second time in my life, he doesn't choose me.

"I guess I'll go."

My heart sinks. I shouldn't have expected more. I should have known better than to think I mattered in any capacity beyond my job.

"Yeah. Okay."

He slides Akili off his lap and pushes himself to stand. She barely acknowledges the movement. Meanwhile, each step he takes closer to the door makes my chest hurt more.

Until he's out the door, reversing out of the driveway, and speeding off down the street. Then the pain becomes unbearable.

A loud knock at the door startles me as I struggle to fall asleep on the couch. I've reached a new level of pathetic, lying on the throw pillow that smells like Caleb.

"Hannah? It's me."

Caleb? I grab my phone and check the time. It's 2:19am. Unsurprisingly, he didn't call or text first. It appears he's content giving me a minor heart attack.

I walk over to the door to find my boss standing on the other side. I hesitate to open it, because I look like I've been crying for the last two-and-a-half hours. Which I have.

"Please, can I come in?"

Curiosity wins out and I swing the door open. "You really need to start calling first."

He steps inside, closing the door behind him. "We need to talk."

"I thought we just did that."

"We did, but that was about the future. I want to talk about our past."

That startles me more than the knock at the door did. I step back, tripping on my own shoe that I was too distracted to put away. Caleb lunges forward to stop me from falling—which is a contrast to when I fell in the stupid hibiscus plant on the day of my interview, and he just watched.

"Why now?" I ask once I'm steady, ignoring the sensation his touch creates.

"If we don't learn from our history, we're doomed to repeat it."

I stare at him for at least thirty seconds, trying to decipher that one sentence. Finally, I blurt, "Do you want a drink?"

"Yeah. That'd be great." He slips his shoes back off, then follows me into the dining room. "Where's my girl?"

I freeze a few feet from the liquor cabinet. "Uh…" Thankfully, I realize what he's asking before I say something stupid. "She's asleep on my bed. She has a strict routine."

"Did you wash her skin folds and do her eye drops?"

I turn around, holding a bottle of Bahamian rum, to find Caleb smirking. "Mm-hmm. I told you, a good skincare routine is important."

Caleb takes the bottle from my hand, inspecting the label. "What are we having?"

"Dark N' Stormy." I grab the bottle back and walk into the kitchen to find the stash of ginger beer I know Dad brings back with the liquor. "Here's to a night of drunken debauchery sponsored by Warren Parker."

"Just like our teenage years. Seems appropriate."

I pop the cap off of a bottle of ginger beer, topping up the rum. I guess we're really doing this blast from the past thing. A topic we've generally avoided over the past three-plus months. I pass Caleb his drink and take a long pull from mine. Actually, I might need a refill before I even get back to the living room, so I grab both bottles.

We head to the sofa, where Caleb sits closest to the fireplace, and I sit with my back toward the foyer.

"I owe you an explanation. I have for a long time, but I never knew what to say."

Another gulp. "But you do now?"

"No." Caleb brings his glass to his lips, taking an easy sip. "But I'll try."

I drain my glass, then set it on the table to refill it. "Okay. I'm all ears."

He waits until I'm leaning back, clutching a pillow, resting my drink on top of it.

"I never wanted to leave. That's the first thing I need you to know." He leans his head against the back of the couch. "I didn't leave *because* of you, Hannah. I left *for* you."

It's impossible to gauge the meaning of that when I can't look into his eyes. "What does that even mean?"

He opens his eyes and turns his focus on me, allowing the dim lights from the kitchen to shadow his troubled face. "You stood up for me, and that meant more than I can ever tell you. More than that, you gave me the courage to stand up for myself. But Henry didn't take well to that. He threatened to ruin your life if he ever saw you again. I knew I couldn't just break up with you… because I loved you too much."

I take another sip of my drink, swallowing down the "L" word he just uttered. I don't miss the fact it was past tense.

"He doesn't forgive people who stand up to him. He'd destroyed business associates for a lot less than calling him out as a deadbeat father and husband."

Now I feel a rush of guilt for confronting Henry. After all these years, I never felt regret for standing up to him. The way he treated his kids was terrible, but if what Caleb is saying is true—and I have no reason to doubt him—I only made a bad situation worse.

"I'm so sorry. I didn't know—"

"No, it's not a problem with something you did. It's him. And when I was nineteen years old, I didn't have that same courage to take him on. So one day, when he was telling me what a loser I was and how I'd never be as successful as him, I applied to schools in Europe on a whim. I really didn't think I'd get in."

Whim or not, he still did it behind my back.

"But you did, and if you had talked to me about it, I would have understood why. I wish you had told me you were applying to these places and considering going. It takes months between applications and acceptance letters, then between acceptance and getting on a plane, and, the whole time, I had no idea. You waited to tell me until your bags were packed. That's what hurt. For a good two months before that, you stopped wanting me to come to visit and made excuses to get off the phone when we'd talk. I knew something was wrong, but you never said a word."

He leans forward, resting his elbows on his knees and his face in his hands. Silent.

"If you wanted to break up with me, you should have just done it when you applied."

He pops his head up to meet my eyes with an intense gaze. "I never wanted to break up with you. Never. I didn't even know if I could go. I had no way to pay for it and couldn't ask my parents for help. I didn't want to leave Sophie or my grandparents..."

Ouch.

"... or you. Leaving you was the hardest. I kept hoping I'd find a way to make it all work out, but I couldn't. Immature me thought if you hated me, it would be easier."

Now, looking into his eyes, I see sincerity. Kindness. Regret.

"I've spent a lot of years trying to hate you. Trust me. But I can't; not even a little." And sometimes I hate that about him. He's impossible to hate and too easy to love.

He leans in closer, and it looks like he's going to kiss me. It surprises me when I realize I wouldn't hate that either. He exhales through his nose until his shoulders are several inches lower. I push the throw pillow away and lean in, letting my heart make a decision. Caleb reaches one hand out and takes hold of mine, resting on my thigh.

Instead of kissing me, he adds, "I didn't want you giving up on your plans to follow me somewhere you didn't want to go."

"Caleb, there was nowhere in the world I wouldn't have followed you."

35

CALEB

Since U Been Gone

Thank God for this alcohol to settle my nerves. I'm such a wreck, I'm surprised I haven't spilled it everywhere from my shaking hands. Now Hannah makes me regret the last decade of my life with one sentence.

"You didn't even ask me. If you loved me like you said you did, you would have asked. And you know what? I would have followed you. Yeah, I had a year of school left, but I would have come once I was done. It never occurred to you to ask if I wanted to go to France."

I inch closer to Hannah, so now, instead of just being connected by our hands, my thigh is pressed against her bent leg. "You shouldn't have had to follow me, though. I didn't want that for you. Leaving everything and everyone you knew to follow a coward across the globe who couldn't deal with his father? Nah, you deserved better than that."

"And better was breaking my heart without letting me choose for myself?" She lets go of my hand, using hers to clutch the pillow against her again. "If you had told me you wanted to open a restaurant on an iceberg floating around Antarctica, I would have bought snowsuits and lifeboats and battery-powered heated socks and made it happen."

I listen to her confident voice, believing that everything she's saying is true. "How would that be fair, though? Following me and giving up your dreams? You deserve so much better than that."

"We had the same dream," she shouts, spilling some of her near-empty drink. At a more reasonable volume, she adds, "Look, ten years later, we're working in the same place. There was no difference between me following you and following my dreams, Caleb."

I wanted to come back here tonight to clear the air between us. To let Hannah know what she meant to me and means to me still. But the more we sit here and talk, the more I feel like I royally screwed up. "I wish I could undo it all."

Hannah gives me a half-smile and downs the last of her refill. "After you left, I was a mess. I finished high school, but took a year off when I was done to figure myself out. Though I never figured out anything." She chuckles, and as much as I prefer that over her shouting, I don't get the impression she's joking. "For almost that entire year, I resented the idea of going to culinary school because that was something we said we'd do together."

How many times can I kill her passion? I want to tell her how I feel, but a huge part of me says that's selfish. She should be able to follow her own path without having to consider mine.

"But after that year of reflection, I realized nothing else made me happy. I couldn't see myself doing anything other than cooking. So I enrolled in college to start during the winter semester, and here we are."

Ever since the encounter at *Henderson Market*, I've been curious about one thing and haven't had the opportunity to ask. "How did Todd come into the picture?"

She winces, making me immediately regret asking.

"Um… quietly. He was going to the same college in a different programme. We just started running into each other randomly during my last year, and he'd strike up a conversation. As you may have noticed, he doesn't take no for an answer, so eventually I gave in and went on a date with him."

I clench my jaw and grit out, "I noticed, yeah."

"By the end of my final year, he convinced me to move in with him, so I did. I thought it was the next logical step because things between me and my parents were strained."

"Why? What happened with your parents?"

"Todd. My parents could see him for who he really was, and I didn't want to hear it. They warned me, and like an idiot, I let Todd convince me they were just being controlling and trying to ruin my life." She scoffs and turns away to face the black TV screen.

Meanwhile, I clench my hand around my glass, but I'm trying not to let Todd get a rise out of me again.

"Things were fine for a few months, but slowly, he kept planting doubts in my ear, and eventually, I had no one else left in my life. I didn't talk to my parents for almost two years." She chokes out that sentence, cracking my heart wide open.

I hate him. I've been in his presence for ten minutes, and I hate him with more passion than I've ever hated anything or anyone. Henry included. Maybe that's because I share his DNA, which prevents me from reaching that level of loathing, but I think it's more to do with someone breaking Hannah more after I already broke her.

"I'm so sorry," I whisper, leaning in closer.

"The past is in the past, remember? There's nothing we can do about it now and you are not responsible for bad decisions I made. That's on me. I should have left the first time he hit me. Gosh, I should have known long before then, but I was too stubborn... too stupid to see it for what it was."

"You're not stupid, Hannah. People like him manipulate to get what they want. They thrive on power and they'll take it however they can get it. I'm just glad you got out."

She nods and gives me a small smile. "Eventually. I stayed for three years."

Three years? I stare off into space for several seconds, imagining what her life would have been like for all that time.

"He insisted I be a kept woman; said I didn't need to work and he would provide for me. But that stubborn person inside me knew if I allowed that to happen, I'd never escape him. So I applied at a restaurant by our apartment and worked there for a few months. Todd made me deposit my paycheques into a joint account, but I had a backup account from when I was a kid, so I put all of my tip-out money in there."

Every time I think I couldn't hate this guy more, he reaches a new low.

"He found out about my account and, needless to say, he wasn't happy. Though I think he was trying to distract from me confronting him about his other girlfriend I'd discovered. That's how this happened." She traces the scar on her cheek, and I can't stop myself from putting my hand over hers to trace it with her.

I feel sick knowing what she's been through. "He never deserved you." I meet her eyes, and staring into her incredible hazel irises makes me realize something else. "Neither did I."

She drops her hand, flinging mine away. "Don't you dare. Don't play this game like I'm some prize." She stands, rubbing her hands down the fronts of her thighs. "If anything, I wasn't good enough, since I'm the common denominator."

"No!" I stand, grabbing both of her hands, pulling her against me. "That wasn't it at all, Hannah. That was never the problem. *You* were never the problem."

The contact between us creates a buzzing through my veins at an intensity I haven't felt for years. I know where my heart stands, but I won't use that to manipulate her into staying if she doesn't want to. After everything I've done, and how I left, pursuing my own plans without consulting her, I owe her the same courtesy to decide for herself.

"You were always enough. I didn't leave because I didn't love you; I left because I did."

But my words stop short before I tell her I still do.

"If you're looking for forgiveness, Caleb, then you have it. I'm not mad at you anymore. I was never really *mad* to begin with; just hurt. But I understand why you left, so thank you for giving me that closure."

He sucks in a breath through his teeth, then blows it out through pursed lips. "What if... Maybe... I should probably let you sleep."

We've already said so much—opened so many old wounds that we needed to clean the grit out to start healing—but he still looks like he has more to say. His eyes are bouncing around, unable to settle on me. His hands are fidgeting, moving from clasping each other to being shoved in his pockets.

What surprises me most is the fact I don't want him to leave. Yet, there's no reason for him to stay. Not when everything we were is in the past. Everything beyond boss and employee. Regardless of why he left, he still did, and life looks too different now. I am too different.

"Yeah, we've got a busy day tomorrow. New Years." I'm not sure why I add that, like he doesn't know the date.

"Yeah. Okay. Want me to pick you up for work?"

"I don't start until two."

"Oh. Right." He starts walking toward the foyer with slow, hesitate steps. "See you tomorrow, I guess?"

I trail behind him until we reach the front door. "I guess. See you tomorrow, Chef."

Caleb lowers his head and his voice, "G'night, Hannah." Then he disappears into the light snow falling outside and disappears once again.

"Thank you," I gush, pulling my friends in for a hug. "Come in."

Angel and Vida walk inside, each with their dogs in tow as a black Range Rover backs out of my driveway.

Akili is bouncing, happily greeting her best friends too. She's had a lot of alone time over the past ten days since my parents left for their trip, but they're set to come home on Sunday. Akili will be happy to have her servant back, and I'll be happy to have company again. Turns out, I'm not cut out for living alone, either. Which I have been since Caleb was here seven nights ago.

Cosmo, a fluffy white Maltese, and Genie, an American bulldog, follow Akili into the living room, each finding something new to sniff.

"Well, they're happy to be reunited too," Angel declares, tugging off her coat. "Seriously, why do we live here? These temperatures are outrageous."

"I know. I was hoping it would be a little warmer so the dogs could play outside, but such is life in Canada. At least I didn't have to shovel the driveway."

"I'll forever live in a condo just to avoid that job." Angel shakes out her gorgeous spiral curls that are now back to her natural dark colour after being blonde for a while.

Vida tugs off her scarf and combs her fingers through her equally impressive curls.

I've always envied their voluminous hair, but I know from their complaints before, the grass is always greener. Still, I find myself asking, "Can you guys do my hair?"

They both tilt their heads and Angel pairs that gesture with a raised brow.

"Us? Do your hair? Like how?" Vida asks.

"I don't know. Curl it? Cut it? Colour it? Whatever. I just... I need something different. It will be a good distraction while I pour my heart out and you guys give me amazing advice that will steer my future."

"No pressure or anything," Angel replies. "How 'bout we work on curling it, and we'll book a salon day soon for the rest? I will not be responsible for ruining your gorgeous hair."

"Ha! Gorgeous is a stretch. It's just... boring. Brown and straight and... plain."

Angel puts a hand on my arm, ushering me into the living room. "There's nothing plain about you, Hannah Parker. What's really going on?"

I drop into the chair Akili normally sits in, but since she's off chasing her friends around, I doubt she'll care. Then, once Angel and Vida are settled on the sofa, I tell them everything.

About my job search and how I know at least one has contacted Caleb.

About my conversation with him last week and the conflicting feelings I've been battling.

And my need to try something a little different before I can consider a massive change, like leaving home again and moving across the country.

"Oh-kay..." Vida drawls. "So let's start with your hair. Then I'll make us some drinks and we'll be in better shape to dive into the other stuff."

So that's what we do. My girls spend the better part of ninety minutes curling, setting, and spraying my hair. It's so pin-straight that the first few attempts literally fall flat. I think now they've discovered the right amount of hairspray per curl to make it stay... which I estimate to be half a can.

After we've inhaled a sufficient amount of ozone-destroying chemicals and my hair can double as a helmet, Vida goes into the kitchen to work her magic. My cocktail-making skills are limited to three ingredient drinks, but Vida takes things to a whole new level. Considering it's minus twenty-two outside, she opts for hot buttered rum—with the same rum Caleb and I drank in this exact spot seven days ago—which she sets on the coffee table when she's finished.

"Okay, this rum is *bomb*. Can your dad bring me some?" Vida asks while sitting down.

"Sure. Just take the unopened bottle in the cabinet. I'll tell Dad to bring another one back. My treat."

We spend the next two hours talking about everything. We start out serious, doing our best to hear each other out and guide each other in the right direction, but after a few ounces of rum, we're giggling, arguing who is the superior songstress between Kelly Clarkson and Christina Aguilera—though Vida refuses to be the tie-breaker—and snuggling our dogs. I even broach the topic of letting Sophie join our friends-with-dogs group, because I would love to reconnect with her.

The entire evening is so relaxing and helps to bring my world back into focus. Just because something was in the past doesn't mean it has to stay there forever; does it? Maybe there are things I can find space for again, even after all the time and changes that have happened.

When it's time for them to leave, it's nearing midnight and the dogs are all exhausted.

"I love you girls. Thank you for listening and distracting me... and making it so I can go horseback riding without any extra gear." I pat my head, feeling the crunch of my hardened curls.

Both of my amazing friends chuckle as they zip up their coats.

"Whatever you decide, we'll support you, but promise me you'll make your decision based on what you want and not what you're afraid of," Angel says.

"I will. Promise."

With one last hug, the girls and their furry companions run back out to the waiting SUV, jump in, and disappear down the street.

My buzz is wearing off, but I'm tired and hoping I can capitalize on the contentment my friends' visit left me with and get a good night's sleep. Their presence, paired with my parents' absence, made me realize how lonely I am when all I have is work and Akili. She's a great companion, but I'm not sure I'm cut out for moving away on my own.

Even walking down the hallway to my bedroom feels lonely.

But a knock at the front door stops me mere inches from my room. Akili can't be bothered to put on her guard dog act this late at night, so she turns back to look at me, then carries on and jumps onto my bed.

"Thanks," I mutter, before walking back to the foyer.

Instead of Angel or Vida, whom I expect to find, I see the face of the one person whose presence continues to overwhelm me.

I pull the door open. "Hi. You really need—"

"To call. I know. But I didn't know I was coming here until I pulled into your driveway." He looks like he had a hard day. With all the hours he's been working for the past four months, he's still never had dark circles under his eyes until now.

"Wanna come in?"

"Yeah." His face relaxes as he steps over the threshold. "Where's Akili?"

"You know her drill. She's clocked out."

"Oh. Sorry it's so late. I..." He exhales a deep sigh, shrugging off his coat. "I just wanted to talk to you for a minute."

"Okay. Well, I've got to go do Akili's bedtime routine, so you can talk while I do that." I wave him along to follow me down the hallway. Not until I'm halfway there, do I realize I'm inviting him into my bedroom. My embarrassing bedroom I haven't redecorated since I was sixteen.

"Uh… I'll just be a minute if you'd rather wait—" I don't get to finish my sentence before Akili hops out of the bed and rushes over to Caleb, jumping at his pant legs.

A smile brightens his tired face. "Hey, girl. Did you miss me?" He bends down to scoop her up, and, without hesitating, walks over to sit at the end of my bed. "Let your mom do your skincare routine, okay? We have to take care of this beautiful face." He kisses her on her nose, and I just about die from the cuteness. Swoon-induced heart attack.

I have to take a few breaths to steady myself so I can grab Akili's skin wipes and eye drops. My hands are shaking from anticipation, rather than fear, which hasn't happened to me since I was fifteen, and Caleb kissed me for the first time.

Relax. It's just my teenage love sitting in my teenage bed-room, loving my dog. Nothing to get worked up over.

He holds Akili still while I do her eye drops and clean her skin. He doesn't say a word; instead, watching each movement I make.

The parallels between this moment and where I thought we'd be at this point in our lives is alarming. But I still have so many unanswered questions, I ask the most pressing one. "Why'd you come over?"

37

CALEB

Let Me Down

My entire day consisted of stressing over Hannah leaving and wavering between telling her I don't want her to go or staying silent. When I got in my car at the end of my workday, I wasn't even sure where I was headed. But, I guess my heart decided for me, because I ended up in Hannah's driveway.

Now I'm seated on her double bed with her parents still away, acting out the beginning of a teenage fantasy. A few adult ones too. Everything right down to her curled hair and flushed cheeks are things I've dreamed about.

Minus washing Akili's skin wrinkles.

And while this might be how some of my fantasies started, I know it's not going to work out the same way they ended.

"Your hair looks good like this. It's… different."

She sets the eye drops and wipes in a basket on her dresser, then starts straightening random items. "My friends came over today. Angel and Vida. They're the ones with dogs that I said Sophie should tag along with."

"Right. I did give her your number, but…"

"So you *do* still have my number. Yet you don't know how to use it." She spins back around to face me, having run out of things to tidy. "You didn't answer my question, Caleb. Why did you come over?"

Thank God I did that one day of yoga, so I know how to take a cleansing breath. Maybe I need some more practice, because it doesn't work all that well. "I called the executive chef of *Ponderosa Pines* today. To give him a reference." I think I say it convincingly enough, I don't betray how much I hate the possibility of her leaving.

Nothing. No change in her expression at all. Until she takes a deep swallow, steps back, and averts her eyes. "What did you say?"

"I told him you're an amazing chef, and he'd be lucky to have you. That not only are you talented, dedicated, a great team player, and passionate, you're strong, fierce, independent, and… beautiful."

She lifts her wide hazel eyes to stare at me. "You did not."

"Okay, no. I didn't say the last few, but that doesn't make them less true."

"Caleb…" She lifts her arm behind her neck and sweeps all of her long, curly hair over her shoulder. That leaves her left shoulder fully exposed under the thin strap of her tank top. "I… I don't know what to say."

Sophie's question from weeks ago keeps bouncing around in my head, seeking an answer. *Am I okay with disappearing from her life again? Now that she's here, can I walk away a second time?* That answer, if it were just up to me, is an easy one. But I'm not the only one whose feelings are involved here.

I shift myself forward, adjusting Akili as I move. "Please don't go. I told myself I'd never ask that of you. If you want to explore new opportunities, you have every right to go, but I can't live with myself if I don't tell you I don't want you to leave."

She plays with the length of her hair, twirling a curl around her finger. "Why?"

Apparently I haven't been obvious enough if she doesn't know by now. Or maybe she just doubts me too much after leaving her heartbroken before.

I lift Akili and place her on the bed beside me, then stand to approach Hannah. "You're the best part of my day. If that's not obvious by me showing up here whenever you have a day off, I don't know what is." I huff a laugh, trying to stop my voice from shaking. "I want you to be my sous chef. Jorge is going to be the head chef, and before you ask, it's not because I don't think you're capable. It's because I know your passion is in creating food, not directing people. So I want you to have that role and be able to keep living that dream."

Hannah's face falls and her shoulders drop. "You came to my home—to my bedroom—to give me a job offer and beg me not to take a different one?" She scoffs, then walks out the door, disappearing into the hallway.

I glance at Akili and swallow deep because I know I screwed this up again. I swear, when I look at her, she tells me to man up and say what I need to say. She doesn't want to move to British Columbia because she could get eaten by a mountain lion or a grizzly bear.

"We can't have that. Let me go try to make this right… again," I whisper.

Hannah is standing in the foyer, holding my coat, when I reach the end of the hall. "If that's all you came here for, Chef, I'd appreciate if you kept work talk between work hours."

"Please, can you give me another minute? Let me try again?"

She glares at me, returning to the fire-breathing dragon Hannah I'm coming too familiar with. "Sixty seconds."

I breathe a literal sigh of relief. "First, I only told you about the job because I don't want you thinking you can't have your dream job here. I wanted to tell you that first so you can decide if you want to stay for you and not just *because* you're the best part of my day." I'm not sure if she didn't hear me when I said that earlier or if she wasn't interested in that confession, so I feel the need to repeat it.

Her hand drops, letting my coat drag on the floor. "Are you offering me the sous chef position because you don't want me to leave or because you think I deserve it?"

"Of course you deserve it. I wouldn't even consider it if you hadn't earned that spot, Hannah. There's no one in that kitchen I trust more than you to deliver perfect food every time. No, I don't want you to leave, but the job is not a bribe." I step forward and take my coat from her hand, hanging it back on the knob in hopes she'll give me more than sixty seconds. I'm sure that timeframe has passed already. "Your dreams are important to me. *You* are important to me, and I never want you selling yourself short or giving up on something you can absolutely achieve. Not for anyone." Me included. Perhaps me most of all.

"I wouldn't." Her eyes flick over to my coat. She pauses for a moment before turning toward the living room, nodding for me to follow. "A dream job isn't the only reason I applied somewhere else. I told you that already. This"—she wags her finger back and forth between us as she sits—"dynamic is hard to handle. My head is a mess, and my heart is..."

She stops herself short, but the mention of her heart being affected gives me hope that she has feelings for me, too.

I lower myself onto the couch beside her, intentionally not putting a full seat cushion's distance between us. "At this point, I've been an idiot so many times in my life, it's embarrassing. I could write a book about being an idiot, and the longest chapter would be about when I left you. But I don't want there to be a chapter about how I didn't tell you how I feel." I hold her eyes, hoping to relay how genuine my words are. "I'm not the same stupid kid I was when I walked away the first time. This time, if you decide taking this new job is for the best, it won't be because I was too much of a coward."

"Why are you telling me all this?" she asks, her voice quiet and hesitant.

Mine couldn't be more clear. "Because I love you, Hannah. I never stopped loving you."

38

HANNAH

Second Hand Heart

I gape at Caleb, trying to find a hint of regret or dishonesty. I don't see any of either. "No, you don't. You can't love me. We're not the same people we were before, and too much has happened. You're confusing love with… familiarity or exposure."

He deflates, slumping into the back cushions. "Do you honestly think I don't know the difference? I'm familiar with Jorge and Tyson too, but trust me, neither of them are on my mind every waking minute. I don't think about a future with them, or about kissing them, or what our kids would look like."

I choose to ignore him admitting he thinks about kissing me, because I won't lie and say I don't think about that too. "Well, to be fair, that's a biological impossibility. You could always adopt or get a surrogate, but Tyson said he never wants kids, and Jorge already has four."

"Hannah." Caleb smirks, which softens his tense jaw. "That wasn't my point at all. I don't want Jorge's kids." He leans closer, resting his hand on mine. "I know you despise scallops, but you can cook them to perfection every time. You hate baking and prefer fruit-based desserts because you think chocolate is overused. You prefer making side dishes over proteins, and I think that's because they often get overlooked and you want to make them spectacular. Which you do, by the way. The day that made you fall in love with cooking was your parents' twentieth wedding anniversary, which was also the day I fell in love with you. Having you around again, I thought it made me fall in love all over, but looking back, I know I never stopped."

If this is supposed to be a confession of his undying love, it isn't exactly what I've been dreaming of for ten years. "You don't even see how everything you said just proved my point? Everything you know about me is related to food, Caleb. To my *job*. It has nothing to do with who I am as a person. You know Chef Hannah, not Hannah Parker."

"You're kidding yourself if you think that your job isn't a huge part of who you are. You didn't choose this path because it's easy work. You go in there and give your all every day because that is who you are."

He shifts a few inches closer, so our hands are no longer our only point of contact. His proximity is enough to make me shiver from the sensation rushing across my skin.

"If you want me to prove my point, I will, and I'll keep proving it until you can't doubt how much I love you."

Those three words again make my throat go dry. I could use another drink, but I drank so much buttered rum today, my arteries will be clogged for the next three to six months. So, instead, I stare at Caleb, allowing his presence to give me the same buzz. Though I fear he's much more dangerous for my heart than clogged arteries.

He clears his throat and gently squeezes my hand. "You always wanted a pug because you read that they're great family pets and are good with children. You're a diehard fan of Kelly Clarkson and you'll fight anyone who says she isn't one of the best vocalists of our generation. You still love The Powerpuff Girls, though you'd never admit it out loud. Side note, I will admit your Powerpuff Girls pyjamas are *by far* my favourite, and the fact your dad still calls you Buttercup is adorable." He smirks again, causing my cheeks to burn hot. "I know you'll stand up to fight for everyone else before yourself. You're the type of person who gives her all to everything. And right now, you're giving your all to resisting me. But I don't think you want to, Hannah. So why can't you fight for yourself? For what you want?" He lifts his hand and grazes his thumb along my jaw.

It's not fair he has these historical tidbits of information in his memory bank to draw on. And as much as his last point is accurate, my fear that he'll hurt me again makes me disagree. "You're wrong."

His eyebrows raise, but he keeps his eyes locked on mine.

"I love The Powerpuff Girls and Kelly Clarkson, and I'm not afraid to admit either. But I'm insecure and indecisive. I drive myself crazy being a perfectionist because I'm so afraid of letting people down. I'm uncertain in my own decisions because I've repeatedly made the wrong ones—especially where my heart is concerned. So you can say you love me, but the truth is"—I stop, taking a deep breath because I don't want to hurt him, but I have to be honest—"I'm afraid to love you back."

He studies me for a moment, still skimming his thumb along my jaw, sending hordes of butterflies right to my core. "Then can you let me love you until you can trust me again?"

Can I? For ten years, I've thought about the possibility of having Caleb back in my life again. Now he's presenting me with that reality on a silver platter, and I'm not sure I'm brave enough to take it.

"I told you I forgive you. And I mean it... I do. So it's not a matter of me not trusting you. I can't trust myself."

He finally drops his hand. My confused heart releases a surge of regret, making me want to beg him to put it back. But I wasn't kidding when I said I can't trust myself. I know how I *think* I feel about Caleb. That's the main reason our back and forth over the last few months has been so taxing. Whether I can take the chance is another matter.

Caleb surprises me by saying, "Tell me what you know about me. Who am I?"

That's a loaded question. Because, like him, I have a lot of history to draw on. "Caleb McNamara. Chef extraordinaire. You… you know what? I don't even know much about who you are now. You used to like running. Now, I don't know. You used to love watching baseball, but I haven't heard you mention it once. Your sister used to be your best friend, but that could have changed too. See, so much has changed, I don't know you anymore."

"Baseball isn't as popular in France, so I kind of lost interest. I stopped running when I finished high school but now I do muay thai with Oscar… sometimes. Not as often as he wants me to."

Suddenly, his handling of Todd makes more sense. "That's how you gave Todd a bloody nose."

He turns away, looking down at his lap. "I'm pretty sure even without any training, I'd have done the same thing. But I never started working out with Oscar so I could beat people up." He lifts his eyes to meet mine.

Logically, I know that. He's not the type of person who feels the need to physically intimidate people to gain control. Even when he's shouting and dishing out colourful criticisms over someone's work, I've never been afraid of him. His presence has overwhelmed me, not terrified me.

"Okay, so you're a bit of a hot-head sometimes, but that comes from being so passionate. That same passion makes you intense and laser-focused, and when you really want something, you…"

"I, what?" he asks, locking his gaze on me.

"You… work hard at it."

With a renewed intensity I haven't seen for over a decade — not even in the kitchen—Caleb concludes, "There's nothing I want more than a second chance, Hannah. If you want to take this other job, take it. If this is the opportunity you've been waiting for to follow your dreams, I won't stand in your way for a second. In fact, if that's the case, I *want* you to take it. But I'm not afraid to work hard to prove how serious I am about you. This time, the only person who will keep me from you is you."

CALEB

A Moment Like This

Yoga is probably a smarter choice today, but once again, I find myself wanting to pour my frustration into a punching bag. Actually, frustration isn't even the right word for how I'm feeling. I'm just… lost. I left Hannah's house three nights ago with her promise she'd think about everything. At least I know I laid everything out there. If she takes this other job, it won't be because I was too afraid to tell her. It will be because I was an idiot ten years ago.

In all the years between, my work kept me going and helped me find confidence in something. But it's not enough anymore. More importantly, it's not what I want most. I'd flip burgers at a fast-food restaurant if it meant Hannah could see herself how I do. If I could help rebuild the fire in her that Todd and I both had a hand in dousing, I'd shuck oysters in a seaside shack.

I struggle through Oscar's "warmup", trying to explain what happened on Friday night. How my nineteen-year-old cousin became my go-to person for advice, I don't know, but he's a lot wiser than I was at his age. Nineteen wasn't a good year for me in terms of life choices.

"You told her?" he asks, standing a metre away in the training ring.

"I did. Flat out said that I love her and have all this time." I sigh, letting my shoulders droop. I'm an easy target, and I know it, but Oscar doesn't capitalize.

"What did she say?"

"Paraphrasing? First she said she was just familiar to me and I've mistaken that for love. Then she told me she's made so many bad decisions concerning her heart, she doesn't trust it anymore, so she can't love me back." Saying those words out loud twists my gut even more than they did when they spilled out of Hannah's mouth.

"So, what are you going to do?" Oscar takes a lazy sweep at my legs with his feet, but without any resistance on my part, I go down like a bag of bricks.

And decide to stay there.

I stare up at the flickering fluorescent lights suspended from the twenty-foot ceiling, looking for answers. "I don't know."

The light above me becomes obscured by a shadow and, once my eyes adjust, I see Oscar reaching his hand out to pull me back to my feet.

"Can I just stay down? You win, man." I tap the mat for emphasis.

"That's not how this works. I don't care if you're bleeding from every orifice of your body, you get back up. If one leg is broken and you can't stand on it, you use the other. We are not training anyone to get knocked down and stay there."

I deflate into the mat, understanding his point, but not knowing *how* to get back up. "This is my own fault. I should have never left."

Oscar toes my ribs with his foot. "Get up."

"Seriously, man. I think this is my… What's the word? Comeuppance or something. You reap what you sow. You get what you give. All that jazz."

"Get. Up," Oscar repeats with a new level of irritation in his voice. "You won't figure it out down there. I haven't been wasting my time training you, so you can quit when things get hard."

"Just let me stay here," I beg, feeling every bit as pathetic as I sound.

"No. I said get up!" he shouts. More playful than angry, but I don't want to hear it a fourth time.

"Fine!" I roll until I can get on all fours, then force myself to stand. "I'm up. Happy?"

"Nope." He smiles and starts bouncing on his toes. "I didn't mean get up off the mat." He sends a right hook to my temple, but there's no heat behind it. "I mean, you get knocked down, you grapple back to standing. Or do you want me to put you in a figure-four leg lock and you can see what it's like to be totally stuck?"

"That's not even muay thai."

"Doesn't mean I don't know how to do it. Point is, old man, you will not tap out. You will get up."

I want to be frustrated with him for relating every life experience to kickboxing. If I could solve every problem with a right hook, things would have been great after I broke Todd's nose.

But to appease my very stubborn, freakishly strong cousin, I agree. Also, because everyone in the gym is staring at me and this is one of the last places you want to appear weak.

I attempt a sad knee strike, which Oscar blocks and starts laughing. Heaven help anyone who ends up in a fistfight with this guy, because he's slicker than an oiled skillet. But the important thing is that I'm back on my feet.

Now, I just need to figure out how I'm going to fight for the love of my life.

"Can we talk?" Hannah asks at the first opportunity we've had to speak all day. At least about anything other than the thirty-two person wedding party that occupied our dining room for the better part of four hours tonight.

"Yeah. Here or…?"

"Your office is fine."

That reply leaves me with a marked feeling of disappointment. If she wanted to discuss personal matters, she'd have asked to talk somewhere else. This is business. Something that, months ago, would have filled me with relief. Now, I don't know what to think.

"Okay. We've got a few minutes while the dining room gets put back together." I nod for her to follow me into my office.

We walk in and she scans the space. It's a slight improvement since she last saw it, but it's still not somewhere you'd want to spend any length of time.

I settle in front of my desk, leaning back on my hands and crossing my ankles. "What can I do for you?" I forcefully keep the grimace off of my face as I berate myself for making this seem so casual.

"About that new job."

My heart stops beating. Actually stops. It might have fallen out altogether, but my focus is on Hannah and I refuse to look away, so I can't check the floor.

"I'm not going to take it. If it's okay with you, I'd like to stay here. At *Hibiscus.* As your sous chef," she rambles.

This is the answer I was hoping for. More than anything, I didn't want her to leave. I *don't* want her to leave. But I ask the same thing she asked me. "Why?"

She furrows her brows and glares at me for several seconds. "Is that not okay with you now?"

"Of course it is. I told you I want you to stay. I guess what I'm asking is, *why* do you want to?"

She exhales and starts fiddling with a button on her jacket. "If you think I'm going to give you some declaration of my undying love, that's not why..." Her words trail off and she scrunches her face.

Well, that's a hit I won't recover from for way longer than any Oscar has landed.

"I love this job. I love our menu and the location. There's so much potential in this place, and I feel like we can reach it under your leadership."

Again, even with the professional approval, all I feel from her words is pain in my chest. My heart is still there, turns out. It's currently breaking.

"But the truth is, if that's all I wanted, I could find that anywhere."

In a move that steals the breath from my lungs, like a squarely landed gut punch, Hannah steps forward. Her eyes are level with my chest, but she's looking upward at me through her dark lashes.

"It's not all I want, though."

I suck in a long inhale through my nose. "What *do* you want?"

She pulls her bottom lip between her teeth, continuing to stare at me without tilting her head. "Were you serious... about what you said?"

"Which part?"

She bites down on her lip until it loses colour. "That you never stopped loving me?"

I didn't realize that from everything I said, I had left any room for doubt. But, given our history, I can't blame her for needing more reassurance; which I'll happily give. "Not for one second. I might not have realized that for a long time, but I never stopped." I inch forward, testing if she'll pull away. "Hannah Parker, I love you. Still; now; always; forever. Whichever way you want me to say it so you believe me, it's true. And not because of who you were or what we had. I love you for who you are today and who you'll be tomorrow. And every day after that."

She finally tilts her head up so I can look straight into her eyes, and I notice a single tear trickling down her scarred cheek.

I trail my thumb over her scar and wipe her tear away. "Let me prove it, because there's never been anything I've wanted to work harder at in all my life."

We stand in silence for several seconds as I wait for her reply. Something. At least a slap would be an answer, but she's not hinting at anything.

Finally, she replies with two simple words that say a lot: "Kiss me."

That response never occurred to me. I've wanted to kiss her for months, and now that the opportunity is in front of me, I hesitate. Until I see the doubt in her hazel eyes that makes me afraid she thinks I didn't mean what I said.

I place my hand at the base of her neck and pull her toward me as I lean down to meet her lips with mine. Our flesh colliding together provides an instant bolt of euphoria that spreads through me, head to toes.

In between frantic kisses, I mutter, "I'll never hurt you again," and "You're perfect." I'm so dumbfounded by this reality, I don't know how much time passes before I remember we're at work. That I'm her boss, and there's an abundance of activity happening outside my office door. But the importance of that all fades away a little more with each brush of Hannah's lips against mine. The way she clutches the back of my jacket makes my entire body itch with anticipation. How she moans into my mouth makes me weak; so strong, but so, so weak.

And I promise myself in this moment that I'll never let her doubt how much I love her again.

HANNAH

Dirty Little Secret

Things with Caleb have been great since we decided to give "us" a second chance. We've managed to keep our personal and professional lives separate—at least, I think we have—and now that the kitchen is functioning without any major issues, he's been able to keep more manageable hours. Over the past three months, he's made a genuine effort to focus his time off on me.

And it feels nice.

Really nice.

Maybe too nice.

Like the calm before the storm that gives you a false sense of hope, then the levees break and you're washed away in rushing waters you stand no chance of combating. Or maybe that's just my past experience making me jaded.

My middle name *is* Jade.

That thought hangs over me like a dark, looming shadow, though.

"How's the hottest chef in the kitchen?"

Oh, it's not the thought. It's Ivan. Standing next to me with his arms crossed and a scowl marking his awkward features.

I scan the room for Caleb… really, for anyone, hoping someone will intervene, but Adriano has disappeared, Jorge and the other chefs are occupied with their tasks, and Alejandro is washing dishes with his headphones on.

"You're not supposed to be back here. You should leave."

He steps forward, crowding my space even more. Of course, he couldn't have approached me while I was filleting a fish again. He had to wait until I was whisking crepe batter. Not that I would have gutted him, but it would have looked more intimidating.

"Now there's where you're wrong. I *am* supposed to be here. It's you who should be fired. If it wasn't for your pretty little boyfriend threatening to quit if my uncle fired you—"

"What?" I pause my task and turn to face Ivan. "What are you talking about? I don't even have a boyfriend," I choke out, though I'm pretty sure that's a lie. I think I do. Probably. Yeah, he is, isn't he?

"Don't act like you don't know. No one in their right mind would give up a job for a chick, even if she's hot."

So much of what Caleb has told me before replays in my head. His voice telling me not to be a doormat. That it's not drama if I'm sticking up for myself. But I don't get to reply to Ivan's words before he's off on another tirade.

"Now I have this stupid job where Alec is constantly busting my balls, making me clean people's disgusting food off of their tables. I didn't know you were such a prude, or I wouldn't have given you the time of day."

I clench my teeth. "Yeah, if only you had spoken to me like a human being, you could have kept the job you *clearly* loved so much." I roll my eyes, intentionally turning my head so he can see.

"You're a real bi—"

"Hey!" Adriano yells from behind us. "Get out, man. You're not supposed to be here." He wastes no time getting in between me and Ivan, shielding me with his body. "Go," he orders the kitchen crasher.

"This is none of your business. All you pretty boys in here, thinking you run the place."

He really is delusional if he doesn't see that the other higher up chefs *do* run the place. Despite what his shared last name has made him think, he's not in charge of anything. Short of scraping gum off the bottom of chairs.

"Just get out. I'm sure if you look hard enough, you can find someone who actually wants to talk to you," Adriano retorts.

That would require a search far and wide, but I don't add that input out loud.

Mercifully, Ivan decides to walk away, but based on the glare he sends me, I can expect him back. Again. Why am I a magnet for this? Why can't I just come to work and focus on food? Is it some prerequisite for women in this industry to cook while fending off unwanted advances? I wish they had warned us of this in culinary school, because I would have found a different job.

Seconds later, Adriano turns to face me, so I finally look up. Ivan is gone, thankfully.

"Are you okay? He's such an idiot."

As much as I thought I was okay, Ivan's presence just brought a rush of memories to the surface. I stare off at a spot behind Adriano until it blurs and my mind goes completely blank.

Adriano wraps his arms around me and pulls me in for a friendly hug. If Ivan had tried that, I would have kneed him in his busted balls so he'd realize Alec hasn't been so bad. But I count Adriano as a friend. Someone I can trust. So I welcome his comfort.

Until a throat clears behind us.

"Get back to work," Caleb barks.

I haven't heard that level of anger in his voice for months.

Adriano attempts to speak, but Caleb cuts him off, repeating his order. Adriano leaves me with a gentle pat on my shoulder as I try to blink my vision back into focus.

"What happened?" Caleb steps forward, but I put a hand out to stop him.

We are not blurring professional lines any more than we have. Just because Adriano gave me a hug, doesn't mean Caleb should. Adriano isn't my boss, and everyone in here knows how much he loves his girlfriend. No one will read into it. Caleb is a different story; according to Ivan, we haven't been as covert as we thought.

I clear my throat, which helps to chase my threatening tears away. "Let me finish these crepes so I can get the batter in the fridge."

"Han—"

"Chef, I'll come to your office in two minutes."

With that, he leaves me to get back to my task.

I place the batter in the fridge and proceed to Caleb's office. The door is open a crack, so I slide it open an inch and peek inside. "Chef?"

Caleb tugs the door open, pulls me inside with an arm around my waist, then closes the door behind me. "What happened? Why did I walk in to find Adriano all over you?"

The accusatory tone of his question infuriates me. "Excuse me? You mean a friend giving me a hug because Ivan showed up and refused to leave?"

"Ivan?"

"Yes," I shout, but lower my voice so we don't attract attention through the door. I continue to tell Caleb what happened and exactly why Adriano was giving me a hug. "Not that I should have to explain any of that to you. Are you really that insecure that after a few months, you think you can control who touches me? Because I hate to break it to you, Caleb, but I spent enough of my life being controlled by an insecure man, and I'm not willing to do that again." My anger doesn't even allow me to think straight as I step to the door to open it.

Caleb clears the distance from his desk before I turn the knob, placing a hand on the top of the door to stop me. "Please, don't go. That's not what…"

Despite his down-turned lips and drooping eyelids, I don't have the patience to feel sorry for him right now. He can look sad all he wants, but that doesn't change what just happened.

"I think you need to learn where to direct your anger, because even *if* Adriano was being inappropriate instead of being a good friend, I was reciprocating. So if someone were to deserve your anger, it would be me. And clearly you haven't paid much attention, because he's in a very happy, committed relationship."

"You're right. I'm—"

"I'm taking the rest of the day off." Without waiting for him to reply, I open the door and leave.

Adriano gives me an apologetic smile when I pass him, and it takes every ounce of energy to relax my face to send one back. He has nothing to apologize for, but I sincerely hope Caleb will.

I'm so distracted, I nearly crash into this stunning blonde woman waiting at the hostess station. "I'm so sorry," I utter, pausing to make sure she hears me.

"Oh, 'tis no bother, *ma chérie. 'Scuse.*"

I force yet another apologetic smile and continue on my way out the door.

My blood pressure and heart rate lower as I approach ground level, and even more so as I near the bus stop.

Did I overreact? Was I justified in getting so upset?

What kind of idiot am I, leaving my job over something so stupid? My work ethic matters, and here I'm compromising that because of a lovers' quarrel.

No. I'm better than this. Caleb and I can talk this out like rational adults, and I can let him know his alpha-male possessive nonsense won't be tolerated. We've been back together for the same length of time I was on probation, so I can't expect everything to be smooth sailing from the start. There's a learning curve.

Before I reach the shelter for the bus, I decide to turn around and go back.

The elevator dings for the twelfth floor, where me and four others exit. They head to the right for the hostess station, and I veer left back to the kitchen. As soon as I enter, I scan the space for Caleb, but I don't see him anywhere. Everyone else is so busy shouting out orders and timing for their respective dishes, I don't think anyone notices me.

I walk toward his office, noticing the door is open a crack, and the light is on. As I approach, I hear his voice, but can't understand what he's saying.

The female voice, on the other hand, is quite recognizable. The French woman I bumped into not ten minutes ago. "We are good *togezer*. I *mees* you, *mon amour*. Won't you come back?"

I glance in the crack of the door and spot Caleb leaning against his desk with his arms behind him. His usual relaxed pose. The gorgeous woman steps forward, stopping between his legs and tugging on the collar of his jacket.

"You want me to come back to France? With you?" Caleb asks.

That's all I need to hear before I turn back around and once again leave *Hibiscus*. Perhaps for good.

44

CALEB

Let Your Tears fall

As if having an argument with Hannah wasn't bad enough, this day became infinitely worse when my ex-girlfriend walked into my office. Someone is getting fired for letting her back here. She's the type to cause a scene if she doesn't get what she wants, so I can't exactly kick her out, though.

She's not even close to my priority right now, but I have no choice but to deal with her. Our proximity makes my skin crawl when she steps forward and touches my jacket. I attempt to appease her for about thirty seconds before I completely run out of patience.

I place one hand on either of her shoulders, gently moving her backwards. "I'd rather sit on a rhino's face than go back to France. Largely thanks to you and your father. Whatever your reason is for coming here, I don't want to hear it. Now, if you don't mind, I have work to do." I glare at her to help solidify my point, and in doing so, I ask myself how I ever found anything appealing about Madeline Laurent.

Her mean-spirited, selfish behaviour is hidden well behind her flawless alabaster skin and sapphire eyes. Probably, what I found most appealing about her was how different she was from Hannah. Not because I didn't love Hannah, but because I couldn't bear to be reminded of her at every turn. So I ended up with someone who couldn't be more different.

Madeline disregards my clear refusal, insisting her father will give me a new role as executive chef, and that she and I can pick up where we left off. But her presence hasn't only made it clear leaving France was the right choice for me; it also makes me understand just how serious I am about Hannah.

"Time to go." I step to my door, swinging it open wide. "I'd say please tell your dad I said hi, but frankly, I don't care."

Her eyebrows pinch together for a fraction of a second before she relaxes her face to neutral. A trick she has practiced to protect herself from premature wrinkles. "I'll be at *ze International 'otel* until Sunday." She blows me a kiss, then sweeps her hair behind her shoulder.

I follow her to the exit for two reasons. One, I want to make sure she leaves. Two, I want to see if anyone hints at having any familiarity with her who would have let her in my kitchen.

Lo-and-behold, Ivan sends her a wink when we walk past. If he hadn't already sealed his fate today, that would have done it. Now I'm just glad I don't have to fire two people.

Madeline leaves without any further drama, thankfully, but I'd bet her father sent her here with strict instructions not to cause a scene. Again.

Now the only thing on my mind is speaking to Hannah. I need to talk to her. I want to be honest and explain what just happened, because now, more than ever, I understand I had no right to get frustrated when I found Adriano hugging her. Actually, I owe him a thank you for getting rid of Ivan. Though that situation is far from dealt with.

Why won't she answer the phone? After I try three times, I start to get worried, so I send her a text.

Caleb: Hey. You ok? Can you call when you get this? We need to talk. Love you.

While I wait for a response from Hannah, I pick up my office phone to call Sergei.

He answers on the first ring and I waste no time voicing my demands. Ivan needs to find a new job out of this restaurant immediately or I will notify the labour board of the behaviour that's being allowed here. I don't care how hard I've worked to rebuild the reputation of this restaurant; I will drag its name through the mud to protect Hannah from dealing with Ivan again.

Sergei resists, utters some words in Russian that I suspect I wouldn't appreciate, but eventually complies. In Sergei's case, profit margins trump freeloading family members. He's finally seeing the profits he expected after his extensive renovation, and he's not willing to give that up for his brother's entitled son.

With that settled, I am more eager to talk to Hannah. I try calling her one more time, and when she doesn't answer again, I leave her a voicemail. "Hey; it's me. I wanted to check and make sure you got home okay... and apologize. I'm sorry about earlier, but I took care of it and Ivan won't be a problem again. Please call me back so I can tell you that in person. I love you... and I'm sorry."

Before the screen of my phone dims, a text message pops up.

Hannah: *Not really in the mood to talk. LOL.*

Her saying she's not in the mood to talk would be concerning enough, but the ironic 'emotional support LOL' concerns me even more. I have to fix this. I unbutton my coat and toss it in the laundry bin on my way out the door—for no other reason than I can smell Madeline's obnoxious perfume on it.

"Jorge, I'm headed out for a bit and I don't know how long I'll be. Can you handle things here?"

He nods. "Sure, Chef. Got it covered."

That's all I need to hear before I run to the back of the kitchen and press the button for the service elevator. I'm not going through the restaurant and risking an encounter with Ivan right now.

Thirty minutes later, I'm standing in front of Hannah's house, knocking on the door. Her dad's new car isn't in the driveway, but it's possible he's away. After my third attempt, I hear rustling on the other side, though I can't see anyone through the window.

"Hannah?"

Like a total creep, I press my ear to the door. I hear Akili tapping around the foyer. Otherwise? Silence. I make a last-ditch effort to call her one more time. A second after my phone rings, hers echoes inside the house. At least I know she's home.

"Hannah, please? Can you open the door? I'm sorry for overstepping earlier."

It's not like her to ignore me like this. We haven't had an actual fight since we reconciled, but this is so unlike her. That's one thing that has changed since our whirlwind teenage romance. Now, we're in a trust-rebuilding phase. I only hope she knows I would never hurt her on purpose. I've learned from my mistakes.

I hear a sniffle from inside, and that drains the last bit of my calm. "Hannah, open the door. Please." I knock repeatedly until Akili starts barking and the door finally swings open, revealing a puffy-eyed, red-faced Hannah.

"Babe, please, don't cry. I'm sorry for being an idiot." I step forward to give her a hug, but she presses her hand to my chest.

"Stop. No. Not until you tell me who that woman was."

A million thoughts flash through my head. I assume she means Madeline, but how does she know about her? Did Adriano text her? Did Ivan somehow tell her? Before I can ask my own question or answer hers, she clarifies.

"I came back to tell you I was sorry for overreacting; so we could talk about what happened. The way Ivan blamed me for his problems took me back to years with Todd when everything that went wrong was my fault. I was on edge and upset, and I shouldn't have left. By the time I got to the bus stop, I realized that, so I turned around. What a surprise to find you in your office with another woman standing way too close to be a business contact, begging you to return to France."

I don't want to be one of those people who blames someone else for their mistakes, but if I see Ivan again, I'm afraid he might need those dentures. If he had never approached Hannah, this wouldn't be happening. If he had never let Madeline into my office, this wouldn't be happening. Basically, if Ivan had a decent bone in his body, *this wouldn't be happening*.

There's only one thing I can do to fix it.

"Let me tell you everything."

That seed of doubt I've been carrying around has flourished into a hungry woman-eating corpse flower. My instincts are terrible when it comes to protecting my heart, and no one has the power to shatter it like Caleb McNamara. But I couldn't *not* open the door.

I don't think I'm a complete idiot. He wouldn't have shown up here or left text messages and voicemails, telling me he loves me if he was going back to France. Then again, last time, he told me he loved me every day until he broke up with me, and he knew he was leaving then, too.

"I'm listening," I prompt.

He bends down to pick up Akili, who can't seem to read the room. For such a wise little creature, she can be kind of daft sometimes.

"Can we go sit down? It's a long story."

"Fine." I walk to the sofa, settling into the seat farthest from the fireplace.

Caleb and Akili get comfortable at the other end.

"You're watching *Chopped*?" Caleb asks, glancing at the TV.

I reach over to click the power button on the remote instead of answering.

"That show makes me question my skills as a chef. I don't know if I could make anything edible out of pork rinds, cactus pears, and grape soda."

"I'm sure Akili would eat it," I retort with full confidence.

Caleb laughs, but it's lacking any humour. The tension in the room is intense. There's no way he doesn't feel it too.

Before he explains anything else, there's one other thing I want to know. "Did you really tell Sergei you'd quit if he fired me?"

"How did you find out...?" He pauses for a second, continuing to pet Akili. "Ivan?"

"Yeah. I don't know if he thought that would make me mad or something, but it didn't. He was using that as a guilt trip to prove how I ruined his life."

Caleb shakes his head and rolls his eyes. "Well, we don't have to deal with him anymore. Sergei wasn't too keen on the idea of a labour board dispute, so he agreed to send him to one of the other family businesses. Hopefully, in Siberia."

That's a relief. Ever since the encounter that resulted in Ivan being moved to the dining room, I haven't seen him much. I could handle the odd glare when he dropped dirty dishes in the dish pit, but for the most part, things have been civil. I was fine with that arrangement until today.

Caleb absentmindedly strokes Akili's back as she curls up in his lap. "I'm sorry I wasn't there to handle Ivan. I'm even more sorry for how I reacted. I didn't think Adriano was making a move on you... I was worried you looked freaked out and I didn't know how to fix it."

"That's ridiculous, Caleb. You can't always be the person to come in and 'fix it'." I add air quotes for emphasis. "Most of the time, I need to fix things myself. All I need from you is support. You can't be going around breaking noses of everyone who upsets me. You're not a neanderthal."

"Maybe a bit neanderthal. I can't promise there will never be a day when I throw you over my shoulder and take you to my cave."

I laugh, picturing that scene. "Oh great. A cave man and an idiot all rolled into one. I'm a lucky girl."

His playful smile disappears and morphs into a straight line.

"I am a lucky girl. You know I believe that, right? I love that you want to protect me, but all I'm saying is that I don't always need you to."

He nods; a hint of a grin reappearing. "Now that we have that settled, can I explain who that woman was?"

My shoulders tense, preparing for the weight of this conversation. "Please."

"Her name is Madeline Laurent. Uh... I guess you could call her my ex-girlfriend. Truth be told, we were never serious. Or at least, I wasn't. Her dad owned the restaurant I started working at three years ago. He's a well-connected politician in Paris, and also came from a powerful, wealthy family, so he had his hand in everything."

In all the months that have passed since Caleb and I reconnected, or even the few since we started dating again, we haven't talked much about France, other than in passing conversations. To be honest, I was afraid if I did, he'd keep feeling guilty over leaving, and I didn't want that hanging over our heads. So this conversation has to cover a lot of unknown details.

"What was your job at that restaurant?"

"Head chef. The executive chef was operating four different restaurants, so he was only there once or twice a week. I thought it was my dream. The menu was incredible, and a lot of the staff had graduated from *Ecole de Cuisine* too, so it was a top-tier group. Madeline was the dining room manager, which kind of like Ivan, was a pity job she was unqualified for but got because of family connections."

"Dating someone at work is never a good idea, huh?" I chuckle, trying to bring a smile to Caleb's face.

Thankfully, a small one appears.

"In that case, it was a terrible idea. I don't even know how we got to that point, really. It started out with her showing me the sights. Then I ended up tagging along as her plus-one to a bunch of political functions. Mostly a bunch of people just like Henry, so I hated every single event. I guess that's what made Madeline seem more tolerable than she was. Compared to the other people around..."

"Sounds similar to me and Todd. Very few redeeming qualities, but wore me down from repeated exposure. Like arsenic. Micro-doses make no difference until you eventually die from the accumulation."

Now Caleb chuckles, startling Akili and prompting her frantic tail wagging. "Something like that, yeah. She was ready to get serious, and I knew I didn't want to be with her, so I broke things off, which she didn't appreciate."

I'd say some people need to have some dignity and move on; if someone dumps you, they're not *the one*. But when Caleb left me, I was a mess. I'm hardly in a position to judge Madeline for struggling to let him go.

"Sophie came to visit maybe four or five days after I broke up with Madeline, and even though she knew I had a twin sister, when she saw us together, she went berserk. I'm talking screaming in the middle of the street, crying, grabbing things from passersby and throwing them. I felt serious second-hand embarrassment, but it was hard not to laugh when Sophie whispered in my ear that I dodged a bullet." He releases a short, deep laugh again and a full smile appears.

"That's... quite a scene." Now I feel a little better about my reaction, because at least I just cried alone in my room, listening to sad Kelly Clarkson break-up ballads.

"Made the local news that evening… and the paper. As you can imagine, her dad wasn't impressed, so to save herself from her father's wrath, she threw the blame on me. That I took advantage of her. I cheated on her. The whole nine yards. Anything to justify her reaction."

As soon as Caleb says those things, I know I don't even have to ask if any of it was true. Neither the Caleb I knew or the one in front of me now would ever be capable of anything like that.

"I'm sensing a theme with people we seem to attract into our lives. Why do you think that is?" Really, between Todd, Henry, Madeline, and Ivan, we're filling up a narcissist short bus pretty fast. It would have to be short because they'd all want to be in the front row, so they could say they're number one.

"I don't know, but I'm pretty sick and tired of it. I'm not wasting any more time or energy on people like that. Not even Henry. Him and Madeline both tried to ruin my life, and both times I fled the country." He looks down at Akili, breaking eye contact with me. Even from this angle, I can see the sadness in his eyes.

"Hey, don't go there. Into that downward spiral of blame and guilt. It's not going to help anything, and you did the best you could in bad situations. I think it takes a lot of courage to pack up everything and move somewhere else. Look at me. I've gotten complacent and stayed where I shouldn't have because it was easier than leaving. You, Caleb McNamara, had the courage to leave."

He turns to face me again, gifting me with a sweet smile. "I'm so freaking proud of you for getting out, Hannah. I'm sorry I ever left and—"

"Nope. I've told you this already. You are not to blame for my terrible choices. I understand now why you left, and as much as that might play with my head sometimes, I'm not mad at you for it." I focus on Akili to say my next words. "When I heard you in your office, you said something like 'You want me to come back to France?' I panicked that you were going to leave me again."

"Babe, I promised I'd never go anywhere without you again, and I meant it."

I don't know how he does it. He takes me from raging mad to forgetting why I'm angry in six-point-four seconds flat. As much as I'm afraid of having my heart destroyed, I trust him not to this time.

"Good. Because if you made me fall so in love with you again just to leave with my heart, I don't think I'd recover."

His eyes light up, and he takes a sharp inhale. "Yeah?"

I nod my head as tears spill out of my eyes again—though, this time for a different reason. "Of course, I love you. I spent an entire decade trying not to love you, and the minute I saw you again, I knew I had failed."

He picks Akili off his lap and sets her on the floor. Her wide eyes look at me like she knows it's my fault and I'm going to hear about it later. Caleb shifts himself forward, so he's hovering above me. His lips are mere inches away from mine, but it's his eyes I'm focused on.

"I love you so much, Hannah. I know you've forgiven me and that's all that matters, but I'll never forgive myself for losing ten years with you."

"Luckily we have several decades left," I whisper, because my heart is buzzing so fast, my words come out in a breath. "I love you too, Caleb."

He closes the gap between us, tilting my chin so his mouth can capture mine with its heart-stalling softness and heat. Each movement confirms how much I love this man, because he can never be close enough. Aside from how physically attracted I am to Caleb, it's his passion, his tenderness, and his vulnerability he shares with me that makes me love him more each day.

"Thank you for coming back to me," I whisper between kisses.

"I'm never leaving again."

"Oh, Hannah!" my mom calls from the foyer.

Caleb pulls back, allowing me to lift my head and see both of my parents standing there wearing massive grins.

"Don't mind us. We didn't realize you'd be home. We'll be going." Mom turns around and swats Dad's chest, forcing him back out the door. Before she walks through the threshold, she leans back in. "Hang a sock on the door next time." Then she disappears.

I drop my head against the back of the sofa. "We should really start going to your place more."

Caleb laughs, lowering his mouth against mine again. After a few quick kisses, he pulls away. "You also need to stop eavesdropping at my office door, yeah? Next time, just come in."

My cheeks flush hotter than they already were from kissing Caleb and getting caught by my parents. "Lesson learned. You promise to never leave me. I promise no more eavesdropping."

And with that declaration, Caleb dives forward again, putting his love in action through his lips.

43

CALEB

My Life Would Suck Without You

The more time passes, the more certain I am that Hannah and I were meant to find each other again. The past four months have been the happiest of my life. Even happier than the two years we were together in high school, because now I don't have to deal with Henry. Or so I thought.

"Son."

I follow the sound of his voice and find him standing beside the fresh delivery of produce that just arrived. "What are you doing here?" I ask again. Clearly, he didn't get the point last time.

Maria stands wide-eyed with her hands clasped together in front of her like she's pleading for forgiveness. I send her a soft smile to let her know I understand. Henry's bull-headed ways are a lot different from the flirty smile Madeline no doubt used on Ivan. There's a difference between being threatened or bullied and being winked at.

Henry avoids my question, staring at me with a satisfied grin. "It seems you've had some difficulties getting in some products you wanted to order. That's a shame."

I grit my teeth, biting back what I really want to say. My staff members are unloading our shipment, and I won't undo the progress I've made over the past few months by losing my cool. I unclip the packing slip and scan my eyes down the list of items. The swordfish and tuna I ordered are missing.

Judging by Henry's expression, he knew that before I did.

"Congratulations, Henry." I slap the paperwork down on an empty prep surface. "You've prevented me from making fish. If that's the greatest satisfaction you have in your sad, miserable life, then I feel sorry for you. Because guess what? I don't need them to keep this place running. I don't need them to *continue* to be successful. And I don't need *you* for anything."

Henry's eyes flare, but he reins in his fury before he exposes his true self to my employees. "This is just the beginning, boy. You and your sister want to test me. I hope you're ready for the consequences."

Mention of Sophie concerns me for a split second. She's currently organizing my office, but I don't think there's any way Henry could know that. I send Adriano a look that I hope portrays *call security*, because I don't know how far Henry is willing to take this little episode.

But I will not back down like I used to. I'm not afraid of him or his childish tantrums. I step forward, bringing my chest within inches of his. "Try me."

Truth be told, our little local promotion five months ago proved something critical. We may rely on international products to create our menu as it stands, but there's nothing Henry can do to stop me from producing stellar food with local ingredients.

"You and your useless sister are a couple of ungrateful, spoiled brats. I should have made your mother terminate her pregnancy. Oh, I tried, but she insisted on trapping me and refused. The three of you have been nothing but leeches."

It doesn't bother or surprise me that he didn't want me, but the thought of him so willingly bringing harm to Sophie infuriates me beyond reason.

I open my mouth to launch a tirade that will have Henry McNamara cowering in the corner, but before anything comes out, our two security guards appear, halting my words. Their appearance saves me from reacting exactly how Henry expected me to.

Adriano directs them to the man I once called my father.

The only words that leave my mouth are: "Make sure he never comes in here again." Then I turn and walk away. This time, it doesn't feel like running. It feels like a victory.

Security escorts Henry out through the service elevator. The thought of Henry McNamara being removed from the premises through the doors we use to deliver raw meat brings a smile to my face. Just one small gesture that will make him realize he's not as important as he thinks he is.

I come to a stop beside Adriano. "Thanks for that. He's…" I pause, not wanting to disclose my sordid family history to an employee. But Hannah views him as a friend and he just had my back, so there's no shame in the truth. I don't have to appear as the unshakeable boss. It's okay to be human. "He's a night-mare."

"No worries. I've got a mom who's the same way. Trust me, man. They're never worth it because they'll never change. All you can do is protect your own peace and find your own happiness." He claps me on the shoulder before stepping forward and hoisting a crate of produce to unload in the fridge.

And that's all that needs to be said on the matter.

At least, until I walk into my office and my sister's focused gaze lifts from her paperwork to me.

I close the door behind me and settle into the chair on the opposite side of my desk. "So, Henry just showed up."

She drops her pen. "What? Here?"

"Don't worry. He's gone, and he won't be back. He tried to sabotage my shipment." I scrub my jaw with my right hand and grimace. "Well, I shouldn't say 'tried to' because he did, but it's really not as much of an issue as he seems to think. It's a minor inconvenience at worst."

"I'm so sorr—"

"Don't be. If there's one thing I've learned over the past few years, it's that no one else is to blame for Henry's actions. But how 'bout we promise each other we'll stop letting him have any control over ours?"

Sophie takes a deep swallow, sliding her glasses down her nose to peer over them. "I think that's a good place for us to start."

I smile at her, letting the tension from Henry's appearance roll off my shoulders. "I'm glad Hannah had the day off. He'd have had a field day if he saw her here. I'm assuming Mom hasn't told him, because if he knew, he would have asked about her."

"Well, that's one decent thing she's done, huh? Let's send her a thank-you card." Sophie rolls her eyes.

I think back to Henry's comment. "That's not the only thing, Soph."

We may have had a miserable childhood—and several years of adulthood—at the hands of Henry, but it was thanks to our mother that we had a chance at life at all. And maybe she's not the spineless villain we've made her out to be. Maybe she's a victim too.

Sophie and I sit and talk for about fifteen minutes, rehashing the past and discussing what we each want in the future. What we both want most is the freedom to be happy.

So, like Adriano said, I'm going to find my own happiness. And I know just where to find it.

Today was draining. So when I opened my unread messages twenty minutes before the restaurant closed and found a selfie of Hannah and Akili sitting on my couch, I couldn't wait to get home.

When Hannah swings the door open and smiles wide, it hits me right in the chest. Add to that, Akili dancing at my feet, happy as ever to see me, and coming home no longer feels like returning to the desolate, lonely bachelor pad it once was.

"I could get used to this," I say, pulling Hannah in for a kiss.

The stress of the day melts away as she wraps her arms around my neck and whimpers into my mouth. The feel of her soft hands clutching the back of my head, pulling me closer, fuels the neanderthal ways I try so hard to rein in. But this time, my love for her takes over.

I walk her backwards until her back is against the wall, and she responds by jumping up to wrap her legs around my waist. It gives me perfect access to her bare collarbone, so I sweep her hair over her shoulder, then trail my lips along her soft skin.

"Caleb," she breathes, throwing her head back.

Before I can think, I'm carrying her into the living room and laying her on the couch. I stand to look at her as I pull off my T-shirt that smells like the accumulation of a thousand restaurant meals. "I love you so freaking much, Hannah Parker."

Her eyes glass over, halting the heat of the moment. "Thank you for loving my broken parts and helping me trust myself again."

Those words mean so much more than *I love you*. At least, they do at this moment.

"You're perfect. But if by loving you, I've helped you love yourself again, then that's the best gift I could ever ask for." I lean forward to give her another quick kiss. "Let me go shower and change, then we can pick up where we left off."

She sticks her bottom lip out in an adorable, exaggerated pout.

"What?"

"Please, don't change. I like this outfit." A wicked grin replaces her pout. "But yes, you need a shower."

I laugh, snatching my shirt from the arm of the sofa, then walk past Akili, giving her a quick ear scratch. But before I head to the shower, I turn back to Hannah. "Thank you for loving my broken parts."

44

HANNAH

Don't Rush

Ever since Henry's reappearance at *Hibiscus* three weeks ago, Caleb seems lighter. Happier. Like he's finally closed a chapter in his life that he's content not revisiting. Having Sophie around more often has also been good for him, because after years apart, they're finally able to spend time together regularly. I've also been able to reconnect with her, and it made me realize how much I missed her, too.

With the kitchen staff working like a well-oiled griddle—smooth and efficient—Caleb has officially turned *Hibiscus* into a success story. Not only am I proud of him, but I'm grateful to have been a part of turning it around. Finally, I've found things worth the effort to salvage.

But now that he's achieved what he set out for, I get the impression the excitement is wearing off. He's worked out quarterly menus to capitalize on as much local ingredients as possible based on seasons. He's settled into a routine with full days off. And thanks to Sophie, even his office is organized and clean for the first time since he took over nine months ago.

Tonight is the first night we've both been able to leave early enough to have a date night. And of all the options, we settled on picking up Akili and coming to Caleb's place with *à la carte* meals from *Hibiscus.*

Now that Caleb has fed half of his *Boeuf Bourguignon* to Akili, she's fast asleep on the sectional's ottoman.

I try to ignore those lingering questions as I lean in until my lips meet his. Kissing Caleb overwhelms my entire system and makes all the fears and worries fade. My nerves are alight, firing through my entire body. My muscles tense and relax, begging for his touch. Even my bones feel like they curve around him to pull him closer. Each touch of his lips fills me with a high-powered torch that welds my broken pieces back together. I get lost in him until I'm laid back on the sofa, oblivious to anything else around me but him.

With a groan, Caleb inches his head away, tilting his head to either side to stretch his neck. "Oscar did a number on me today."

I run my hands up his shoulders, stopping at the base of his neck and squeezing to loosen his muscles. "I want to come watch one of these workout sessions."

"No way," he grumbles, collapsing against me.

"Um... Caleb? You're squashing me."

He presses himself up again with a silent chuckle. "Sorry. That feels amazing."

"Get up for a second. And take your shirt off." I waggle my eyebrows at him, then wink.

"Heard, Chef." He tugs his T-shirt over his head with a groan.

I stand and instruct him to lie down on his stomach. Once he's settled, I straddle him, positioning myself so I can reach his shoulders.

Slowly but confidently, I knead his upper back muscles until I feel the tightness ease. I do the same, working my way up his shoulders and neck. Caleb's groans of satisfaction make it easy work. He goes completely silent for a minute, so I assume he's fallen asleep. I lift myself to get off of him, but he reaches a hand back to grip my thigh. With one foot on the floor and the other stuck in the back of the couch, I'm hovering over him, unable to move. He drops his hand and flips himself over in a fluid motion he likely learned from muay thai.

Which reminds me. "Why don't you want me to come watch you work out?"

He reaches his hands around my back, pulling me down on top of him. He's unbothered by me landing with a thud, not nearly as graceful as he is. "You'd think a lot less of me if you saw how badly Oscar whoops me every time. And he looks way better with his shirt off. It's not a fair fight, really."

"Don't be ridiculous." I trail my fingernail up his obliques, across his chest. "When I look at Oscar, I still see the troublemaking nine-year-old kid who used to spy on us."

"You knew he spied on us?"

"You didn't? He wasn't exactly stealthy. That's why I'd swat you away sometimes, because I could see him peeking around the basement stairs."

"That little..." His eyes flick to the left—like he's strategizing how to get payback—then focus back on me. "I was worried you didn't find me completely irresistible."

"Now that is ridiculous." I lean forward, trailing my lips up his neck, across his stubble.

"Hannah," he hisses.

I torment him further by continuing my path to the corners of his mouth. He keeps twisting, trying to make our lips connect again. Each time he does, I find a new route until he's begging me to kiss him. Mercifully, I put an end to the torture for us both.

By the time we stop, I'm heated from the inside out. Every inch of my skin is flush, sensitive to the touch. My breaths come in short pants, making my chest heave. I probably look like a hot mess, but Caleb doesn't tear his eyes away from me.

My way of making my body temperature plummet and entirely kill the romantic vibe is to ask: "Are you stuck in a rut?"

"A rut?" He sweeps my hair out of the way that was brushing his chest. "You want me to spice things up a little?"

He'll never take me seriously in this position.

I shift backward, out of his reach, then settle myself next to his feet. "I mean with work. Now that you've done what you set out for, is the thrill gone? Are you still happy there?"

"I'm happy wherever you are," he answers, pushing himself up to sit beside me.

"No, we can't do that. I love you, Caleb, but I don't want you thinking that your happiness lives and dies with me. That's a lot of pressure on me, for one. And two, you deserve more than that. So what I'm asking is if you see yourself being happy at *Hibiscus* forever, or if it was the challenge you loved?"

"I did love the challenge. But I love you more, and that's more important to me."

"What do you want, though? Out of life? Where do you see yourself in the future?"

He pounces forward, tackling me back on the couch so I'm lying flat with him overtop of me in the reverse of the situation I just got us out of. "Married to you. Have a whole litter of kids. What are you thinking? Seven? Maybe a baker's dozen? A few more dogs."

There's no way he can't feel the warmth that just bloomed from my core outward at the mention of getting married and having children. My career is established. I've found the man I love more than anything. I've moved on from the mistakes and trauma of my past—even if they will always be a part of me. That's what I want too.

"Well, I was thinking two kids, but we can figure that out another time. Akili is not willing to discuss more dogs, though. She has made that very clear."

Caleb chuckles, lowering his head to the side of my neck again, repaying me for my torture minutes ago. I arch into him, desperate for his touch, but not wanting to give up on this conversation.

"So where you work doesn't matter to you?"

He pulls his head back, leaving my neck cold from the air conditioning latching on to where he kissed. "No. For a lot of years, I thought my career was my priority. But it never made me truly happy. You, Hannah Parker? You make me happy."

"You make me happy too," I whisper. "You're meant for great things, Caleb, and I don't want to keep you from them."

"I don't want to see my name in lights or in any history books. I want a simple life… with you. That will be the greatest thing I'll ever do." He gives me an irresistible wink, then returns to making me regret torturing him. He doesn't play fair.

"If you keep this up, we probably will have thirteen kids," I mutter once I can catch my breath. I literally feel dizzy from the euphoria buzzing through me. Like I'm drunk on Caleb, and it's better than any Bahamian rum.

"Then we should probably hurry and get married," he retorts, beaming at me.

I pinch my top lip between my teeth to suppress my smile so I can determine if that was a rhetorical statement or a terrible proposal. "Why the rush?"

"Hannah, I've loved you for more than half of my life. Trust me, this isn't some harebrained idea that's come to mind in the heat of the moment. If you want to know what will make me happy, step one is having you as my wife. My life partner. Falling asleep next to you every night. Waking up to you and our girl." He glances behind my head, where Akili is snoring, really adding to the overall ambiance. "Proving to you how much I love you every single day."

I don't even need to think about my answer. As much as I was afraid to trust myself again—afraid to accept that I was and always had been in love with Caleb—I trust *him* with my whole heart. I trust him not to break it.

"Then make me your wife."

The smile reaching his eyes tells me all I need to know. As does the way my face hurts from my own impossibly wide smile. He could check my gums for gingivitis right now. But judging by the hungry look in his eyes, that's not what he's thinking.

And it's not how we spend the evening.

Ready for Love

"What are you doing here?" I ask my mother.

She is not the person I was expecting when I heard my doorbell ring. I run through different scenarios why she'd show up at my house and, for a second, I worry something happened to one of my grandparents.

She puts my fears to rest by stating, "Everything is fine. Can I come in?"

I've lived here for almost ten months, and neither of my parents have ever stepped foot inside. Safe to say Henry never will, but after my last interaction with him, I have more sympathy for my mother. Reluctantly, I agree.

She steps inside just enough to close the door, and comes to a stop, clutching her purse in front of her. "I came here to apologize, Caleb."

My feet stick to the floor like they're suddenly made of concrete. "For?"

Forgive me for being naturally suspicious of my mother and her intentions. Her track record for doing things out of the goodness of her heart isn't stellar.

"I didn't do right by you and your sister, and I know it's too late to fix that now, but you need to know how much I love you both."

Ah, love. The arbitrary emotion that is supposed to forgive even the most horrific transgressions. Like "I love you" is enough of a bright point to combat the darkness that suffocated you for years. Obviously, people love to different degrees, because I couldn't allow people I love to suffer at the hands of a man who is incapable of the emotion to *any* degree. Her version of love and mine are very different.

But my journey with Hannah has made it clear that it's never too late to fix things. Not when there is real love to experience. When, coupled with action and forgiveness, love *can* drive away that darkness.

"It's not too late, Mom. If you want things to be right, we can work on it." I take her purse and set it on the table inside the door. "Come in."

She gives me a weak smile, which is either lack of actual emotion or Botox. It's hard to tell. Regardless, she follows me.

"Have you talked to Sophie?" I ask.

"Not yet. She's not speaking to me. I'm trying to give her space."

I can't say I blame my sister for not wanting to open that door of communication again. Our mother hasn't exactly been a reliable support system and felt more content to feed Sophie to the wolves than stand up for her. But healing has to start somewhere, and me holding onto resentment won't make matters easier.

"What's all this?" Mom asks, pointing at the ingredients organized on my kitchen counter. "Oh, are you expecting someone? I just assumed..."

"Uh... yeah. Hannah."

Now a smile wide enough to confirm Botox is not a reason for my mother's otherwise stoic face appears. "You're seeing each other again?"

After how things went in the past, I never imagined that would make my mother happy. I was sure she'd advised Hannah to apply at *Hibiscus* to throw a wrench in my plans. But looking at how happy she is, I don't think that's the case.

"We—"

The doorbell rings for the second time in ten minutes.

"One second. That'll be her." I leave my mom standing in the kitchen and run to open the front door.

On the other side stands my gorgeous fiancée and her wiggly pug. Correction: *our* wiggly pug.

"Hi," she greets. "Is someone else here? There's another car—" Hannah's words stop dead when she locks eyes on something behind me.

No doubt it's my mother. I turn around to confirm that she's standing a few metres away.

"Come in." I take Akili from Hannah's arms, tucking her under mine like a football. Then I grab Hannah's hand and pull her inside. "She just wanted to talk."

"Oh, I can… um…" Hannah hooks her thumb behind her, gesturing that she can go back outside.

"No, it's fine. What better time to make yourself at home?"

Not to mention, forgiveness of my mother will require her accepting Hannah as part of my life.

We stand in awkward silence for a minute until I let Akili down to break the tension. No one can be upset when they're watching a curly pug tail wag back and forth as her squatty little body scurries around sniffing everything.

I follow Akili to the kitchen, hoping the other women will join us. I opt to get to work on what I was about to create before my mother interrupted; comfortable multi-tasking—cooking and conversation.

Sure enough, both women walk into the kitchen and each drop onto a stool at the edge of the counter. Neither of them say a word.

"To answer your question, yes, Hannah and I are engaged," I say without looking up from cleaning an artichoke.

My mother gasps and claps a hand over her bright red lips. "I'm so happy for you. Really, I am," she replies, surprising us both. "I knew as soon as Catherine mentioned Hannah was unemployed that you two could get your second chance."

I drop the artichoke on my cutting board and look at Hannah. Her lips are parted and her eyebrows furrowed, staring at my mother.

"You… told her to apply to give us a second chance?" I ask.

Mom releases a long breath and starts picking at her fingernails. "What you guys had—I guess have—is a once-in-a-lifetime love. I knew if you just had a chance to explore that again, you'd find your way." She looks up from her hand and glances at Hannah, then at me. "Trust me, that's not the kind of thing you ever want to throw away. But I knew if I told you that from the start, you'd doubt my intentions. Which I don't blame you for."

I look over at Hannah and wonder to myself what would have happened if my mother hadn't intervened. Would we have found each other again? Was our love strong enough to span a decade and heartache and trauma, yet still find our way back? Chances are slim. Which means I have my mom to thank for leading Hannah back to me. Or me back to her.

Instead of just saying thank you, I do something I haven't done for a long time. I walk around the counter and wrap my arms around my mother.

She starts weeping in my arms, and it's the first time I've heard her cry in decades. Maybe ever. She might cry in private, but she's always prided herself on being a poised, composed woman who never let anyone see her cracks.

"I'm so sorry, Caleb. I'm so proud of you for following your dreams and being strong enough to do what I never could. More than anything, I just want to see you happy."

There are so many questions around that declaration. Why couldn't she find the strength to walk away? What about Sophie? Why wasn't her happiness a priority? Why did we have to get to the point as a family that we were fractured before any of this came up? And as much as I want those answers, I look over at Hannah and none of them matter right now.

I get to spend the rest of my life with her. Sophie is fine and happy in her own life. The journey wasn't always easy, but we're both in good places now. Everything else can come in time.

"It's not too late for you to be happy, either. You don't owe him your life." I step back to release her, hoping she can see the sincerity in my eyes.

She reaches over to the counter, grabbing a napkin to wipe her eyes. "I'm too old to bother with fairy tales now."

She doesn't get a word out before Hannah says, "I never meant to hurt you, you know? What I said… back then… I was immature, and I didn't understand. But I do now, and I'm sorry."

Both women smile at each other as my mom reaches a hand out to place on Hannah's arm.

"You were wise beyond your years, and you stood up for my children when I didn't have the courage to. I was jealous you were more brave than I could ever be."

"That's not true," Hannah replies instantly. "Because when I was in your situation, I realized how hard it was to leave." She rifles through her bag and pulls out a section of the newspaper.

I scan the section title, assuming it's another critic who visited *Hibiscus*, but it's not.

Hannah points to an article on the bottom half of the page. "This is my ex. He destroyed my self-confidence. He alienated me from my family. He beat me," she says, her voice cracking.

My hand clenches tighter around my knife, and I force myself to take a breath. Until I realize what the heading of the newspaper says and why she brought him up.

Twenty-Nine-Year-Old Toronto Man Charged With Aggravated Assault.

"Todd?" I ask, my eyes widening.

"Yep. He assaulted an undercover officer. After his history of reports when charges never stuck, this one finally did." She turns to face my mother. "I brought this here to show Caleb because I felt like it gave us some closure. But I think I was meant to bring it here to show you. So you'd know that I understand how hard it is to be in your position, but it is possible to get out and find happiness again."

Mom's puffy eyes start leaking again, trickling tears down her cheeks. "I'm so sorry you had to learn how awful it is. You always were so much stronger than me, Hannah." With that, she stands, not acknowledging anything else Hannah said.

It's not that I assumed she'd hear a few things she's been told a hundred times and all of a sudden walk away from a thirty-five-year marriage, but I wish she wasn't so dismissive of the idea.

"I'll leave you two to your plans. I'm sorry for cutting into your time." She walks toward the door with her shoulders slumped and her head hung low.

"Mom?" I call after her. "We're getting married at City Hall tomorrow. Two o'clock. If... uh... if you want to come."

She turns around with a wide smile. "I wouldn't miss it."

After we say goodbye to my mother, we stand at the front door, watching her leave.

"Do you think she'll ever leave him?" Hannah asks.

"I don't know. But I don't want to worry about their marriage ending, because tomorrow, ours starts."

The Sun Will Rise

The sunrise is absolutely beautiful here. I stare out over the oceanfront balcony, listening to the water rhythmically lap at the shore as beach-loving birds squawk overhead. Tourists are already strolling the beach, searching for seashells and other souvenirs to take back to wherever they call home.

"You're up early," Caleb says, walking across the tiled floor toward me. He wraps his arms around me from behind, pressing his bare chest against me and kissing below my ear. "Something on your mind, Mrs. McNamara?"

"Just thinking about going back to the grind in a few days. The escape has been nice."

Our last-minute Bahamian honeymoon adventure was only possible because my dad got us on his flight and set us up in a villa owned by a friend of his, but we've made the most out of every minute.

"Let's not worry about normal life just yet. We still have two full days left to enjoy paradise." He leans down and kisses me in the same spot again.

I spin in his arms, coming to face him and running my nails across his torso. "But in Canada, you have to wear layers and layers of clothes all the time."

He growls, tightening his arms around me, pulling us flush, and capturing my lips with his. Each time I kiss Caleb, I get a rush of butterflies that I never want to stop. We get lost in each other until we're breathless and need to pull away for oxygen.

I take a greedy breath of salty ocean air, studying Caleb's features. "Something on your mind, Mr. McNamara?" I repeat.

"You have a point about all the layers. I could get used to you in a bikini every day."

He leans in to kiss me again, cradling the back of my neck in one hand and adjusting my lips for easy access. The smile on his face as he breaks away floods me with happiness I never thought I'd find.

"Let's get dressed and grab breakfast. We have to make the most of our time left."

The sadness that chases away my surge of happiness catches me by surprise. Normal life holds a lot less appeal after five days in paradise with my husband.

We get ourselves ready to head out for breakfast and experience a few more adventures before we have to return to the cold weather and our gruelling work schedules. At least we still work together, so we see each other often. Plus, the heat and decor of *Hibiscus'* kitchen almost feels tropical.

Caleb leads me down a cobblestone street, trying to find somewhere to grab a bite to eat. The storefronts and restaurants are so colourful and adorable, everywhere you look is like a postcard. On top of their unique style, the crystal blue sky framing each building makes for breathtaking views in every direction. I'm busy taking it all in when Caleb stops abruptly.

"Look."

I glance up, squinting against the sun, and spot the distillery that makes the rum my dad loves. The same rum I still owe him a bottle of from more than six months ago. But when I follow Caleb's pointer finger, I see a "for sale" sign in front of what looks to be a bed-and-breakfast. "Do you think they serve food to people walking by?"

"Not for breakfast. For us. To buy."

"Since when do you want to buy a bed-and-breakfast?"

"I didn't until I saw it. But picture this," he says, grabbing both of my hands and turning me to face him. "Us, living together in paradise, running a small kitchen, still getting to create what we love, but also having time for ourselves. For our thirteen kids and five dogs. We'd get to see people enjoying our food instead of just cranking out one dish after another, never seeing our hard work pay off."

"Caleb, we agreed on two kids and no more dogs." I chuckle because the excitement on his face is adorable. "But we can't just give up everything and move halfway around the world."

"First, we're a four-hour flight from home, and your dad flies here almost every week. Second, what are we giving up? Long work days, snow, and barely seeing each other outside of the restaurant? Our friends and family can come visit whenever they want, and you know Akili hates the snow. We can hire staff for housekeeping and give back to the people here." His words are picking up speed the more he presents me with his spontaneous list of pros.

"What about Sophie? She'll be heartbroken if you leave again. Or Oscar? He'll miss beating you up during training. Or your grandparents? And your mom? You've just reconciled."

"Sophie will understand. She'll be thrilled to come visit here, just like France. Oscar has other trainees to punish. We can go home to visit my grandparents, or they can come visit with Sophie. They'd love that. And I can still have a relationship with my mom from here."

Even thinking about moving away from Angel and Vida makes me sad. But the truth is, they're both busy with their own lives, and with our work schedules, we see each other less and less as the weeks pass. Moving somewhere that people can come for a vacation could be a way to combat that. It would force a break for everyone we love.

"What about hurricanes? You'd rather hurricanes than snow?"

"We'll get storm shutters and keep emergency supplies."

I chuckle at how easily he dismisses that major possibility. "Just that easy, huh? We don't even know if we can afford anything here. I don't know what the real estate market is like, but I didn't bring much of a nest egg into this marriage."

"We'll sell our place and have more than enough for a down payment. As long as we keep it up and running, it will cover our costs. Maybe this isn't the right one for us, but we can look to see what options there are. Just tell me you'll consider the possibility."

He's so excited by the idea, it's hard to find any more points to argue with him. Can I walk away from everything? I was prepared to do that when I was searching for a job before. The only difference now is that I wouldn't be going alone. I'd have the love of my life by my side. And with my dad nearing retirement age, my parents always talked about moving somewhere warmer, too.

"When we get home, we can look into it. See if it's possible and what it will take. I'm on board if we can make it happen."

Caleb smiles so wide, his eyes crease behind his sunglasses. "Let's just look." He pulls me toward the bed-and-breakfast he has his sights set on.

"Now? I'm in a bikini." I'm wearing a thin cover-up, but it still feels weird to discuss a business transaction without pants.

"I know. Maybe they'll give us a better deal." He winks and leads me up the short pathway, past a sign that reads *Oceanside Escape B&B*.

We walk into the stunning yellow colonial building with a wraparound verandah and a red clay roof. The windows and doors are a vibrant white, but I notice the absence of any storm shutters. We enter the main door and absorb the interior. The gleaming, colourful tiles and well-lit entryway make the home feel welcoming.

An elderly woman with short grey hair appears, wearing a wide smile. "Good morning. Can I help you?" Judging by her accent, she's not native to the Bahamas. Her tan, weathered skin suggests she's been here for many years, though.

Caleb introduces us to the woman, who informs us her name is Cecily, then explains that we're newlyweds looking for a place in the area... like this has been a lifelong goal and not a spur-of-the-moment decision. "We noticed the for sale sign out front and were just wondering if we could learn a little more about the place. But if now isn't a good time..."

"No, no." Cecily waves a hand for us to follow her. "Come in. The staff handle the daily duties around here. I'm just a pretty face who talks all the guests' ears off." She giggles as she leads us into the dining area where six couples appear to be enjoying breakfast.

Before we know it, we've taken a tour of the entire two-acre property that has its share of citrus, coconut, and banana trees, as well as an abundant vegetable garden. The bed-and-breakfast and staff accommodations are in the main building, but there's a separate three-bedroom home next to it. There's also a small chicken coop at the corner of the property where they collect fresh eggs each morning. It's a self-sustaining homestead in the centre of paradise.

"This is a dream come true," Caleb whispers. "A dream I didn't know I had."

I nod in agreement on both points. When we decided to take this trip, it was enough of a headache to arrange things at *Hibiscus* so we could both leave. It was a daunting task and a realization that our time off together would be minimal. Not just for now, but forever. As much as I love cooking, I want a family—a life—outside of a kitchen more.

Cecily explains the pros and cons of moving to the Bahamas, having come from Maine with her husband when they were merely thirty. She claims they had a very happy life until he passed away six months ago. Now she'd like to move back home to be closer to the rest of her family. My heart hurts for her hearing the sadness in her voice over the loss of her husband and leaving the place she's called home for almost forty years. I can't help but offer her a hug, which she kindly accepts.

"You two are meant for this place," she declares, wiping her eyes. "So many people have come through these doors wearing suits, carrying clipboards, talking about the changes they can make to maximize profits. I turned them all down because Harold and I wanted to run a place with heart. Somewhere people could come and feel at home. We treat our guests like extended family, and I didn't want everything we'd worked for to become another mass-produced tourist trap."

Caleb and I look at each other, both nodding in acknowledgement of Cecily's wishes.

A chicken clucks from the coop to my left, drawing my attention to the path leading to it. Each stone laid in the pathway has two handprints and is marked with a new year. But what tugs at my heart the most is the initials *C & H* etched into each one.

I follow the individual stones, counting thirty-nine in total. Finally, I reach the end, which isn't quite all the way to the chicken coop. "I think you're right," I say to Cecily. Tears pool in my eyes when I imagine Caleb and I continuing this tradition, making our own mark on this slice of paradise, completing the path Cecily and Harold started decades earlier. Carrying on their legacy. "Caleb, I want to do this."

He looks at Cecily, who is beaming, then turns his focus back to me. "Yeah? For real?"

"For real. I think we were meant to find this place, too. Just like we found each other again."

He jogs the several steps to reach me, sweeping me into his arms. "You know this wouldn't be paradise without you, right?"

"Does this mean you can cook topless every day?" I ask, giggling away my threatening tears.

"As long as I'm not cooking bacon." He laughs, setting me down on the stone dated seven months earlier. "There's nowhere in the world I'd ever want to go without you again. I love you, Hannah McNamara. I've always loved you, and there's nothing I won't do to make sure you know that every day."

"I told you before, there's nowhere I wouldn't follow you. I love you, Caleb."

And standing here, on top of a piece of concrete that marks the end of one love story, we mark the next step in ours.

THE END

If you enjoyed this book, please consider leaving a review on Amazon or the retailer's website where you purchased the book from. I love hearing from my readers.

If you'd like to hear from me, find all of my links here: linktr.ee/TiffanyAndrea.

SPECIAL THANKS

Thank you for making it this far. If you've gotten to this point, I sincerely hope you enjoyed Caleb and Hannah's story.

I promise not to ramble on, as I usually do, and skip right to my gratitude. Thank you to my dear sister duo, Sarah and Rebecca, who provide so much support and encouragement, I'd be lost without you. I appreciate you taking the time to read Caleb and Hannah's story and provide me with helpful feedback.

To Sara, you really are a superstar. I appreciate your feedback endlessly. Your notes make me laugh, and your pointed questions make me really dive into my characters' motivations. They wouldn't be the same without you.

Finally, to Elena, your encouragement always comes at the exact moment I need it most. I appreciate each and every kind word you send my way. Thank you for helping Caleb and Hannah come to life.

Lastly, thank you to real life Hannah, who is a book reviewer who supported me way back when I had no idea what I was doing. (I still don't.) I appreciate you humouring me and being so kind when I desperately needed it.

As with most of my books, I chose a musical artist for inspiration. This story has transformed so many times since it was first a concept, and eventually, thanks to a little help from Sarah, I finally settled on Kelly Clarkson. Her music provided the perfect material for second chance romance inspiration.

So, here is my ultimate playlist for The Pugly Truth. You can find it on Spotify through my website at linktr.ee/TiffanyAndrea.

(Please note, I do not make any claims to any of these songs. All rights belong to Kelly Clarkson or the record label. I'm merely sharing my inspiration.)

Don't You Pretend
Behind These Hazel Eyes
I Don't Think About You
Trying to Help You Out*
Standing In Front of You
Breaking Your Own Heart
Dance With me
Creep – Radiohead cover
Haunted
Don't Let Me Stop
I Hate Myself For Losing You
Don't Waste Your Time
Because of You
Walking After Midnight – Patty Cline cover*
Just Missed the Train
(Stronger) What Doesn't Kill You
Bad Reputation
Catch My Breath
Heat
Dark Side
I Dare You
Never Again
Happier Than Ever

Love Goes On
Not Today
Walk Away
Nostalgic
Mr. Know It All
Hear me
All I ever Wanted
How I feel
Honestly
Impossible
The Day We Fell Apart
Since U Been Gone
I Forgive You
Let Me Down
Second Hand Heart
A Moment Like This
Dirty Little Secret
Let Your Tears Fall
Piece By Piece
My Life Would Suck Without You
Don't Rush
Ready For Love
The Sun Will Rise

A few special mentions:
Miss Independent
Broken & Beautiful

*Indicates song is not available on Spotify Canada at the time of publishing

You Are Enough Series:
We're All a Little Broken: Book 1 (Zara's story)
We're All a Little Overwhelmed: Book 1.5 (Zara's extended epilogue)
We're All a Little Guarded: Book 2 (Chelsea's story)
We're All a Little Tired: Book 2.5 (Chelsea's extended epilogue)
We're All a Little Scared: Book 3 (Isla's story)
We're All a Little Determined: Short Story Collection (Available free on my website)

This women's fiction series focuses on various aspects of mental health and overcoming trauma. It addresses anxiety, depression, panic disorders, miscarriage, adoption, grief and loss, racism, discrimination, and more, but in a light hearted way that will also make you laugh. The entire series is set in Muskoka/Bracebridge, Ontario.

A New Leash on Life Series:
This series will consist of twenty interconnected standalone romances of various genres, each featuring a cuddly canine companion.

Total Bull (Angel and Damian)
Ay Chihuahua (Dina and Holden)
Tell-Tail Sign (Sophie and Boyd)
The Pugly Truth (Hannah and Caleb)
Pitty Party (Frankie and Oscar) *Coming 2023*
Chemistry Lab (Hollis and Myer) *Coming 2023*

Dear Sister, Never Again: This women's fiction novella was shortlisted in Wattpad's annual novella contest. It explores the journey to realizing DNA isn't the only thing that makes family.

Suburban Watchdogs: This nonsensical comedy features four longtime friends and their slobbery dog on a mission to save their town from being overrun by a trio of bumbling criminals.

Con Artist: This standalone romantic comedy follows the story of an FBI agent tasked with investigating an art theft ring. The only thing his number one suspect makes away with, is his heart.

Trip and Fall: This standalone road trip romance follows two twenty-somethings who each have a different reason for wanting to leave town and explore the countryside. One out of a sense of wonder; the other, a sense of desperation. Will they find more than the adventure they were looking for? *Coming 2023*

Sign up for my newsletter, access my website, or follow me on social media to keep up to date with new releases and sneak peeks.
Linktr.ee/TiffanyAndrea